Shaman: The Awakening

Shaman: The Awakening

V.R. McCoy

COPYRIGHT (C) 2014 BY V.R. MCCOY
LAYOUT COPYRIGHT (C) 2014 CREATIVIA

Published 2014 by Creativia
Paperback design by Creativia (www.ctivia.com)
Second Edition, Edited by Simone Beaudelaire
ISBN: 978-1499181968
Cover art by http://www.thecovercollection.com/

This book is a work of fiction. Names, characters, places, and incidents are the product of the author's imagination or are used fictitiously. Any resemblance to actual events, locales, or persons, living or dead, is purely coincidental.

Dedication

I would like to dedicate this novel to my mother, Margaret Ann Gibson McCoy. She was and always will be my inspiration, guide and biggest fan. She introduced me to the world of mysticism.

I would like to thank the brothers of Kappa Alpha Psi Fraternity, in particular the Xi Chapter of Howard University; Invictus Forever

Thank you to my sister, "Hey Trae, here's another one!"

Thank you to my partner in crime and by the hip brother J. George Mullins. "Yo Nupe; if memories are to be treasured, we have a pirate's chest full of great things! Miss you brother.

I would also like to say thank you to all who supported me throughout this journey; especially the cast of characters for their indulgence in this work of fiction; Dr. Gregory Banks, MD., Ms. Gracie Mullins, Max Maurice, Joaquinna D. Green and my eternal brother and friend Carroll Hughes. I wish we had spent more time horseback riding, my brother, but we will ride again someday (RIP).

Prologue

The nightmares never cease. Since I was a child I've struggled to deal with them. Every night there is a different horror. I see them taking shape as if I was there. Then I wake up sweating profusely from these horrific dreams. I use to dream of another world in which I was running from the strangest creatures. Creatures that only can exist in nightmares, yet they're all too real to me.

Some nights I dread going to sleep, as if I was in one of those Freddy Krueger films; "A Nightmare on Elm Street," except I don't bring any of the horrors back with me. For years now I've survived every last encounter. At least those kids finally received some peace or rest from the nightmares.

Chapter 1

The Gift and the Curse

I was alone at a table in the corner, playing chess in the activities room. The other patients were watching television, playing cards or some other board games. The television seemed to remain on *Law and Order* whenever I was in there. I had learned to block it out. We were all here for multifarious mental disorders or breakdowns and required psychiatric assistance in one form or another. This wasn't an institution for the criminally insane, but for voluntary admissions. It was a privately run institution and their patients were affluent or from affluent families.

This wasn't the first institution in which I had been a patient. When I was a child I had been in and out of these types of facilities. The psychologists and doctors attempted to treat me for my sleep disorder and strange nightmares. I was poked, prodded and placed under the close scrutiny like a lab rat. I was humiliated and treated as subhuman; someone without feelings or a soul. There psychobabble didn't really help much as you can see.

I have this gift or curse, whichever way you want to look at it. It has been in my family for years; trickling down through the generations. My grandmother, a Cherokee Indian, had the gift and her father, a

3

Medicine Man, had it also. He had acquired it from his mother; and so on and so on. My mother didn't have the gift, but her sister, my aunt, acquired it. I consider it a curse, because it has been tormenting me for years. The Cherokee's name for it, translated in English, is 'Vision Quest'. It is the ability to have foresight in dreams, but not only to read dreams; to manipulate them. Historians and scholars refer to it as Shamanism.

These dreams were just nightmares I had as a kid. When I became a young adult and learned how to control the nightmares, the dream manipulation became something else. I worked with Dr. Gregory Banks, a renowned Psychologist, for years. He guided me and helped me to focus my nightmares and turn them into positive dreams.

Women who wouldn't ordinarily give me the time of day would show interest in me. If I dreamt of them in certain romantic scenarios, it was like I implanted my dreams or subconscious suggestion inside their heads, but it was much more than that. It was like the actions or scenarios actually took place! I would catch them blushing around me the next day, as if they had experienced the same dream. Of course I couldn't confront them about it, but soon dating became extremely easy! Dr. Banks called it dreamscaping.

It got to a point where I could have any woman I wanted, and I did. I had orgies with two to three women. I even had happily married women leaving their husbands' bedsides at three o'clock in the morning to visit me for sex. Then the nightmares came back! I had grown weary of the sex games because it felt like I was cheating, no; I was cheating! Would these women really be with me if it wasn't for my dream implants?

As soon as I stopped dreaming of the women, my mind went other places at night. Dr. Banks stated that my unusual subconscious mind was stronger than normal. They couldn't find any physiological differences between my brain and others', but I utilized more of my frontal lobe than they did. He also explained that at night, when the rest of my brain is asleep, my frontal lobe goes into overdrive.

The Gift and the Curse

I was always a bit of a scopophiliac. I would rather observe than participate; not like a peeping tom, but more of a voyeur with permission. So, of course I watched a lot of television news. It let me into the lives of others. This is what really began my quest into what landed me here in the loony bin.

I began to dream of these cases of people getting murdered. Unlike my previous nightmares as a kid, now I had actual faces and events I could put together in a dream. I could focus as Dr. Banks taught me. I attempted to notify the police on these cases to assist them and ended up their prime suspect, until they caught the actual killers or perpetrators with my assistance.

Once again I was poked, prodded and placed under the bright lights of their endless deprivation interrogating techniques, or 'interviews', as they would call it. It was a mild form of torture. They were no better than the childhood psychologists who did the same thing when I was younger. I felt like I was at Abu Ghraib, when all I was attempting to do was help. Still, to this day, there are some who think I'm a cohort in some of the crimes. They can't wrap their minds around the fact that someone has the abilities I do.

This gift that I have has been around for years in different cultures and forms. The Native American Medicine Man, the Celtic Shamans – druids, witches and others throughout history have displayed this ability, but modern man views this as a threat. Most can't even believe in a higher power than themselves, and consider anyone with advanced abilities as a threat; thus the witch burnings throughout history.

Once my assistance was beginning to prove valuable to the local authorities, the FBI became interested in my abilities as well. I was hired as a consultant with the FBI's National Center for the Analysis of Violent Crime in Quantico, Virginia. There are several departments that fall under the NCAVC. The particular section I was associated with was a Special Task Force called the Violent Criminal Apprehension Program (ViCAP) which was under the auspices of the Behavioral Analysis Unit. Our task was to solve the unsolvable when it came to kidnappings, abductions and serial killings.

In the beginning, I didn't know if they wanted to study me or just keep their eye on me. I thought perhaps their intent was to prevent me from being involved in any further high profile cases. There were still those out there who wanted me locked away somewhere with the key destroyed instead of being thrown away. I was an anomaly that a lot of authorities and people in general weren't ready to accept. Therefore the FBI kept my abilities under cover.

The FBI placed me in a section of ViCAP with others who had special gifts. Most of the Bureau referred to us as the X Files and the rest just called us the Freak Show. It truly was a circus of characters. Say what you want about the Freak Show, but our section had one of the best case closing records of the entire Bureau. We weren't celebrated or paraded around due to our unorthodox methods, but numbers don't lie. We were invaluable consultants and the textbooks were thrown out the window when it came to our section.

The teams were assembled with one special ability consultant. There were usually five to six person teams including a consultant and a SAC (Special Agent in Charge). The SAC for our team was Steven Weiss. He was a very cerebral, calculating and analytical agent. He was a born multi-tasker. As a child he was a chess prodigy and graduated from Stanford University at the age of 15, when most kids are going to high school. The FBI was lucky to acquire him.

Agent Weiss' parents were murdered when he was a youngster and the killer was never found. It was their deaths that brought him to the FBI. Perhaps it was a personal crusade, but he was still one of their best and brightest. The other agents comprising the team were Dianna Samboro, Amber Carson, Max Maurice, Paul Woodward and me, the special abilities consultant; Christian Sands.

Agent Dianna Samboro was an Italian American and former Olympic archer. She graduated from American University in Washington, D.C. with a B.S. in Psychology and remained in D.C. after

The Gift and the Curse   7

graduating. Born and raised in Sacramento, California, her family was originally from Sicily. She was a marksman with firearms.

Agent Max Maurice was a star Linebacker for LSU, until he tore his ACL. He graduated from LSU with a double degree in Psychology and Social Studies. After college he enlisted as an officer in the Marine Corps before joining the FBI. His family was originally from New Orleans, Louisiana.

Agent Paul Woodward graduated from the University of Texas with a degree in Criminal Justice and a post Jurisprudence. Being from an affluent family in Houston, Texas, his parents didn't condone his career choice. He was supposed to become a lawyer and work in the family business. Paul was married, with five kids and a beautiful wife.

Ms. Amber Carson had graduated from Howard University School of Law and had a license to practice law in D.C., Maryland and Virginia, but chose to walk in the footsteps of her father, who died in the line of duty as an FBI agent. She also had an undergrad degree in Psychology. Her family was from Washington, D.C. She was a divorcée with one young son, who was born before she attended college.

Then there was me; I had a musical degree from the University of North Carolina. My family was originally from Clinton, North Carolina, and I just happened to be paired with these psychoanalytic experts. As much as I had been examined and prodded by psych experts, I guess I had a long range of experience in psychoanalytic techniques as well.

In the beginning, it all seemed so surreal for to us. Most of the teams took our team for a joke. I was nicknamed Freddie Krueger behind my back, but as the results of my consulting began paying off, they began to take me more seriously. As the caseloads increased and the criminal profiles became more vicious and violent, my dreams became the same. That's when things really became creepy and weird.

At first I was just an omniscient observer in these reenactment dreams, but eventually I began communicating with the killers and seeing things that could only be described as supernatural. Even my team looked at me like I was crazy and in need of medical care. I was officially considered weird and insane at that point. The FBI abandoned me after that last uncanny job and placed me in here to receive psychiatric treatment, but I wasn't insane and they knew it. They just couldn't accept the facts of what happened. Hell, even I must admit looking back that the events which occurred would seem a bit strange and unbelievable, if it hadn't happened to me.

Chapter 2

A Dream Within A Dream

It was the beginning of winter in D.C. The snow and the cold came early this year. The talk in the city was that Global Warming had everything screwed up. Apparently Washingtonians had become accustomed to mild winters lately, and the inclement winter weather didn't really appear until the middle of January, or even late February. That year the cold weather started in early November, and there was snow on the ground by Thanksgiving.

There was even a nor'easter dumping its bitter snows on the city and the rest of the Northeast in early December. This weather was actually average for this time of year in this region. If anything, we should have been happy it wasn't warm! That's the true sign of Global Warming and the melting of the Polar Caps.

I owned a nice condo in Foggy Bottom, just west of Georgetown. It was an old apartment building which had been renovated. I had two floors, a fireplace and a balcony. I had to have a fireplace and hardwood floors wherever I lived. I enjoyed everything about a nice fireplace; the warmth, the crackling sound, the smell and the look of a fire burning, just as much as I enjoyed winter.

9

I didn't have a lot of furniture in my place, but I did have several instruments. I had a baby grand piano in the living room, a guitar, a stand up acoustic bass and a cello. I used to teach music before I became involved with law enforcement. The piano was in the middle of the hardwood floor and the acoustic bass with the bow beside it was standing up in the corner of the living room under a track light. The cello, which I loved and played often, was in the middle of the wall with its track light pointed at it. Then there was my vintage Les Paul guitar, which accented the other corner of my music wall, standing up within the glow of its lighting. The living room almost looked like a museum. I had spent a lot of money on my instruments. They were original works of art in themselves.

The rest of the living room consisted of one leather sofa, an accompanying leather chair, and a coffee table on a circular rug in front of the fireplace. I had a bookcase to the right of the mantle with several books. The stereo case was opposite the music wall. It contained a Bose stereo surround sound system with a CD player and a turntable for the vintage vinyl records I collected.

I didn't have any paintings or sculptures. I loved art and visiting the museums, but I could never decide on what artist, period or genre to place on the wall. I liked so many different styles of art, but I did lean towards Impressionism with its abstract and indistinct lines. All of my doctors agreed it was my subconscious mind that influenced this. I almost felt like Jekyll and Hyde the way they spoke of my dream state or subconscious, as if it were completely separate from me.

I loved the solace of winter. There were fewer people on the streets and fewer crimes committed. The snow was serine and pure. Snow could make any hellhole or ghetto appear pure, even the hardened streets of D.C. It covered up a lot of deficiencies and made the city look better, at least for a little while. Everything seemed so peaceful in the winter.

Perhaps my introverted personality also played a small part in my outlook when it came to winter. I really had become a bit of a

A Dream Within A Dream

recluse - always felt self-conscious, like I was being judged. Besides, the less contact I had with people the fewer dreams I had to worry about or manage. Sometimes my dream focus would stray if I became extremely tired. I was getting at least four solid hours of sleep per night, when I wasn't working complex cases. I shut myself off from the external world during that time.

I didn't watch any television or listen to talk radio. I preferred to listen to my jazz records, play chess, read poetry and play the piano or the cello. The music helped me to relax. Whenever I worked cases, I would go for days without proper sleep. You would think my dream state would be considered resting, but it wasn't. A part of my brain was working overtime while my physiology, nervous system and muscles, reacted to everything my mind was experiencing. It's like when you kick, punch or talk in your sleep, but more intense.

When I was younger, I used to sleepwalk while in these dream trances. My mother had to use double key-locked doors to prevent me from leaving while I slept. I've learned to control all that now.

I didn't have any friends; just associates from work, the team. I liked it that way because it was less complicated and weird. The team members would call and check up on me now and then. Sometimes the SAC (Special Agent in Charge), Steven Weiss, would visit the condo. I also heard from Dianna Samboro often. She liked me more than the other team members. Under different circumstances I could have seen us having a relationship, but it would have been too awkward while working together and her knowing what she does about me. She didn't seem to mind or treat me as though I were weird; neither was she indifferent to me, but you never know what lies beneath a person's psyche until you really dig deep. You don't need special abilities to figure that one out!

I was spending a normal evening at home, cooking and listening to jazz, when the telephone rang. I was expecting Weiss to be calling me in, since I really didn't have any friends. It was Dianna on the phone.

"Hello, Chris, are you busy?" she asked

"No, just cooking dinner," I replied.

"Hey, I was in the neighborhood and wondered if I could stop by?"

"Yeah, sure. Come on over," I urged.

She arrived about 15 minutes later.

"You really were in the hood," I stated when I opened the door.

"Yeah, I was doing some last minute shopping in Georgetown. Did you complete your shopping already?" she inquired.

"Yes, what little I had."

"Well, I'm a simple girl. I hope you didn't get me anything too expensive," she replied with a smile as I took her black pea coat.

"Wow, you look totally different without your Clark Kent glasses on, Chris. You should show those beautiful green eyes of yours more often from," she said, staring me in the eyes. I hadn't really thought about it, but she was used to seeing me with my black rimmed glasses on while at work. I hardly ever wore them when I'm at home.

"So, I'm in time for dinner," she further stated, engaging me with a smile. Dianna was very forthcoming and out front. She wasn't shy at all.

"Yes. I'm cooking some pasta with lobster and sauce."

"Can I help," she inquired with excitedly? "Sure," I replied.

I had a huge, modern kitchen, with an island range and hood. The kitchen was large enough to eat in. I had two bar stools and a small, upright table that I usually ate on. I didn't really have guests over for dinner, so it was all I needed.

"What a coincidence? You're fixing Italian cuisine and having an Italian girl over for dinner," she said, laughing, as I escorted her to the kitchen.

Dianna was a beautiful and vibrant woman. She had killer curves and a dynamite smile. Her hair was shoulder length and curly, like a lot of women of Italian descent. She was of darker complexion like the Sicilians. As she was a comfortable 5'7 and weighed about 140 pounds, she was in perfect shape. She had on jeans which appeared like a second skin, the way they hugged and accentuated her curvy, voluptuous body, and a white blouse buttoned down to the point where I could see just enough cleavage; not slutty, but sexy. There

A Dream Within A Dream   13

is a fine line between the two. She had on the sexiest black boots that came almost up to her knees. Dianna was fine from head to toe, with or without clothes.

She assisted me in the kitchen. She turned it into a sensual experience. There were several moments shared in the kitchen when we were close. She was flirting the whole time and I was enjoying every minute of it! She was fun to be around. We opened a bottle of wine and enjoyed our dinner with light conversation. She was like a schoolgirl, asking questions about me and my abilities.

"So, what if someone was dreaming about you; could you tell," she inquired? I started to smile. "Are you laughing at me," she asked with a small giggle? "No, it's just refreshing. Most people feel uncomfortable talking about it with me."

"Oh, so you're the boogey man now, huh?" she said, teasing me and smiling.

"No, from what I hear, I'm Freddy Krueger," I replied while making a gesture with both my fork and pasta spoon. We both had a good laugh at that one.

"But really, can you tell if someone dreams about you?" she insisted at last.

"No. It would have to be what the doctors and I call 'Invasive Dreamscape'. That person would have to have the ability also," I replied.

"So you can invade others' dreams without them invading yours?" she asked.

"No. When I'm in Dreamscape, I share the dream with them. They know and experience everything I do, but to really answer the question; I don't know. If I feel a strong enough connection with the person, I guess anything is possible. I mean, who would've thought any of this is possible," I replied.

She smiled and continued eating.

I wondered if she had been dreaming about me, or was going to dream about me. I never really gave it much thought since we worked together. I promised Steve that I would never invade the dreams of team members unless it was under critical circumstances and their life was in jeopardy. Thus far I had kept my promise and respected the boundaries and privacy of my team on a professional level. Perhaps Dianna was just testing me to see if I was invading her dreams, or those of the other team members.

After dinner we took our glasses and the bottle of wine into the living room. She viewed the books of poetry I had on the mantle and requested a reading. I just knew she was going to ask me to play something on the piano or one of my stringed instruments, but once again, she proved herself unpredictable. I read Poe to her in front of the fireplace. Since the theme of our evening conversation was centered on my Dreamscape, I followed in kind by reading her "A Dream," "A Dream within a Dream" and my favorite, "Dreams". She stated that she understood and could see why "Dreams" was my favorite.

She asked that I read more of my favorites, which I obliged until she fell asleep. It was a hypnotic trick I learned from Dr. Banks; how to set external moods. I wasn't trying to manipulate her, but I could tell she needed the sleep. It was obvious by the way she nestled in the glow and warmth of the fireplace. I let her rest on the sofa and placed a blanket over her. I sat on the floor beside her, thinking about what to do with my newly acquired friend.

Dianna was vibrant and full of life. She was an extrovert, the complete opposite of me. She had lots of friends and stayed active. That's why it wasn't really a stretch of the imagination to find her in the neighborhood. Although sometimes she over-exerted herself, being so active. This was one of those times. It was the holiday season and she had been out all day, visiting and shopping. I still didn't understand her interest in me. Although she had made it quite clear that she was attracted to me. She was a flirt at heart and a very attractive woman, but there was no mistaking her attraction towards me for mere teasing friendliness.

I fell asleep on the floor beside Dianna, and when I woke up she was gone. There was a note on the sofa which read, *"Hey Chris; thanks*

A Dream Within A Dream 15

for a lovely evening. Next time it's on me. See you in my dreams. Dianna. "She had left the door open for another dinner date, although this one had been spur of the moment. Or had it?

It was midnight when I woke up. The stereo was still playing jazz and the fire in the hearth had subsided to barely glowing embers. I poked them and placed some more wood on top. I wasn't sleepy, so I cleaned the kitchen and washed the dishes. While cleaning, I thought about her note, especially the last part of it. I wondered if she was making a joke, or if she was soliciting an audition for a demonstration. I dismissed such thoughts and went back to the living room. It wouldn't be appropriate to engage in such activities with a colleague.

The next day I went for an early run through Rock Creek Park. It was a crisp, cold morning, but I had dressed well for it. I enjoyed jogging in the park and swimming at the YMCA, because they were solitary sports which didn't require team effort. I could be left alone to my thoughts. After the run I went directly home for a shower, breakfast and a cafè mocha latte. I wanted to use the Christmas gift I got for myself; a Geneva Gourmet Coffee Maker. It was an expensive machine I had been observing for the longest time, but it had just gone on sale for the holidays. I didn't particularly care for the season; it always made me depressed, but I did enjoy the sales. I also enjoyed the Christmas spirit: what it meant and what was brought with it. *'Good Will To Men'.*

After breakfast I was attempting to enjoy my cafè mocha latte when the telephone rang. I was an old fashioned guy who still had a home telephone. It was of the antique black stand up variety, with the horn-type listening device. I was a bit agitated when I answered, because I was looking forward to enjoying my cup of coffee in peace.

"Hello," I answered in a perturbed voice.

"I'm sorry for disturbing you, Chris," Dianna said, clearly having noted to the tension in my voice, "But did I lose my flash drive over there? I usually keep it on my keychain, but I couldn't find it this morning."

"I didn't see it, but I'll look for it," I replied.

"Ok, call me if you find it. And by the way, thanks again for a lovely evening."

"It was my pleasure," I replied. "I mean it; the next time it's my treat. We can either go out to eat or I can prepare dinner for us at my place," she said.

"Sure, thanks," I replied.

"So which will it be," she asked?

"Whatever you prefer," I replied.

"Oh, you're easy, huh? Ok; I'll cook dinner for us at my place. What are you doing for Christmas Eve?"

"Nothing special," I replied.

"Ok then, you can come over to my place and we'll have dinner together."

"Alright," I responded.

"I'll talk to you later," she said before hanging up the phone. Now I was certain she was interested in me. *I need to see if the Bureau has a fraternizing policy.*

I hung the telephone up and went back to enjoying my gourmet cup of coffee. I looked for her flash drive afterwards and discovered it between the cushions on the sofa. I called Dianna to notify her of my discovery. She inquired if I would be in later this afternoon, so she could pick it up. I informed her that I had a doctor's appointment at 2:00 pm. She asked if she could pick it up later in the evening, to which I agreed. My new doctor was Joaquinna D. Green, M.D. Dr. Banks felt it was time for me to move on and continue my therapy sessions with a fresher perspective, since I was in control of my dreams and doing well.

The real reason was of a more personal nature. He could no longer take the harassment from the police department and the media, when I was considered a prime suspect in the prostitute abduction case. I later vindicated myself and helped the police find the killer, but the damage had been done. I didn't blame him. He had a family with kids to consider.

A Dream Within A Dream

When Dr. Green took my case, she was well aware of the publicity and high profile that came with having me for a patient. Although I was proven innocent, or should I say proved my innocence, there were still people who had their doubts. This was before the FBI took an interest in me. Dr. Green was young and single, with a new practice. Her having a high profile patient like me would do wonders for her career and resume. The publicity wouldn't hurt either.

It was early when I arrived at Dr. Green's office. She was still with another patient. I waited in the sitting area and read through the National Geographic on her table. She had better magazines than any of the shrinks I had visited and played dream games with. There was Sports Illustrated, Car and Driver, Vogue, Gentlemen's Quarterly and Time, just to name a few. Even better, they were all up to date; how I abhorred reading a Sports Illustrated article about an event that had happened several months ago, like articles about the past Superbowl in June!

I had been hooked up to just about every CAT scanning device and REM machine out there. I'd been hypnotized and traumatized by their science, but I'd come out standing tall. My mother had wanted me to have a normal life, free of the nightmares and sleep walking. Without her concern and help I would have never met Dr. Banks, who assisted me greatly in controlling this ability of mine.

Dr. Green didn't need proof of my abilities. She was well briefed by Dr. Banks, a leader in his field, who also published several books and publications for medical journals. He was a highly recognized, award-winning doctor. He had taught Dr. Green at Harvard Medical School.

Dr. Green had two employees working in her office. There was a middle aged woman, who handled most of the general receptionist duties. She answered the telephone, greeted the patients, checked them in and did filing. The other employee was a muscular young man, who worked on the computer and kept the office in order. I believe he was there for security purposes as well. He was the reason why so many of the magazines were geared towards men. He looked like a former jock of some sort.

A young woman exited the Analysis Room (AR) with Dr. Green. She was in her early twenties and extremely thin; perhaps anorexic. I could see her clavicle bone clearly through the blouse she was wearing, and her facial bones protruded sharply, as though shaped with a chisel.

"...Continue with that and I'll see you again next week," Dr. Green said to the thin young lady as they approached the receptionist desk. She then turned her attention towards me with a smile.

"Hello, Christian. How are you?"

"I'm doing well, Dr. Green."

"That's excellent. You can go in; I'll be right with you."

She had a folder with the young lady's name on the label; Audrey Bynum. Dr. Green remained at the receptionist desk as I walked towards the AR. I had heightened my profiling and investigative skills after working with the police and the FBI, but even before then my vigilance was quick and accurate. I could walk into a room and describe everything I saw at a later date. It was a side effect of the dreamscaping. I learned how to pick apart and memorize visual scenes from my dreams, with the assistance of Dr. Banks.

Dr. Green's office was very comfortable, as most analysis rooms, except she didn't force her patients to lie on a couch or anything. I could walk around or do whatever I felt like at the moment. Her office looked like a living room. There were three leather recliner chairs and a plush leather sofa, all black, a coffee table in the center and lamp tables on each side of the sofa. She even had a flat screen television with a DVD player.

There were no clocks on the wall, or anywhere in her office. There was a huge window which she kept covered by automatic shades and curtains. The shades were designed to completely eliminate the daylight from outside. I had seen this before in the more expensive psychoanalysts' offices that I'd visited through my childhood.

She had two typical portraits on the wall; a rendition of Whistler's painting; 'The Nocturne in Black and Gold: The Falling Rockets and Van Gogh's 'Starry Night over the Rhone', which I found to be quite

A Dream Within A Dream 19

interesting. The theme of both of these paintings was dream states. The word Nocturne suggests a tranquil, dreamy mood. She also had a 1919 copy of 'The Interpretation of Dreams' by Freud in a glass case on the wall. It must have cost a fortune. It was clear Dr. Green, like Dr. Banks, had a particular interest in dreams.

She also had an expensive, black wooden desk in the corner of the room with Newton's Cradle which some call Pendulum Balls, on the desk. I always found this applied physics apparatus interesting. Dr. Green was not only smart, but had a very interesting mind of her own. She explained the Pendulum of Life with Newton's Cradle which was so insightful. I looked forward to our meetings; especially since the Bureau paid the bill. It was a stipulation of my agreement, which they had no problem in supplying.

Dr. Joaquinna Green was an African American woman, about 35 years of age, with long black hair which she wore pinned up in one of those modern, feminine hairstyles. She was a tall, about 5'10", with a curvy, athletic body. You could see that she worked out. If I was to describe a celebrity who looked similar to her, it would be the actress Paula Patton. Dr. Green was wearing a grey power suit with a pink blouse and black high heel shoes, which accented perfectly sculptured calves covered by smoke grey stockings.

She didn't wear jewelry; no necklace or watch. She used her cell phone to time sessions inconspicuously. She wasn't worried about going over the allotted time, but she was concerned about other patients waiting. I was usually scheduled for an hour. As I stated before, I was her star patient and she had an added interest in dreams. That's why Dr. Banks referred me to her. This was her specialty, just like his.

"So, how's everything with you, Christian?"

"Everything is well, Dr. Green."

"How's work?"

"Well, you know how that is. I'm induced into a dream trance and I live inside the dreams of psychopaths. No, I'm sorry; problematic individuals."

She smiled when I corrected myself. "And how are you coping? Are you still doing yoga and meditating?"

"Yes," I replied as I paced the room.

"What's bothering you today? You seem a little edgy," she said She could tell I had something on my mind. Usually I'd play with the Pendulum Balls while we talked.

"I did want to speak to you about one of my colleagues."

"Okay, tell me about it," she replied while sitting on the sofa with her legs crossed.

She had my folder next to her while the recorder captured the session. She was polite enough not to write while we were in session. She gave the clients her full attention. That's what she liked referring to us as, instead of patients. She wanted to eliminate the stigma which accompanied the use of the word patient.

We discussed my relationship with Dianna for the rest of my session. Dr. Green provided me with a lot of food for thought. She thought it was a good thing to have Dianna as a close friend and encouraged it, but stated that we both needed to really think long and hard about taking it further than just friends. She pointed out all of the ramifications of having a relationship with someone you work with. She gave the pros and cons, but as usual left the decision making up to me. After our session she gave me a Christmas gift. This I hadn't anticipated. She must've had given one to Ms. Bynum when I came inside the AR, or on some other occasion.

"Thank you, Doc, but I didn't get you anything."

"It's alright, Christian. The point of Christmas is to give without expecting to receive."

The Doc had a way of putting everything into perspective and making it seem better. I still felt a little guilty because I didn't buy her anything. Now I had to purchase two additional gifts; one for the Doc and one for Dianna. I couldn't show up for dinner empty-handed on Christmas Eve.

When I left the Doc's office in Bethesda, I went directly to the Mazza Gallery on Wisconsin Avenue to shop for gifts, but was over-

A Dream Within A Dream 21

whelmed by the mob of people who were there. It took time and effort to find parking, so I gave up. I could only imagine how crowded it was inside! I continued down Wisconsin Ave. and stopped in a jeweler's. I saw a nice pair of diamond studs that I purchased for Dianna, and a Moldova watch for the Doc since she didn't have one.

I had only purchased one gift for Christmas before, and that was for Talayah, my niece in Atlanta. She was in grade school and we had a special relationship, since I was her only uncle. I didn't have anyone else to purchase gifts for, so I spent a little over my budget. I always sent my mother and sister cash; they had just about everything they could ever want.

It was late in the day and I didn't really have the time to spend looking for gifts. I also couldn't bear the crowds. The Doc has some big medical text book term for the condition; she calls it enochlophobia. I'd never heard of the word until she presented it to me. All I know is that I don't like being around a lot of people.

While on the way home I received another call from Dianna. She wanted to know if she could come by to pick up the flash drive. I told her I would be home in twenty minutes. She said she'd see me in two hours, so I stopped in the music shop on Connecticut Avenue and picked up some sheet music, vinyl albums and some CD's. I was thinking about getting back into teaching music again, but private lessons.

When I arrived home I was tired from dealing with the traffic and shopping, so I put on some jazz and lay down on the sofa until Dianna arrived. I was contemplating my discussion with Dr. Green about Dianna and me. Then I picked up the cello and bow, and began to play. It always eased my mind and helped me to think. I would close my eyes while playing and just go to a special place without dreams or the outside world. It was my private place. After about 45 minutes of playing, the doorbell rang and my serenity was shattered. Dianna had arrived for her flash drive.

"Good evening, Dianna; come in."

"Good evening, Chris; please, don't stop playing because of me," she stated, smiling as she entered.

"I was just trying to relax a little," I replied.

"It sounded great! Take Five?" she inquired, correctly naming the piece I was playing.

"Yes," I responded.

"Can I hear more?" she asked.

"Sure," I stated and continued on the cello. I completed 'Take Five' and then went into my rendition of 'Summer Time', all on the cello. She was incredibly impressed, and smiling from ear to ear.

"I had no idea that you could play like that! I mean, your profile stated you taught music, but you can really play," Dianna said smiling with enthusiasm.

"Thanks Dianna. Do you play?"

"No; not at all, but I do love jazz."

"Excellent; that's something we have in common," I replied.

"We have more in common than you know," she replied with the most beautiful smile, still amazed. I returned the cello and bow to their designated place on my music wall and brought the flash drive to her.

"It seems you have the advantage on me. You read my file, but I haven't been privileged to see yours," I said.

"Yeah, I know; you have to be an agent to get that privilege, and even then it has to be approved. All consultants' files are open for review," she replied.

"I see," I said, smiling.

"So, are we still on for Christmas Eve, because I purchased everything for our dinner?" she asked.

"I'm looking forward to it."

"Good; then I'll talk to you later," she said and leaned in, kissing me on the cheek. We were proceeding slowly but surely, and I liked it. I walked her back to her vehicle, and said goodbye as she departed.

Chapter 3

Silent Night

It was finally Christmas Eve. I had been anxiously anticipating its arrival to have dinner with Dianna. She was the first woman who had shown interest without me implanting or suggesting interest through dreamscape. I was totally hyped about seeing her again!

It was a perfect winter's evening. There was an expected chance of snow in the forecast, and all was well. I telephoned my mother and wished her a Merry Christmas. She was living in Atlanta with my sister and her family. My sister and I didn't get along very well. We'd had a falling out several years ago, and the relationship never seemed to repair itself. I spoke to my niece and wished them all a Merry Christmas. Usually families are very busy on Christmas Day, opening gifts and visiting each other, so I decided to get it out of the way in advance.

I had already dropped off Dr. Green's gift yesterday and had Dianna's wrapped and ready to be presented. I also purchased an expensive bottle of wine and placed a bow on top of it, just for dinner. I called Dianna later in the afternoon to check on her, and to see if she needed anything for the evening.

"Good afternoon, Dianna. How are you?"

"Hello Chris. I'm fine, how are you?"

24   *Silent Night*

"I'm doing well. I was calling to see if you needed me to bring anything besides the wine this evening."

"No, I have everything we need, except I neglected to inquire about what type of foods you eat? Are you allergic to anything, or are there any foods you don't eat," she asked.

"Yes. I'm sorry, but I don't eat pork."

"Well, that's good to know. I don't eat pork either. I told you we have a lot in common," she replied.

"What time should I arrive?" I inquired.

"Is 5:00pm good for you?" she responded.

"Yes, that sounds great."

"Ok, then I'll see you then," she said and hung up the telephone.

I didn't have a Christmas tree or any decorations around the house, just a wrapped gift from Dr. Green and six Christmas cards. I received cards from my mother, my sister's family, Dr. Banks and family, Dr. Green, Steve Weiss and one from the Guitar Store on Connecticut Avenue. I spent a lot of money in that store and was on their mailing list.

I lived modestly on my consultant's salary. The only expensive things that I owned were my instruments, which also doubled as decorations. I drove a black, two door, 1964 Volvo P1800. I called it a classic, but most would just refer to it as junk. She was worth about $4,000.00 but purred like a kitten, and the interior was perfect. Up until now it all had sufficed me without a problem. My FBI salary with benefits and perks was excellent, but I wondered if I had gone overboard spending for Christmas. I wondered if the gifts I purchased for Dianna and Dr. Green were too much, and if the ladies would take offense at them. I didn't want them to read something else into those presents. Or was that just my paranoia running away with me again?

I arrived at Dianna's house on time at 5:00pm. She lived in Vienna, Virginia. It was nice out here in the suburbs. She lived in a brick three story town house with a parking garage. She had a Christmas Wreath on the door and on the doormat was a picture of the Magi's following the Star of Bethlehem. I rang the bell and she came to the door in

Silent Night 25

the most stunning attire. She was wearing a Christmas red velvet dress with black high heeled shoes. The garment was made to hug her body and show off her curves. It rested far above her knees and displayed her voluptuous thighs and sexy legs. This outfit screamed sexy! I was in awe and couldn't stop staring at her.

"Wow," I exclaimed as soon as she opened the door. She flashed a giant smile and attempted not to blush, but I guess I gave her the greeting and response she was looking for.

"Thank you very much. You look nice as well. Please come in," she replied.

"This is for you. Merry Christmas!" I said, handing her the bottle of Dom Perignon with a bow and her wrapped Christmas gift.

"Thank you; I have a gift for you under the tree as well, but we have plenty of time for that," she stated and kissed me on the cheek. Apparently she has a full itinerary for the evening.

"Dinner is ready and warming in the kitchen, but I wanted to ask if you would accompany me to church this evening before dinner?" She surprised me with that one.

"I haven't been to church in years. I'm Catholic and believe in the Trinity, but there has been some distance between me and the church lately," I replied.

"It's never too late. I'm a Catholic school girl. So, will you escort me to church this evening, Mr. Sands?" Her eyes twinkled as she flirted with me.

"It would be my pleasure, Ms. Samboro." I played along, feeling my face spread into a teasing grin.

"Thank you very much," she replied with a smile, and grabbed her coat.

We drove my vehicle to her local church, which was only 20 minutes away. It wasn't as crowded as I thought it would have been. They had a special service for the coming of Christ. It was great!

"I enjoyed that immensely," I stated to her on the way back to her house.

"I'm glad you enjoyed yourself, so did I."

We savored a lovely dinner together back at her place. She prepared an exquisite five course meal. She had Christmas jazz songs playing on the satellite stereo station. We opened a bottle of champagne in front of her wood burning fireplace and talked.

"I must inquire, Dianna; why aren't you spending Christmas with your family?"

"Well, they decided to go back to Sicily for Christmas and I preferred to stay here. I wanted to get to know you better. Is that alright with you?"

"Absolutely, and thank you. Everything has been wonderful," I replied, and then she kissed me. I reciprocated.

Later, she read the works of some of her favorite poets for me. We opened our gifts after midnight and began kissing again. We started making out in the living room and ended up in the bedroom. We remained there for the rest of the night. Then, around 03:00 AM while we were asleep and snuggled in bed together, our cell phones rang. That ended our silent night. It was a message alert from the FBI. The entire task force would be alerted when it was time to come in for an assignment. The timing couldn't be any worse.

We got up at the same time to check our phones, which wasn't necessary. The message was the same on all phones. It simply stated, *Please respond to the Task Force conference room today, December 25 at 0900. Wheels up at 1100.* The message alert never went into details about the emergency or assignments. We always packed clothing for a week's stay at the destination. This didn't give Dianna and me much time together this Christmas, but at least we had been able to spend a wonderful evening and night together.

"Good morning, bright eyes. How are you," Dianna inquired with a smile? She replaced the cell phone on the nightstand and made her way to my side of the bed.

"I was doing excellent until the phone rang," I responded.

"Well, let's see if I can make it better," she said as she moved herself on top of me in the bed and began kissing me.

Silent Night   27

I still found it hard to believe she was here with me. She was just as gorgeous waking up in the morning as she was later in the day. She didn't wear much make up, perhaps a little gloss lipstick but that was about it. She had natural beauty and didn't need to fix herself up with makeup. I guess that's why she looked perfect even after waking up.

"So, who did you get those beautiful cat eyes from?" she inquired.

"My mother has green eyes," I stated.

"Do you look like her or your dad?"

"It depends on who you speak to. What about you?" I asked.

"I favor my father," she replied.

We continued making love for about an hour, and that was cutting it close. I still had to drive back to Foggy Bottom and get my luggage for the trip. Most of us kept a suitcase packed and ready, because we never knew when that phone call was going to come or how much time we had to respond. The good thing was that it was Christmas morning and there shouldn't be any traffic on the road. Only the lonely and the weary would be traveling this early a major holiday.

When she got out of bed, all I could do was watch and admire the shape of her. The curvature of her shape was exquisite! It was like watching the Venus de Milo. She was perfect from head to toe. I got excited all over again just watching her walk from the bed, and she knew it. She turned around smiling, knowing I was watching, and asked, "Well, are you coming or what?"

She wanted me to join her in the shower. It did make sense, since we were in a rush. We could save a lot of time showering together. Then I thought to myself, *You truly are a nerd to even consider thinking about saving time, when all she wants to do is continue making love in the shower.*

I finally departed her place at 0600 hours with a humongous smile on my face. Since there was no traffic, I could make it back to D.C. in 30-40 minutes by bending the speed limit a bit... or maybe more than a bit, I hoped. I could use my credentials if stopped by law enforcement for speeding, but I could only go so fast in the old Volvo

28   *Silent Night*

I was driving. There was no traffic, as I had suspected, but it had snowed last night and the roads were slippery. I made it back to Foggy Bottom an hour later. I grabbed one of my recently purchased suits from the closet, and threw it on. I had purchased three suits since I became a consultant for the FBI. I really wasn't a suit wearing kind of a guy. I picked up my prepared luggage and departed.

The FBI instructed us on what to pack while on assignment. Our luggage contained the standard items: one black or blue suit with a tie, oxford shirt and oxford dress shoes which we wore during departure. Two suit slacks to coordinate with blazers, two pair of khaki pants, three oxford button-down shirts, two FBI polo shirts, one FBI sweat suit, a pair of casual shoes, a pair of sneakers and unspecified underwear and toiletries.

We purchased whatever additional items we needed while on assignment. We all had a government credit card to utilize while on in the field, which was restricted to compensation for per diem and expenses. I grabbed two packets of strawberry Pop Tarts and a bottle of Starbucks Cappuccino from the fridge, and departed for Quantico, VA. I arrived in Quantico with little time to spare. Everyone else was already in the conference room, waiting for the briefing.

"Merry Christmas, everyone," I said as I entered, and everyone responded in kind. There was coffee and Danishes in the conference room which everyone was partaking in. I smiled at Dianna and she smiled back.

"Hello," I said, grinning as I sat across from her at the conference table. She was looking as pretty as when I left her earlier that morning.

I sat down next to Amber. Paul, who was usually Amber's partner, sat on the other side of her, and Max was next to Dianna across the table. We were waiting for Steve to arrive, so we exchanged chit-chat.

"So, what did you get for Christmas, Amber?" Max inquired.

"What Christmas? We scaled down this year and just made it more a religious gathering, like it was supposed to be."

Silent Night   29

"Wow, Mrs. Scrooge; you didn't get anything for your son?" Max demanded.

"You asked me what I got for Christmas. He made out like a bandit," she replied.

Amber was extremely funny and cynical. A recent divorcée with one son, she had moved her mother in to live with her. Paul was on his cell phone, texting his wife and kids. Paul was from a big family and had 5 little ones of his own. Max was a bachelor with a lot of female friends. Most of Max's family lived in New Orleans, so he probably spent Christmas the same way Dianna and I did.

Just as I ran out of people to entertain myself by regarding, Steve finally entered the conference area.

"Good morning everyone, and happy holidays. I'm sorry to call you in on Christmas morning, but duty calls. The bad guys never take a break, so neither do we," Steve stated as he walked to the front of the room and began briefing us on our new case.

"Thus far, the local Bureau has had several abductions and no bodies. There is no certainty whether the victims are still alive, but we can hope for the best. The locals are calling the subject the Night Stalker," Steve stated before being interrupted.

"You mean like the old television show?" Paul inquired.

"Yes; they are all women, and they are believed to have been abducted at night. We believe the subject is counting down in sequence, in reference to the dates he's abducting the victims," Steve replied.

"The first abductee was taken on September 5, the second on October 5, the third on November 3 and the fourth on December 3. The pattern is 5, 5, 3, 3 and the locals believe the next projected date will be January 1 and then February 1, if we can't stop him. We're not certain why he or she is counting down this way or what the sub is counting down towards. This is all we have to go on for now. We will work towards constructing our own profiles once we land in New Mexico. Any questions thus far?" Steve inquired, but no one responded, so he continued.

"Paul and Amber will look into the victims' backgrounds and scrutinize the local police department's files. Check to see if we can find any connections that might have been missed. Max and I will visit the victims' families, friends and persons who were in contact with them. Chris and Dianna will visit the victims' residences and places of work, so Chris can do his thing," he said, referring to when I conduct dreamscape.

I hadn't been able to keep my eyes off Dianna during the entire meeting. At first I thought I was making her uncomfortable, until I saw her smile and fling her hair. I think Amber and Steve noticed it, but then again, I was in a room filled with expert profilers. It wouldn't be long before they discovered our secret.

"We have six days before the first of the year, which is the next projected abduction date. At the latest, we have until nightfall on the 1st. Are there any preliminary questions?" Steve inquired.

Everyone responded, "No, sir."

"OK then, I'll meet you at the shuttle bus at 10:30," he stated in closing.

The briefing was over around 10:05. I went to my office to check my email until it was time to depart. I was sitting on the side of my desk, reading some correspondence, when Dianna walked in. She closed and locked the door behind her. She was smiling and shaking her finger slowly back and forth as if to scold me for being a naughty boy, but she was grinning at the same time.

"Look, mister; we have to set some ground rules while at the office. You can't be looking at me that way around the others."

"Looking what way?" I inquired, admiring her beauty and smiling.

"The same one you have on your face now," she replied.

Then she walked over to me. She slowly and sensually ran her hands up my legs and wedged herself between my thighs while I was still seated at the desk. Then she kissed me on the mouth.

"Oh, that look," I responded after the kiss, then kissed her in return and replied, "You were saying something about the rules of the office?"

Silent Night   31

"Never mind," she stated as we continued to kiss.

"Wow," she exclaimed, and then added, "Merry Christmas Chris."

"Merry Christmas, Dianna."

"You left your gift at my house this morning," she said.

"I thought you were my gift," I replied.

"Now, I can really get used to that. You keep on saying the right things and you won't be able to get rid of me," she said while looking me in the eyes.

"Did you enjoy my gift to you?" I inquired.

"I thought we would open them together when we return," she replied.

"Sounds like a good idea," I retorted.

Dianna walked back to the door at that point, unlocked it and said, "I'll make sure to put on a red bow the next time, and have you unwrap me."

I loved seeing her walking away as much as I enjoyed seeing her coming. She had the sexiest walk, or maybe she just had a very sexy ass; either way, I loved it.

I went to the computer to check my emails before departing, and discovered Dr. Green had sent me an email thanking me for the gift, but stating that she couldn't accept it. I knew I was going to hear some squabble over the gift, but we'd talk more about it when I returned. I didn't get a chance to open the gift she gave me, but I was curious to see what it was. Dianna's surprising interest and visits had engulfed me at the time. I sent Dr. Green an email, thanking her for the gift, but didn't respond to the aforementioned gift returning.

Chapter 4

The CROSSROADS

Albuquerque is considered the Crossroads of New Mexico. Most of the
business going to and from New Mexico goes through Albuquerque.
It is situated in the center of the state and is actually at the intersection of Highway 25 and Highway 40; its two major interstates.
Albuquerque has been considered the Crossroads in mystic legends
since the days of route 66, which ran through the city. Even Bugs
Bunny references Albuquerque as the crossroads in the cartoons. It
has always been a place of mystery and the unknown, from UFO
sightings and landings to witchcraft and mysticism. The Crossroads
is the place where the mystical and the underworld meet or perhaps
intersect the world in which we live in. It is the place where legend
says you can cross over into another dimension, and creatures from
there can come in for a visit.

We landed at the Albuquerque International Sunport, Bernalillo
County, New Mexico, a little after 1300 hours Mountain Time. It
took us 4 hours of flight time to reach Albuquerque, but due to
Mountain Time being two hours behind Eastern Standard Time, we
actually gained two hours for the investigation. Every minute was
crucial, since we were on a countdown until what was expected to
be the next abduction.

The weather in Albuquerque was sunny, with a mild temperature
of 64 degrees. This was a gladly expected warm welcome compared

The Crossroads   33

to the bitter cold and snowy winter of D.C. that we had left behind.
Albuquerque is the epicenter of technology and business for the state
of New Mexico. It is located in the center of the state, nestled within
the Rio Grande Valley amongst the Sandia Mountain Range, with
the Rio Grande running through the city. It is the largest city in
New Mexico.

We rented three Chevrolet Transverse SUV's at the airport for the
team pairings. After we checked into the Hilton Garden Inn Hotel, we
immediately went to work. Our first stop was to make contact with
the FBI Headquarters in downtown Albuquerque. It was located at
4200 Luecking Park Ave NE, Albuquerque, NM 87107. This was only
to acquaint ourselves with the powers that be, and hierarchy for the
state's investigative branch. Then it was off to the Satellite Office in
Bernalillo at 505 South Main Street. That is where we would set up
shop and establish a functioning work area within their offices.

When we arrived at the Bernalillo Satellite Office, it was like most
of our receptions. There were mixed emotions about our arrival and
our taking over the cases. The FBI is a very competitive organization.
We all work towards a common goal, but that doesn't mean it's
devoid of egos and temperament. It all came down to this simple
premise; we were the Special Task Force Unit from Washington, D.C.,
flying in on a private jet to fix the problems that the local bureau
couldn't. This wasn't well received by many offices and jurisdictions,
but some welcomed the assistance and looked forward to our arrival.

The Special Agent in Charge of the Bernalillo office was Agent
Alonzo Ortega. He was a native of New Mexico and filled with the
knowledge and history of the State and its surroundings. He had been
the lead for 7 years over the satellite office, and was a very good agent.
The decision to send us wasn't of his volition, or their main office in
Albuquerque. The decision came down from D.C., where most of the
major decisions are made. The satellite office wasn't that big, as to be
expected, but they already had a conference area with several desk
and other office items waiting for us. Like the other jurisdictions,

they were going to assist and make us as comfortable as possible, but it didn't mean they liked it. Or us.

Ortega appeared to be a pleasant man. He welcomed us and showed us around the facility. They had a small building with two floors and several vehicles at their disposal. They were mostly 4X4 vehicles, due to the desert and mountain terrain which surrounded Albuquerque. He wore a suit and tie with cowboy boots. There were only fifteen agents at this location, including the Special Agent in Charge, and they had to cover 8 counties. That was 1.875 agents per county. They were grossly undermanned in a border state, with bandits and smugglers at the gates.

You would think they would have loved the assistance, but it was just like the other jurisdictions. Most of the agents were polite, but not over-eagerly friendly. They wouldn't be inviting us to lunch or dinner anytime soon, but we were used to it by now. I guess that's why the team is so close. The rest of the Bernalillo agents wore regular shirts, unbuttoned, or polo shirts with casual or khaki pants. They wore an assortment of boots from cowboy to Timberland. They weren't dressed in the bureaucratic garb as seen at the main field offices of major cities. I felt right at home.

"So, Agent Weiss, all the records and files are there on the conference table, and if you require any additional support or assistance from us, please let me know," Agent Ortega stated.

"Yes, we're going to need at least two agents to escort us in the field," Agent Weiss informed him.

"OK, I'll give you Agent Gracie Mullins and Agent Trace Burkhart," Ortega replied.

"Thank you very much, Agent Ortega. That will be all for now," Weiss stated, then turned his attention towards us. He was always thinking steps ahead.

"OK guys, you have your assignments. Now let's get to work," Weiss commanded in a medium soft tone.

Agent Gracie Mullins was assigned to escort Dianna and me. She didn't appear to be perturbed about us taking over the case. In fact,

The Crossroads   35

she was enthused to be working with us. She had only been with the
Bernalillo Office for a year, and still felt allied with D.C.

"Merry Christmas I've heard a lot of good things about what you
guys are doing with the Task Force. A couple of friends I graduated
Quantico with are still in D.C., and I asked them about you. They
said your SAC is a genius, and that you have a flawless record for
solving cases. They also said that your department utilizes uncon-
ventional methods to solve the unsolvable. I was hoping I would get
this chance to work with you," Agent Mullins said with a smile that
could light up a room.

Dianna looked at me, and started smiling. Agent Mullins was displaying all the attributes and characteristics of a rookie astonished
by the hype of our reputation. We had seen it all before, but it never
affected us or changed or demeanor towards the job. We didn't get
into all the awards and accolades that were attributed to doing a good
job. They were only distractions, and our team looked beyond it.

"Thank you, Agent Mullins. It's a pleasure working with you as
well. Can you take us to the latest victim's residence?" I inquired.

"Sure thing," she replied.

On the way to the home, Agent Mullins briefed us on her while
in the car. Everything she stated was already in the reports that we
read, but she was trying to be helpful.

"Melissa Sykes was the latest of the four abductees that we know
of. She is a waitress on the evening shift at The Diners. She got off at
2300 Mountain Time and hasn't been seen since. They interviewed
her relations and coworkers, but everyone had an alibi, and no motive
for killing her. Her car was parked at the Diner for days. There were
no signs of a struggle, and no one saw anything at the Diner. They
didn't have any outside cameras either," Agent Mullins said.

"We'll go there after we visit her home," Dianna replied.

Task force protocol dictated we begin at the end. We always started
with the latest victim and worked our way backward. This was done
for several reasons. The first reason was that the last crime or crime

scene was the freshest and most memorable for witnesses, and therefore best for collecting evidence and clues.

The second reason, is that in most serial cases, the earlier victims' chances of survival were minimal compared to the latest. Serial killers were work towards a goal, and each crime represents a sort of rehearsal which was repeated in hopes of achieving the perfect effect. The killer strived to over repeated attempts to realize his goal, and correct wrongs. Serial killers were usually driven by the needs for sex and control, with a consistent evolving signature present in each murder. The further back in time the crime took place, the less likelihood there was of finding survivors. The reason why this subject must have been abducting others was that the previous victims had expired, or were of no more use.

The third reason for working backwards in time was that in the case of serial murders, if you could solve the latest abduction and stop the killings, the murderer would usually lead authorities to information on the other victims. Sometimes they liked to savor their killings and keep it interesting by giving out the details sparingly.

The fourth reason was because of my special abilities. I couldn't use dreamscape with the dead, I could only see through the eyes of the living. I couldn't see through the eyes of someone who had passed away. There were psychics and mediums who did communicate with the dead, but that wasn't a part of my gift.

Serial killers' motives fall under four categories; Visionary, Mission Oriented, Hedonistic and Power/ Control. The visionary killer believes he is someone else when he commits murder. He believes he is driven by a supernatural force; the Devil or God. The Missionary killer is on a mission. He believes he is correcting the wrongs of the world by getting rid of unwanted or deviant persons. The Hedonistic killer is a thrill seeker and gets an endorphin rush from killing. He receives pleasure from killing and suffering. This type of killer has three subcategories; thrill driven, lust (sexual) and comfort (profit/gains). The Power/ Control killer wants to impose his will over the victims and control them.

The Crossroads
37

We drove for several miles until we came to Melissa Sykes' home. She lived in a one bedroom garden apartment. The resident manager let us into the apartment, and then departed. There was still police tape on the door, and a cat waiting outside. It ran in once the door was opened. The local authorities hadn't bothered to take Melissa's calico to a shelter.

We began looking through the apartment. Although it had already been searched thoroughly by the local officers, I had to get a feel of the place. I had to make a connection between myself and Melissa. I had to touch her personal items and get a feel for her; the more personal the better. I don't mean rummaging through her underwear drawers, but items like letters she wrote, a diary or anything of that nature.

Agent Mullins followed Dianna around when we first began our sweep of the area. I attempted to emulate Melissa's actions in the apartment by touching everything in sight. I went to the kitchen where the cat was waiting by its bowl, attempting to draw my attention towards it by meowing. It was hungry and probably hadn't eaten since its master's abduction.

I touched everything as I made my way into the room. I opened the cabinets, looking for the cat food. I searched the counter drawers for a can opener to open the cat food, and then fed the hungry calico. Gracie entered the kitchen at that point, and discovered what I was doing.

"Aww, that's so sweet," she stated, smiling at me. She apparently had a soft spot for animals. I wasn't a cat person, but I knew this would be something that Melissa would do every day. This would be an excellent connection.

Afterwards, I made my way around the apartment, touching everything in sight. I opened the refrigerator. Although the electricity was still on, the food was spoiled and moldy. It had been several weeks since Melissa's disappearance on December 3rd. I opened and closed the microwave oven, turned on the faucet to the sink, and washed my hands.

Melissa was very neat and clean. There were no dirty dishes in the basin. I opened the dishwasher and the few bowls and cups in there were garbage free. This was something I practiced as well. I rinsed all the garbage off the dishes before placing them into the dishwasher. This was a way of protecting your dishwasher from breeding or harboring bacteria and mold odors from rotten and spoiled food. She also utilized the garbage disposal, as I did, instead of the trash can for the disposal of all food items, because neither the trash nor the house smelled like garbage. There was the odor of the kitty litter that needed changing, but even that was tolerable.

I departed the kitchen area and met Dianna in the bedroom, Gracie on my heels. She didn't ask a lot of questions during our sweep, only pertinent and integral ones pertaining to the case. She must have been an excellent student in school.

"They didn't leave much correspondence. There are no bills, letters or magazines. There are some clothes left behind in the drawers and in the walk-in closet," Dianna said.

"We have all those items back at the Office," Agent Mullins replied as I looked around the bedroom and touched everything, as I did in the other areas.

"I think I have everything I need," I informed Dianna and Gracie, then went to the kitchen, picked up the calico and departed.

We were going to drop the cat off at the shelter, but Gracie agreed to care for her, so it traveled with us to the diner where Melissa worked. I kept it in my lap, petting it to deepen my connection with Melissa for dreamscaping while in the vehicle. *I wonder how long it will take Agent Mullins to enquire about my special skill set.*

Not long, as it turned out. She spoke before we left the car. "So, what exactly do you do? I was informed that the teams in your department each have consultants with special abilities. At first I thought it was 'the brain', but it's you, isn't it?" she asked me.

"Who is 'the brain'?" I retorted in a sarcastic voice filled with laughter.

"Oh, you guys don't know your nicknames?" Gracie asked, giggling.

The Crossroads

"Yeah, I've heard it. It's what they call Steven," Dianna interjected with a discontented frown. Then she further stated, "They have names for all of us. It helps them sleep a little better and accept their own shortcomings, by calling us names and labeling us."

"I'm sorry if I offended you," Agent Mullins replied, her eyes cast down into her lap. "I didn't mean any harm. It was just something I heard when I called up Quantico. No one down here refers to you that way. In fact, we're so overwhelmed we hardly even have time to read our bulletins, let alone gossip. Hey, I get it! You guys are the best at what you do, so there's going to be some jealous people, but we are glad you're here."

That ended the conversation and the inquiry into my special ability. *I think Dianna; no, I know Dianna intentionally distracted Agent Mullins with her response to get off the subject.* She was rescuing me from attempting to explain myself, and it worked. My team was extremely intelligent and good at what they did. Dianna was excellent T getting into people's heads, just like the other team members.

There were limited staff at the diner when we arrived, due to it being Christmas Day. We were lucky they were open at all. I did pretty much the same thing I did at the apartment. I inquired about the last section Melissa worked and sat at one of the tables. I ordered some coffee while I was at the table, and inquired if Dianna or Gracie wanted anything. They both declined to order anything. Gracie was completely engaged with what we were doing. While Dianna was questioning the staff one by one, I just sat in a booth enjoying a cup of coffee, or so it would seem.

Gracie remained with Dianna during the questioning, but continuously kept looking my way to see what I was doing. I was examining the surroundings and the staff. I wanted to see what a customer would be doing while Melissa was waiting on them. I looked outside to see what a customer would see from Melissa's section, and then walked outside to see what I could see looking into her section. I also walked the parking lot area. Gracie watched me the whole time; when I got up and walked outside, as well as when I returned. She was completely baffled and looked about to burst with questions about me. Dianna ignored my odd-seeming behavior; she'd seen me do this countless times.

When I returned inside, I spoke to the chef and the rest of the staff, wanting to get a feel for who liked and disliked Melissa. Understanding the emotions of others was critical information I could utilize this during dreamscape. Melissa seemed to be loved by all the staff and they were worried about her. At this point I had officially become Agent Mullins' freak show main attraction. Although I didn't do anything weird or out of place, it just wasn't the normal questioning and interviewing techniques that she was accustomed to seeing.

"Did you find out anything outside?" Agent Mullins inquired?

"No, not really," I responded. I wasn't going to discuss any findings with her until we were back with the team. If Steven wanted to invite her to the brief, she was welcome to participate in whatever I had to say.

On the way back to the office, I sat in the back of the vehicle while Gracie and Dianna claimed the front. The whole time we were driving back, Gracie kept staring at me through the rear view mirror. It was really starting to freak me out and make me feel uncomfortable. I closed my eyes in hopes of viewing something in my sleep, but I couldn't relax knowing that her eyes were glued to me. I smiled and made polite conversation about the past time in Bernalillo. She also found that to be interesting, since this case was on a countdown. I guess I appeared to be inappropriately nonchalant.

We compared our findings as a team back at the office. Steven had already constructed an abductees' board and added what the team presented to him. The board contained pictures and short bios under them, and the locations of abductions. We examined all our findings with a fine toothed comb. We went over scenarios in comparison with the ViCAP Database. We worked until 0400 in the morning, which was actually 0600 hours Eastern Standard Time.

The Crossroads   41

"Let's get some sleep, people, and be back here at 1100," Steve stated and adjourned the meeting. I remained behind with Steve and examined the board further.

"Did you get much to go on?" he inquired.

"Yeah, let's be honest here. If she's still alive, it's been a long time," I replied. "I wouldn't look for a happy ending."

"You know we don't think in the negative. I need you, even more than the other team members, to go home and get some sleep," he stated.

I dipped my chin in acknowledgment and turned to leave just as Dianna walked towards the conference room entrance.

"Need a ride?" she inquired.

"Yes, thank you," I replied.

"What about you, Steve? You riding with us?" she asked.

"No, I'm fine. I'm using one of their vehicles. See you at 1100."

We departed, leaving Steven in the conference gathering his sport coat and briefcase.

"You know he knows," I stated to Dianna, playing with her as we departed down the hallway. In return she bumped me with her hip and smiled.

We drove back to the Hilton Gardens Inn, kissed each other goodnight and retired to our separate suites. There was no time for romance. It was strictly business while in the field. Besides, while Dianna and the others slept, I'll be traveling in the dream realm. I did my usual routine. I took a sleeping pill to assist me in dozing off and staying there. Then I put on my earphones. I was listening to the sound of the ocean waves. I couldn't listen to music because I always found myself counting along with the beat or playing the chords. It was one of the habits of being a musician.

I hadn't experience anything last night. While I received enough external stimuli from Melissa, but I couldn't make a connection. Usually when I couldn't make a connection, 99 percent of the victims are discovered dead. I always woke up depressed after such nights. The sleeping pills exacerbated this condition. They always left me down, even if I didn't have any dream activity. Although we knew the outcome, we still had to catch the killer. I always wondered if I was too late receiving the stimuli.

Dianna was the first to knock on my door in the morning.

"Good morning, Chris. How are you?" She could already tell by my demeanor that I wasn't in the best of moods. "Bad news?" she further inquired.

"I couldn't make a connection with her," I simply stated without going any further.

I used to attempt to make up excuses for why I couldn't make a connection, but it was no use at this point. The team already knew what that meant. My track record was flawless.

Dianna attempted to deflect my mind from thinking about Melissa and being depressed. "Did you eat breakfast yet," she asked?

"No."

"Then let's grab some here at the hotel before we leave. I'm famished," she stated, then kissed me on the cheek and said, "We'll catch him and find her."

She didn't mean *find her alive*. We were tasked with catching the perps (perpetrators) and finding the victims, dead or alive. It made me think of the days of the Old West when the Sheriffs were ordered to bring in the suspect dead or alive.

Dianna always knew the right things to say and do when it came to cheering me up. Her empathy also made her an expert at getting inside someone's head. She was our lead interrogator. She just had a knack for it. I still wasn't sure if she was assigned to be my handler or my partner. It was clear we had crossed the lines when it came to partnership. We were more than just professional partners, but was that also her assignment? I was paranoid when it came to the government and law enforcement, even though I worked for them.

I quickly dismissed this conspiracy notion as a side effect of the sleeping pills. I was depressed and feeling sorry for myself. By the time we completed breakfast, Dianna had lifted my spirits with dis-

The Crossroads   43

cussions about us and our Christmas evening spent together. We also
discussed future plans outside of work.

Agent Gracie Mullins was the first to meet us at the door of the
FBI Office. She was dressed in a blue pantsuit, white blouse and blue
high heels. She had dressed up more than at our previous meeting
when she had on dark blue BDU's and boots. The dress code was
casual at most of the satellite offices. She had dressed up because she
saw us with suits on yesterday, but today we wore casual clothes. We
always wore suits while traveling, but on the ground we preferred
comfort to formality

Gracie was young, ambitious and attractive. She didn't seem to be
thrown by our attire, but it was obvious that she was attempting to
impress us. Steven invited her and Agent Trace Burkhart to join us
for the briefings, since they would be working with us. Steven had
dressed down as well. We didn't have to be advised on what to wear.
We just adapted to the environment we were currently investigating.

The team was assembled in the conference room area. The rest of
the ViCAP team was anxious to see me and get an update on the
missing person. As I entered the room, they could see it on my face.
They knew me well and were some of the best profilers in the FBI. I
didn't have to say it, but I expressed to everyone my unfortunate news
on Melissa Sykes. It was like delivering a death sentence. The team
took it in stride and moved on, but I still felt upset that I couldn't
give them something more to go on. Steve immediately went to the
front of the room and began his brief, without another word spoken
on the subject of my dreams.

"OK, people, here's what we have thus far. We have four females,
all in their twenties. They are of different races and different backgrounds. We don't have any bodies or traces of them. There was no
evidence of a struggle. They were allegedly abducted a night. So tell
me, what's the signature?" Steven inquired.

Then the rest of the team joined in, adding to the profile.

"The subject is a visionary male, a predator who abducts at night;
pretty young females in their twenties. He knows the area very well,

therefore he has lived in this area for an extended period of time. He knows how to avoid cameras and densely populated areas. He has to store the victims, so he's a loner who lives in a secluded place with room to house the women, or he has an unknown disposal site. If he is a collector, then he has abandonment issues or issues with being alone," the team called out in sequence.

"So let's enlarge our parameters today to include the rest of the women, and attempt to discover some sort of link between them. Max and I will continue with victimology. Paul and Amber will look into the local criminals that may fit the profile, and Dianna and Chris will work on the current abductee in line. The clock is ticking, folks," Steve stated as we paired off again.

Gracie Mullins bounced our way, eager to get started. "Here are the magazines and correspondence from Melissa Sykes' apartment, Christian. Do you still need them?" she inquired.

"Sure, I'll look over them later. Let's head to Felicia Holmes' residence and then to her place of work, but first stop off at the diner where Melissa worked, so I can get a cup of coffee," I instructed Gracie.

"It's in the opposite direction and there are better places to get coffee," she replied.

"I know, but I like theirs," I responded. Now she understood that I wasn't going for the coffee. Dianna had known immediately, and didn't question it. She knew I was trying to avoid the inevitable, the realization that Melissa was dead.

I sat in the diner and drank my cup of coffee while opening Melissa's People Magazine. Gracie and Dianna joined me in a cup of java this morning. Afterwards we went to Ms. Holmes' residence. She lived with her boyfriend, who was currently at work, but the landlord allowed us access to the residence while he was away.

They lived on the second floor of a three story apartment building. They didn't have any pets. The place appeared to be unkempt. He was probably still emotionally drained and disorganized due to Felicia's disappearance. Dianna left her card near the door to inform

The Crossroads   45

him that we had been there, and we allowed the landlord to remain as well. I did my usual of touching everything in the place as I made my rounds. The landlord watched me but seemed unsurprised by my unusual actions. Clearly he was not an overly curious man.

We visited the outpatient clinic, where Felicia worked as a LVN. It was a small clinic and all the staff were very close. They were very upset and emotional about her disappearance. Some of the women even cried as they were questioned. Felicia had been missing since November 3, which was 53 days ago. I didn't spend a lot of time at the clinic, because we needed to visit the other missing women's residences and places of employment.

We were finished around 1900 hours and rendezvoused with the other team members at 1935. There were several suspects in the area who had come close to matching the profile. We continued our profiling a composite of the subject until 0100 hours the next morning, and called it quits for the day. We retired earlier than yesterday, and everyone felt good about the progress we were making. I also had a big night in front of me, as I had several women to reach out and attempt to make a connection with.

Another night had passed and I hadn't received anything on my radar. I felt like I was letting the team down. I was usually the main contributor on these killer hunts, but now I wasn't registering anything. Once again, Dianna knocked at my door, expecting something. I opened for her, with only my lounge pants on.

"Another rough night, huh?" she inquired.

"I didn't get anything Di," I replied, and in my frustration, just blurted out, "These women are dead!"

She remained silent, pausing for about a minute, and then retorted, "We still have a killer to catch out there, remember?"

"Yeah, let me shower real quick and I'll be right with you."

While I was in the shower, she took off her clothes and joined me. I was frustrated, but always in the mood for her. The warmth of her naked body pressed intimately to mine chased some of the icy grief from my heart.

Several days went by and we still weren't any closer to finding the assailant. We had questioned numerous felons who fit the profile, but with no results. We even questioned citizens with no priors, but to no avail. The entire Albuquerque office was on board now, assisting in the investigation with us. Catching this subject was the number one priority of the Residence Office. Our teams remained the same size, but we covered a lot more ground with the others on board.

At midnight on New Year's Eve there had been no breaks in the case. Dianna and I snuck away for a midnight countdown and a kiss. There was no champagne or celebrating around here. We were on the bubble and the time was counting down until another young woman would be abducted. There were lives we had been in situations like this before, and were tasked to come in when others failed. We solved the unsolvable, or at least we did up to this point.

Around 0200 in the morning, Steve released the team and told everyone to take a break and come back later in the morning. He would be staying of course, but he was looking after his team. Amber and Paul had families to wish a Happy New Year to. Max had his family down in New Orleans, and I'm sure Dianna wanted to wish her relatives the same. I had already wished my mother a Happy New Year's in advance, and just wanted to get some rest and good news for a change.

Steve stated that he would call us if there was anything new in the case. He was somewhat like me; not a part of a large family and didn't speak much on the subject. In fact, I had never even heard him speak of a lady friend in his life. Steven was married to the job, and it didn't help that he was a young genius and way ahead of his own age counterparts. If it wasn't for Dianna, I would've been alone for Christmas and New Year's as well.

Dianna and I ordered a bottle of champagne from the hotel. They were running a special for the night for couples renting rooms for New Year's Eve. We had already been there for over a week, so we got an even better discount than the regular customers. It was also one of the perks of being with law enforcement. We couldn't have

The Crossroads

slept even if we tried, so we stayed up and enjoyed the rest of the morning with each other. We hoped that all the provisions that were in place would prevent another young woman from getting abducted.

"So, Mr. Sands; I don't have the bow that I promised for our return performance, but I do have handcuffs," Dianna stated while giving me a very naughty look and laughing.

"I don't mind, just as long as I get to do the handcuffing, but I have a better game," I replied.

"And what would that entail?" she inquired, her pretty face a study in curiosity

"Do you trust me," I asked?

"You know I do," she replied.

"OK, let's drink a couple of shots of tequila first, and then I'll show you."

We drank several shots of tequila, then I blind folded her and began taking off her clothes. I fed her different fruits and champagne. I fed her from my mouth to hers. Then I used some honey that I had appropriated earlier and poured it over sensitive spots on her body, licking it off. Then I poured honey over parts of my body and had her lick it off. Then we made passionate love, kissing and caressing each other's body.

After making love for most of the morning, we napped until just before the sunrise. I shared dreamscape with her after she went to sleep, planting sexy scenarios in her subconscious mind and loving her receptiveness to it. This wasn't cheating, since she knew I could do it. It was a sharing of my abilities with someone who didn't fear them. The trust between us made my feelings for her intensify exponentially. As I made love to her mind, she panted and sighed, her body growing wetter while she slept, dreaming about the thoughts I placed in her subconscious. She woke up three hours later, still hot and wet, and jumped on top of me. We continued physically from where we left off mentally in our dreams.

Once her breathing had slowed to normal and my heart stopped pounding, she rested her cheek on my shoulder and said, "Now I see what you mean about the dreams being active. I've never experienced anything like that. It was so real; every bit of it. So you had the same dream as I did?" she inquired.

"Yes, I did. Would you like to compare notes?" Then I started describing the dream to her.

"Wow, that's amazing! You can do that to me every night, if you please," she said with a sigh exhaling, as if she'd just discovered her G spot.

"It would be my pleasure." I replied, and began kissing her again. We settled back to sleep in the morning and decided to stay there until Steve called us. We were hoping that he wouldn't.

Chapter 5

Out with the Old and In with the New

We hadn't gotten much sleep over the last few days leading to the New Year, so Steve didn't call us in until 1100 hours. We had practically lived at the Residence Office for three days straight, while attempting to cross reference our ViCAP databases with NCIC and other databases. We were looking for any type lead to the serial killer, but to no avail. The little reprieve he granted us was much needed, because the team was running on fumes and needed a break.

All of us including all the agents from the Albuquerque Field Office assembled in the Conference Room at the Residence Office on New Year's Day at 1200 hours, , for an all hands on deck meeting. Steven was acting as the SAC of the Residence Office until the subject was captured. Ortega wasn't too pleased about it, but he dealt with it.

"OK people, here's what we have in place for tonight. There is a local curfew for the city beginning at 2000 hours. Agent Ortega and I have coordinated with all local law enforcement to assist," Steven

49

stated. Steven included Agent Ortega in all of his command discussions. He didn't want to take away from his authority. Ortega's reputation was kept intact, so when we finally departed he could continue as the lead without his authority being questioned by subordinates.

"There will be checkpoints throughout the city, especially routes entering and exiting. There will be an all hands on deck for all law enforcement; the local police department, Sheriff's Department, State Police Department and the National Parks Service law enforcement department for Albuquerque. This will all begin at 2000 hours today until 0700 hours on January 2. Hopefully, by then, we will have the subject apprehended."

We continued brainstorming and questioning subjects for most of the day. We knew if there was going to be an abduction, we wouldn't be informed of it until the morning after or a few days later. Most of us remained at the RO (Residence Office) that night, without sleep. We wanted to be there if there was an incident one way or the other, but we were hoping for a capture. I was pessimistic about this outcome. He was very intelligent, and had eluded us completely up to this point.

Instead of waiting at the office for something to happen, most of the teams went on patrol, assisting the locals. Dianna and I drove around with Gracie, as usual. It was better to be active. Gracie was comfortable being around us now, and returned to wearing her BDU's. We decided to stop at the mall to eat and look around. You never knew what you might find at the mall.

We'd caught so many predators at the mall, it was ridiculous. It was the one place where people generally let their guard down. There were so many people present we tended to shun the possibility of something going wrong, but this presented opportunity for predators, who used malls for entertainment, dining and business purposes.

We sat down for a quick meal at Friday's. I hadn't sat down and actually eaten a real hot plate of food since Christmas Eve at Dianna's. We discussed the case while dining. When Gracie went to the restroom, the subject changed.

Out with the Old and In with the New   51

"Gracie and Steve were together on New Year's Eve, you know," Dianna informed me.

I felt good hearing the news that he wasn't alone, but I wondered why she was telling me. What really surprised me was that I didn't notice it the way Dianna had. I guess my mind was just preoccupied. I did recall her mentioning him as being the brain. Apparently, she likes the brainy type.

"She also inquired about you and wanted to know if you were single or not. I informed her that you were currently seeing someone. I hope I didn't overstep my boundaries," Dianna inquired. Now I understood why she was confessing this to me.

"So you hooked her up with Steve?" I replied.

"I wouldn't say hooked them up, but I led her his way."

"And does she know who I'm currently seeing?" I asked?

"She figured it out during our conversation," Dianna replied smiling.

The politics of women has always intrigued me. Men rarely have a say in such matters of the heart. It's best to just go with the flow. I didn't believe Steve, nor I, would have been with such gorgeous women under different circumstances.

"So, what are you thinking?" she inquired, as if she was reading my thoughts.

"I was thinking about what you said and what exactly we would quantify our relationship as being. Are we just seeing each other now and then, as in a casual relationship? Are we just hooking up to have sex or what?" I inquired. Then I immediately thought to myself, *Wow, this is what women usually worry about in a relationship; these sort of insecurities. Man, how the tables have turned!*

"That's so cute," she said and held my hand. "We are together in a relationship. I'm not with anyone else but you, silly," she stated, then smiled warmly and gently caressed my hand where it rested on the table beside her.

"You continue to surprise me, Christian Sands. That is the sweetest gift you could have given me. Most men assume and take things for granted, but I see you are a totally different type of man. You are gentle, sensitive and know exactly what to say and do. I'm a very lucky woman."

"And I'm a very lucky man to have you as well."

We saw Gracie coming back to the booth and let go of each other's hands, and the conversation. I didn't understand why we didn't want to show our affection in front of Gracie, since she already knew about us, but I guess we were just trying to keep it professional. We continued our patrol of the city after dinner and returned to the RO. There still weren't any breaks in the investigation. I knew in the back of my mind that this case was going to get ugly. This particular psychopath was extremely intelligent and organized. He was giving the team a run for their money.

As midnight rolled around, there was still nothing reported from the patrols or check points. Perhaps we got lucky and secured the city so tightly that we deterred the threat. Then, as time moved slower and slower towards the early morning hours, most of the FO agents had fallen asleep on the sofas and lounge chairs, except Gracie Mullins. She was a true soldier. The BAU team remained vigilant and awake, monitoring the radios and hot lines that were set up.

Ortega attempted to stay awake, but finally succumbed to the sleepless nights. He had been up with Steve most nights and wasn't used to theses grueling, depriving cases, which Steve and the rest of our ViCAP team was accustomed to working. We had become coffee connoisseurs over time, playing games in reference to coffee beans and their origins; which country they were from, and the quality of beans from Columbia, Vienna, Ethiopia, Switzerland and Venice. It was just a nerd game to pass the time, and to get our minds off the debauchery and heinous acts we faced daily.

As the sun rose over Albuquerque and a new day was about to begin, the RO agents began waking. They had been napping for perhaps an hour or two. We knew that we weren't out of the woods, as of yet. Early morning is when the bad news comes in. Reports of failure would come around these hours. Someone didn't make it

Out with the Old and In with the New   53

home the previous night or in the morning. Someone didn't make it to work, and no one had heard from them. Some mother, father or spouse would be crying on the telephone about their loved one's absence.

We let the RO agents take over the radio and telephones for the rest of the morning, and took a break to go freshen up and change clothes. They had lockers and showers at the FO. Around 1000 hours the call came in that we had dreaded. Steve received it on the hotline.

"Jessica Juarez was reported missing by her parents," he reported." A single Latino female, 22 years of age, left work at the Wal-Mart at 2330 hours on Jan 1 and there has been no contact with her since. Her car is parked outside her residence. The local police department was allowed inside this morning on the authority of her parents. There were no signs that she ever made it in All the neighbors could say was that they saw a rather large wolf-like dog earlier in the parking area, around the time curfew began. She doesn't have a boyfriend and her friends haven't heard from her either, according to the parents. I've placed Jessica on the board, people. Let's find her and put this perp where he belongs; locked up somewhere in a mental institutional," Steve said solemnly, as if all the life had been sucked right out of him.

Several of the local agents began grumbling and talking about what they would do if they caught the perpetrator. It was totally unprofessional, but Federal Agents have emotions just like everyone else, and theirs were intrinsically entangled with this case.

"We don't need that, agents; just do your jobs and no vigilantism," Ortega said loudly over the agents conversing in the room. "I want the entire ViCAP team at the apartment for processing. Agent Ortega and the RO team will remain here, just in case something else comes forth. Thank you," Steve said and then he dismissed us.

While at Jessica's apartment; Paul, Trace and Amber concentrated on processing the outside surroundings and the vehicle. Steve, Max and the rest of the team, including Gracie, worked the interior of the apartment. When they completed taking pictures and collecting physical evidence; they allowed me to do my thing, which involved touching and opening things; basically, disturbing a possible crime scene.

While I was inside the apartment, the rest of the team went door to door, questioning the neighbors and the building manager. Steve remained behind with me while I got in touch with Jessica's personal things.

I did my usual routine of walking the interior; touching things as I passed by. I opened drawers and closets, turned on lights, and so on. I sat at the dining room table for a while, then went to the living room and turned on the television. I sat on the sofa and just looked around for several minutes. She had several women's health magazines and jogging magazines on the coffee table; she had a subscription. Jessica was obviously into physical fitness.

I got up from the sofa and continued my routine. There were several pictures of Jessica with friends from school and family around the apartment. She had a lot of friends. I saw her in pictures with males, but no reoccurring man who would stand out as a boyfriend. She was a very pretty young woman. All of the victims had been young, attractive females, which was the first connection we could use for constructing a victim profile.

Jessica had health foods in her fridge and in the cabinets, ranging from soy to protein and wheat products. Everything was reduced fat, low sodium, sugar and calories. I spent an extremely long time in Jessica's apartment, as I acquainted myself with her. Afterwards we went to visit her parents, who lived outside of Albuquerque in Luna County.

Jessica came from a large family, who lived on a good-sized ranch in Luna County. Her father was an engineer at the Kirtland Air Force Base. The family was devastated by her disappearance. I was allowed to look around the house and the ranch. I also looked in Jessica's room, which was the same as she had left it when she moved out. I played with their chocolate Labrador while outside. He was extremely friendly and escorted me around while outside. I had this uncanny way with animals which even I didn't understand. Even the most

Out with the Old and In with the New

territorial and viscous creatures had this affinity towards me, and extended friendship.

When I returned inside the house, I informed Steve that I had received everything I needed. I didn't need to speak to anyone else. I had more than enough stimuli to communicate with Jessica if she was still alive. Dianna drove me back to the Hilton while Steve and Max remained at the Juarez residence. Amber and Paul were visiting the girl's friends. We were literally racing the clock, and every minute was critical. If I needed additional information, I would visit her workplace or talk to her friends later.

Dianna remained with me at the hotel suite. She witnessed me going through my routine when I put myself to sleep. I thought it was a good idea to have someone there whom I could trust. She could take notes over the event and what I said in my sleep. I usually didn't have anyone with me, because Dreamscaping is such a personal thing. I went through a lot of emotions and mood changes while under. It wasn't a process I would have revealed to just anyone. I took two sleeping pills, put on my headphones and lay down on the bed. Dianna gave me a kiss.

Several hours later when I had awakened, I was drenched in sweat from the living nightmare I'd been experiencing. I was scared and trembling in the aftermath of the dream. Dianna was holding me and attempting to calm me, to ease my mind. I was panting heavily and out of breath, as though I'd been running. It was from the anxiety of the dream. I had finally made a connection with the horrible incident. I saw Jessica being abducted!

"It's alright, it's alright," Dianna said repeatedly while holding me, and rocking gently. "Can I get you anything," she inquired? "Yes, I have some bottled water in the fridge," I said, agitated. I drank the bottle of water in just a few gulps. My body felt hot to the touch, like I had just got finished jogging several miles. It was 2130 hours. I had been dreaming for 8.5 hours.

"I shouldn't have taken two pills," I said, feeling groggy. Dianna was wiping my forehead with a wash cloth and stated, "It worked. You said a lot in your sleep."

"Was it of any use?"

"I think you were echoing her thoughts," she replied.

"Did you write it down?" I inquired.

"I did even better, I recorded it," she stated, and then hit the playback button on the iPhone.

"Who is this? What do you want? Where am I? Why are you doing this? I'm scared, I'm going to die. Help me! Can somebody help me?" Then I started weeping on the recording.

The FBI never thought about recording me while I was under, because the information that I received in the dreams was already so beneficial. My physicians Dr. Banks and Dr. Deborah always recorded our sessions, but never any law enforcement officials.

"Maybe we should keep a recorder on from now on. It appears that you were echoing her thoughts," Dianna stated.

"Yeah, I used to sleepwalk and talk in my sleep as a child; I thought I had grown out of that. So much for *Out with the Old and In with the New,* for this year. There is something about this case, Dianna, that's different than the rest."

I didn't elaborate to her about the fact that I had never been seen through another person's eyes before. In the past, when I talked in my sleep, it had always been from an omniscient view point. Dr. Banks even let me hear the recordings. Then Dianna snapped me out of deep thought.

"What did you see," she inquired?

I briefed her on the events as they transpired to me, through the eyes and mind of Jessica.

"I'm going to take a shower now. Can you call Steve and inform him that I've made a connection, and see what he wants to do?" I asked Dianna.

"Sure. Are you hungry." she inquired.

Out with the Old and In with the New   57

"I could eat a horse," I responded as I made my way to the bathroom.

"Me too, I'll order some room service."

Dianna telephoned Steve while I was in the bathroom. I felt revived after showering. I couldn't wait to finally contribute to the case. It wasn't much under the circumstances, but I had seen the team dissect the smallest of information and run with it. Dianna kissed me as I exited the bathroom in a towel. She was a very sensual woman, fully in touch with her femininity. It didn't take much for her to turn me on.

"I'm sorry, tiger. You just looked so good in that towel. We don't have the time for that. Steve wants us at the office ASAP," she said and kissed me again.

Alright, we'll finish this later," I replied, grinning.

The food arrived while I was dressing. Dianna ordered some deli sandwiches with cold veggie pasta, coleslaw, potato salad, juice, coffee and mixed fruit. It was a quick pick-me-up energy meal, filled with carbs and protein.

Most of the team was still out investigating the case. Ortega, Amber and a few other RO agents were at the office with Steve when we arrived. We waited for about 30 minutes for Max and Paul to arrive with Trace and Gracie.

"Alright folks, Chris has made a connection with Jessica," Steve said, then indicated I should brief the team on what I had discovered.

"Well, it's correct. She was taken from the parking lot at her apartment complex. When she got out of the vehicle, she heard a large dog growling, but couldn't see where it was coming from. She remembers it being particularly dark out that tonight. She had some bags in the trunk that she went to get out, which is when he came from behind, out of nowhere. He was silent when he placed something over her mouth and nose, perhaps chloroform, and she passed out," I said.

"She woke up terrified in a completely dark place, with no windows or doors that she could see. It was pitch black. She was bound at the wrists and legs. She struggled to move, but couldn't free herself or even scream, as he had her gagged as well. She was lying on a dirt floor. She couldn't hear anything in the background, perhaps due to the terror. Her senses were numb and weren't registering her surroundings. I will continue to monitor her; perhaps she will settle down and give us something more to go on. It is a strong bond thus far," I stated to the team before Steve took over the lead again.

"Alright. Talk to me, people. What can we deduce from this?" The team began our usual profiling session with Steve up at the board, the rest of us collectively spurting out profiling deductions.

"The first thing is that she is alive, so he doesn't immediately kill them, which is a positive. We don't know how long they remain alive, but the next abduction date is February 1. This gives us time for rescue. She hasn't been harmed yet, so he is working up to something. He has her for gratification of a need and is building towards some type of finale. He is a loner, as profiled earlier. He lives by himself in a secluded place. We need to look for houses with unfinished basements or cellars with a dirt floor. Her neighbors had sighted a rather large dog in the neighborhood around the beginning of curfew, and Jessica heard a large dog growling. Maybe the subject hunts with his dog. He stalks his victims before he actually takes them. He knows where they live and work. He watches them well in advance."

Then Steve completed the information sharing session with, "He is very patient, intelligent and well organized. Let's narrow it down and investigate our latest findings. I'll brief Ortega and the rest of the RO."

For the next couple of days, my assignment was to continue dreamscaping, which meant I didn't let any other outside stimuli take away from my connection with Jessica. This wasn't a hard task to do, since I had already conditioned myself to alleviate outside interferences. I didn't watch any television or listen to the radio. I only played music or listened to it. I asked Dianna to take me back to Jessica's apartment. We didn't need Gracie as an escort any longer, which freed her up to do other investigative assignments. From now on, it was just me and Dianna.

Out with the Old and In with the New

While at Jessica's apartment I did my usual, this time retracing her actions as I had seen them during dreamscape, to create an even stronger tie. Then I went inside and spent some time wandering through the apartment, before heading back to the Hilton. I wanted to get a jump start on my dreamscape. I notified Steve of my intentions and departed.

Dianna had an excellent idea while back at the hotel. She knew how the sleeping pills made me depressed and irritable with mood swings, so she prepared a bubble bath with candles for us, and some wine. I couldn't find any flaw in her strategy, and even if it didn't work, I still had the pills to rely on. She cautioned against the addictiveness and side effects of the medication. It was also a good way to ease my mind and for us to spend some couple time together. We relaxed for a while in the large Jacuzzi sized-tub, making love in the water. She literally wore me out. If she wanted to ensure that I fell asleep, she did a good job of it.

We went to the bedroom after making love in the tub, and continued there until I went to sleep. At this point I only hoped she wouldn't fall asleep also, and our findings would not be recorded.

The first thing I recall when I went to sleep was dreaming about Dianna, but then I diverted to Jessica. She was still tied up on the floor, crying. She was wondering about her family and how she would never see them again. She also wondered why this was happening to her, and what she had done to deserve this.

It was still quiet in the area Jessica was being held, but it was warmer inside the enclosed area now than it had previously been. It was daytime. She still couldn't see any light, but t after a while, she saw light surrounding the silhouette of the door, and then heard footsteps. She became more terrified, trembling in fear, curled up on the floor as tears rolled down her face. Her silent crying turned into a low, resonating moan as she heard the doorknob turn.

When the door opened, the light blinded her. She had been in the dark for so long she couldn't see anything for several seconds, and then she took in the silhouette of a person standing in the middle of the door with the light to his back. She couldn't make out his face or anything else. As he approached her, she began yelling through the gag in her mouth, but it was muffled. Then she began squirming and kicking erratically in spite of her bonds, in an attempt to fight back as he touched her. He briefly removed the gag from over her mouth and naturally her screams gained volume. Then he placed the chemically doused rag over her nose once again, rendering her unconscious.

When she woke up she was bathed and naked, with only an adult diaper on. She was on a bed in the dark room now. She hadn't known there was a bed in the room while she'd been lying on the floor. She began to cry again. She was elated to still be alive, but knew her situation hadn't changed much. She felt violated, like someone had raped her. She didn't feel the physical signs of rape, but mentally it felt as if she had been. The thought of a stranger touching her all over and doing whatever he wanted was terrifying.

There was a lantern on a table and a chair rested under the table in the room, but no windows. She was still bound at the wrists and legs, tied to the bed. She was alone now and even more afraid. She was tired and hungry but valiantly struggled to free herself from her bonds, until she fell asleep, exhausted by exertion and terror.

I woke up at that point, struggling as if I was tied to the bed. Dianna was up and had recorded the whole session. She had been up the whole time while I slept —if you could call that sleep. It had been a nightmare filled with anxiety and terror. Dianna was watching over me protectively, and it was nice to see her smiling face as I opened my weary eyes. She gently felt the side of my face. She had the look of a carrying mother. Then she got up to get me a bottle of water from the fridge. I didn't have to ask for it this time, she already knew.

I watched her as she moved through the room like a goddess. I thought how lucky I was to have her in my life. I had never known how lonely I was until she came in and filled the void. I had become used to be being alone and adapted to it. I had been doing all this on my own, and now I felt like I had been missing out on a huge part of life as I watched her. She only had on her work blouse and a pair of black Victoria's Secret lace bikini panties. Yes, I knew they were made by VS, I enjoyed their catalogues like most men. It was better than watching the Sports Illustrated Swimwear Edition. Dianna was looking incredibly sexy in the ensemble.

"Thank you," I said as she handed me the bottle of water.

"You're welcome. Did you get anything else from her," she inquired?

"No; nothing much, but she is still alive. He knocked her out again with the chloroform and bathed her. Afterwards he put an adult diaper on her. I guess so she could use the restroom while he was out? He also placed a lantern in the room where he was keeping her. She's tied to a bed and there's a table and chair in there as well. I didn't hear any distinguishing sounds from the room, and it has no windows," I informed Dianna.

"Well at least we know she is still alive and he is taking care of her for a purpose. I'll inform Steve."

"Alright; did you record anything?"

"Yes, but nothing of significance. It was just the thoughts and reactions of a terrified girl. Here, listen while I talk to Steve."

She handed me the recorder while she got on the telephone. I got up from the bed after listening to myself on the recorder, and slipped into my boxer shorts and pants, which were lying on the chair beside the bed. Then I opened up the curtains. I needed to see some light. I had been in the dark too long. I didn't know if it was a carryover from the dreamscape or what, but I needed to see the sun. I caught a little bit of it before it set. As much as I enjoyed the dark, it was time for some sunlight.

"Steve said good work; just continue monitoring her and keep him updated," Dianna said, and then inquired with a smile, "What made you decide to put your clothes back on?"

"I don't know. I just did," I replied. I really didn't have an answer for her because I really didn't know why. I wasn't going anywhere. I guess I was carrying over some things from the dream; her being naked on the bed and all. Perhaps I was consciously attempting to get myself away from it while I was awake. Dianna came over to the window that I was looking out of and put her arms around me from behind, as we watched the sunset together.

We went down to the hotel's restaurant and ate a good sit-down meal for a change, before I went back under. Gracie telephoned Dianna and inquired about us. She was concerned about her new partners and wanted to make sure everything was alright and ask if we needed anything. Dianna reassured her that all was well and this was just protocol for us. Then we began discussing the case over dinner.

"This perp is doing everything meticulously. He isn't slipping up much," I stated to Dianna.

"I know; it is as if he knows something about investigative techniques," she replied.

"You don't think he is with law enforcement," I inquired.

"Anything is possible and within the realm of reason, I've discovered on this job. You of all people should now that," she reminded me.

"You're right," I stated, but didn't really know how to accept what she just said. Up until now, she had always thought of my abilities as a gift, but that comment didn't sound too encouraging. Maybe I was just being paranoid again.

After dinner we went back up to my suite. I told Dianna that she didn't have to stay while I went under again, and that I could turn on the recorder before I went to sleep, but she wouldn't hear of it and kissed me, telling me to stop acting silly.

"When are you going to rest?" I inquired.

"I'll go to sleep after you wake up the next time. Now go to sleep, my sweet prince," she said and kissed me. I turned on my iPhone and listened to some jazz. I only took one pill this time, and lay down next to her on the bed.

Over the next few days I didn't receive much about Jessica's whereabouts. I briefed the team every day on what I saw, which wasn't much. He basically left her alone. It remained dark most of the time in the area where she was being held. She heard a coyote or a dog in the background at night. The change in temperature and the coyote let her know when it was nighttime.

Out with the Old and In with the New   63

She remained gagged at all times, except when he allowed her to eat. He fed her and bathed her. She had oatmeal and juice for breakfast, noodles for lunch, sandwiches for dinner with applesauce or some other fruit, and water. He was taking care of her, but to what end? There were no signs of the other women. All local law enforcement had joined in on the task force. This subject was very cunning and careful.

"The subject is believed to work during the day, according to the timeline that we received from Chris. Jessica is fed in the morning, and then again in the evening. He feeds her before he goes out and when he returns. Sometimes he returns for lunch and feeds her, but this is random. We need to find a secluded area or home. The subject is believed to have a large wolf-like dog. Jessica hears the sound of a coyote howling at night. It could be the dog that was seen by the neighbors when she was abducted," Steve stated.

Then Agent Gracie Mullins raised her hand, as if she was still in the classroom at Quantico. I found it amusing, based on the information Dianna gave me about their relationship, and smiled. I looked around the conference room at the rest of the team to observe their expressions, and they were all the same. They knew about them, and probably about Dianna and me as well.

"Yes, Agent Mullins," Steve inquired professionally without a hint of his feelings towards her.

"I went back over the CCTV footage when Deseray Johnson was abducted, and there was a large dog observed on the cameras of the parking lot, but only for a brief moment."

"Can you show us the footage," Steve asked?

"Sure, it's right here." She walked up to the command desk and put a flash drive into the laptop which controlled the wall sized monitor. She already had the scene saved at the location.

"The visibility isn't that good due the fact that it was a very dark night and the cameras at the bowling alley parking lot aren't the best, but there it is."

It was in fact a large brown and grayish wolf-like dog. It was only on the footage for a moment and then disappeared, but it was enough to freeze frame it and get a better look.

"So now we know for a fact that this is no longer a coincidence. Our perp owns a dog. Our check of the local veterinarians and animal registries came up nil before, but let's check it again now that we have a good description. Let's also look into licensed hunters registered in the area," Steve said. Gracie was grinning with pride at her contribution and rightly so. It was a good bit of investigative research. I met her at the coffee bar after the meeting.

"Good morning, Gracie; good work on the camera footage," I stated.

"Thanks Chris, but it's nothing compared to what you're doing. I see how valuable your skills are now. We would still have nothing if it wasn't for you," she stated.

"It's a team effort, Gracie, and your contributions have been great. I'm lost without all the investigative brains in that room to put it all together."

I saw Dianna looking from afar as we spoke. I guess Gracie made her feel a little jealous, since she had expressed an interest in me. I think her only questioning had only been due to curiosity about my abilities. Dianna really didn't have anything to be jealous about. Gracie was pretty, but Dianna was even more gorgeous, in fact Dianna and Amber were both extremely gorgeous women, except Dianna didn't realize her beauty. It was totally baffling to me, because she was so outgoing and confident in everything else.

The next day went the same as the previous one. I attended the morning briefing and gave my update. There was no further information pertaining to the case. Steve was one of the most patient people I had ever met; he was truly a cool customer, but I could see the frustration building in him. I would have ventured as far to say that he had never been defeated at anything in his life until now. This perpetrator had him baffled along with the rest of us.

Now I could see the subtle looks and glances he and Gracie shared, since I was privy to the information about their relationship. I hope she was a comfort to him as Dianna was to me. We were all on edge. This case had become a real challenge for the team.

The Note

It was approximately 0610 hours when Steve notified the team to come to the RO. Dianna was lying in bed beside me. *There must be a break in the case,* I thought. Dianna didn't bother checking her phone since they both rang at the same time. We were living together for all practical purposes. It might have been in a hotel suite, but we had been staying together for a solid twelve days. The entire team now knew we were in a relationship, but no one really seemed to care. We were too involved in the investigation. Amber actually encouraged the relationship, she thought we made a nice couple. She said we were each other's Ying and Yang which made it work.

We were totally opposite creatures like the polarity of magnets, but drawn to each other. Steve had placed us together from the start, knowing Dianna kept me anchored and balanced through it all. There was a large price to pay for anyone who profiles criminals, living each day bathed in horror. To actually live out the scenes, see through the eyes of the victims the way I did took an even larger toll on my psyche.

We met Amber and Paul in the lobby before departing for the Field Office. Max, as usual, was already up and had departed. Steve would no doubt already be there waiting with Max. When we arrived at the RO, Ortega and Gracie were present with Steve and Max. We waited a few more minutes for others to trickle in, and then Steve began.

"This envelope was discovered taped to the door this morning, addressed to the FBI. The note inside says, *'I am the coyote. I walk alone. I do not exist in your reality. I roam the plains of both worlds.'* the envelope must have delivered between 0200-0600 hours when it was discovered. There were no witnesses or video surveillance of the deliverer. We received a call from the Albuquerque Journal, they received the same envelope in their mailbox this morning. They agreed not to run the story for now, due to the further panic that it may cause throughout the city. Our subject has upped the ante, now he's added terror to the equation. Ever since we placed the road blocks and checkpoints on New Year's Day, he's been sending us a message daring us to catch him. He's proud of himself, and the fact that he is outsmarting us. He considers himself smarter than us, and is challenging us. He wants us to work for it; to earn it!" Steve exclaimed.

"He has been watching us the whole time. He knows where we work and we can assume he knows where we live. Remember, people: he is a stalker, a hunter; so be aware of your own surroundings and be vigilant! If he wants to play this game, he'll get closer. He was right outside our door delivering this message, saying *come and catch me if you can!* I don't have to tell you what this means. You already know," Steve further stated with a scowl on his face and his brow, indicating he was perturbed by the perpetrator's boldness.

I didn't think some of the RO agents had a clue about the last item Steve was talking about; 'them knowing what that means.' I could see it in their eyes. The ViCAP team understood it meant that Jessica didn't have much time left if he was altering his MO. He might get bored with her and focus his attention solely on us, or go on a killing spree for the attention. It isn't often that a serial killer completely changes his signature, but it does evolve.

"Were there any prints or clues provided by the note," one of the Residence Office Agents inquired.

"There were no prints on the note or outside the office. We are having the note analyzed by Quantico as we speak, for writing profile recognition. Any further questions?" Steve asked.

The conference room became silent at that point. We could feel the uneasiness surround us. This was a bold and calculating killer.

The subject had us looking over our shoulders now, and made us wonder if it was a fellow law enforcement officer or an agent. Steven issued a curfew with the approval of the Governor and the Director of

Out with the Old and In with the New 67

the FBI. This time it wasn't for a day, but until rescinded. The last time something like this occurred was when the D.C. Sniper held Washington under a siege of terror.

The next day, while at the briefing, Steven informed us that the ABQ Journal ran with the story on the front page, stating that it was their obligation to inform the public. There was even more panic and chaos spreading throughout the city. The citizens were calling for the National Guard to patrol the city. Several witnesses in the area of the ABQ Journal building sighted a large dog in the area during the suspected time the note was delivered, but no one else.

"Until a dog evolves a couple of notches up the food chain and grows opposable thumbs, he isn't our prime suspect. The dog is an afterthought, people. If you can link it, do so, but let's get with the bigger picture here. We have a killer that has eluded and out-maneuvered us. We have a young woman to find and rescue, and time is of the essence," Steve stated.

The pressure was mounting and the ever stoic and cool Steve was feeling it from all sides: the Governor's Office, the Director of the FBI, the media and citizens. It was national news now and it didn't take long before POTUS became involved. He was a 'hands on' type of president of the people. The Director sent the Asst. Director and his detail of cronies to overshadow the investigation. It was a circus when Homeland Security arrived to join the party. Homeland was orchestrating all facets of the case and jurisdictions. This was no longer just a ViCAP case.

The only real connection we had on the subject was that he was utilizing Interstate 25. All of the victims had been taken in places near that highway. We also were looking for regions in the state with a large number of coyotes, which was most of New Mexico. Luckily we had more manpower to assist in the investigation, because our parameters and profile had been expanded. It was heading in the wrong direction. Successful profiling was about narrowing down the subjects and parameters, not increasing it.

On January 16, the subject killed Jessica. I heard and saw the whole ritual and briefed the RO on my observations. There was silence in the conference room, as everyone focused their attention on me as I somberly informed them.

"She was blindfolded and naked when he took her outside. She could feel the wind against her bare, vulnerable body. A coyote continuously howled alone in the background. She could feel the warmth of his naked upper torso as he brushed up against her, and she jerked. She was trembling in fear as he continued to touch her body all over, from head to toe. It was if several hands were caressing her all at once as she continued to cringe and jerk erratically; confused and terrified, like a sheep going to slaughter. She knew this was it; the time he had set aside to kill her. She could feel it in her bones," I stated.

"She yelled, but her gagged and muffled screams fell on death's ears. Then she fell to the ground. She could feel the blaze of a large fire nearby. It warmed her as she heard the crackle of the fire. Then she fell unconscious from anxiety and fear. The last things she remembered before going unconscious was the taste of dirt in her mouth," I said and cleared my throat for the rest of the bad news. It felt like I was spewing out vomit or some type of illness, judging by the way the Field Office Agents were staring at me.

"She woke up with some type of oil all over her body. She had been tied to a stake, like they do in witch killings, as she listened to footsteps circling her in the dirt. It was as if he was dancing around her, like in a Native American ceremony. He was chanting in some dialect that I couldn't make out. The blaze from the fire was no longer providing warmth to her naked body; it was uncomfortably hot and getting hotter! It wasn't touching her yet, but the intense heat from the flames was burning her all the same. It was excruciating pain. She became faint from the smoke and the heat. Then the flames became too intense. She was gagged, but it couldn't contain the horrifying screams as Jessica was burned alive. Then the connection was broken," I stated, with all eyes glued on me in astonishment.

Out with the Old and In with the New   69

The entire conference room remained quiet. You could literally have heard a pin drop as their focus remained fixated on me. I drank from a bottle of water I had next to me. My throat had gone dry from the emotional trauma of the brief. It was as if I was visualizing it again, as sweat came to my brow. I could feel the agents' gazes on my Adam's apple as I swallowed the water. Once again I felt like a freak in a circus. Then Steven broke the silence in his ever stoic manner.

"The subject appears to be putting on some type of ceremony that could be a Native American ritual. Although our profile fits the description of a white male, let's not rule out any possibilities. We are still looking for somewhere secluded; places where he could have held such a ritual with a fire outside and not be seen. The constant howl of the coyote and his association with that animal suggests he is close to nature. It could have some religious or mystical significance there as well. He also kept her alive for sixteen days," Steven stated grimly.

"Max, let's see if our ViCAP computer profiling can assist us with any comparisons, differences or significances with our profiling. Amber and Paul will research the local Native American tribes for evidence of fire rituals or dates of significance around the first and sixteenth of January. The rest of us will perform field investigations at the surrounding Native American villages," Steven said, and then further instructed, "We need to disseminate the information that we have to the local enforcement officers; City, County, State Police, National Park and Reservations."

Then Ortega spoke, "We have the Zuni Nation, Navajo Nation, three different Apache Nations and the Pueblos with five different clans speaking different languages, and scattered tribesmen all over New Mexico!"

"Then we have our work cut us for us," Steven retorted. "A.D. Pollin, can you arrange the Department of Interior/ Bureau of Indian Affairs to send us a liaison to assist?" Steven inquired.

"Yes; I'll have them send a team," he responded. He had been watching me the whole time after I addressed the conference room.

It was creepy and uncomfortable. He made me feel paranoid, like I used to a long time ago.

Then Steven spoke to us again, in closing the meeting. "OK then. Let's get on it, people. You know your assignments and what we have to do. Agent Ortega will break down all the main Indian Villages within our perimeter of abductions. We need to also keep in mind that it could be an impersonator, so let's not forget our original profiling." Then Steven turned and addressed the Assistant Director again, "Do you have anything for us, A.D. Pollin?"

Pollin paused, then responded, "No, not at this time."

Assistant Director Pollin's attention was still focused on me. He had questions, but didn't want to pose them at the time. There was a bigger picture to be concerned with. He had to address the media, Jessica's family and his superiors. Then he spoke up, before everyone departed the conference room area. "Wait. I do have something to say to all of you, and I don't want any of this to leak out. We are going to treat Jessica Juarez like the rest of the young women –as a continuing missing person's case – until a body is found. I know of your talents, Mr. Sands, but until I have a body in front of me that we can ID, this case will continue as a missing person / abductee," he stated.

Our investigation wouldn't change one way or the other with the added information. I think the A.D.'s speech was really just a jab at me and my contribution. We still had to find this killer, except this time it was without rescue. We didn't have any of the previous women's bodies either, so we pushed on. We expanded our focus to the surrounding Native American villages and reservations.

The manhunt was in full operation under the auspices of Homeland Security coordination. The team of liaisons from the Bureau of Indian Affairs was very cooperative. They helped smooth the way while conducting interviews. There were a lot of customs that we weren't familiar with that the liaison team bridged for us. The Reservations and villages still weren't pleased with us entering their land and asking questions, but the Bureau of Indian Affairs assisted greatly in diffusing what could have been a very volatile situation. The lead

BIA liaison and investigator was Nina Blackwater, a very intelligent and beautiful woman. She was of Cherokee heritage, like me.

I didn't particularly like the way the case was turning out. I didn't appreciate the profiling of the Native Americans, but the FBI had to turn over every stone at this point in the investigation. It was impossible to investigate such a large number of Native Americans, so we limited our investigations to the bigger villages and reservations in hopes of cooperation from the higher officials and tribal leaders.

Chapter 6

home of the brave

The investigation had been restructured, and grown. This wasn't unusual for a case of the magnitude which was evolving. Gracie was no longer with Dianna and me. Nina Blackwater, the lead agent from the Bureau of Indian Affairs, and two other New Mexico FBI Agents joined us. Gracie was working with Steven and his team. My team had the assignment of investigating the Navajo Nation. It felt like a witch hunt and most of us were in objection, but it had to be done. It reminded me of when the Spaniards came with missionaries and all the atrocities they bestowed on the original inhabitants.

The Apache territory was the largest and most spread out in New Mexico, so Steve and the other agents had that assignment. Ortega and his team were assigned the Pueblos, since he was extensively knowledgeable about them, as he had expressed at the briefings.

We were still getting pounded by the media for the 'witch hunt' as they also put it. This led to a lot of animosity and added fuel to the fire of the already heated tensions from the Native American tribes. They didn't want us coming on what little was left of their lands. They had their own police and politics, and enforced their own laws!

72

Home of the Brave   73

We headed out to the Navajo Nation early that morning, in a Tahoe SUV. The Navajo Nation Council Building was located in Shiprock, San Juan County, New Mexico. It was about a three hour drive, with strangers who had just met. Everyone was already well briefed and there were no questions or conversations about what needed to be done.

"I've heard a lot and read some good things about you guys," Nina stated during the drive to Shiprock. The other two FBI agents showed no signs of interest in what she was saying. Normally, Dianna and I would get a real kick out of hearing such praise, but this case has taken a lot of wind out of our sails.

"Thank you," I said in a low, monotone voice. It seems like I was always responding to that question. Dianna left it to me; rarely would she answer herself. She didn't find compliments necessary, nor did she want to be patted on the back for capturing deviants. I understood this quite clearly, but I also knew from experiencing these horrific crimes that some of these subjects looked at what they were doing as a necessity or obligation to society; the missionaries. This is what Dianna was feeling deep down also.

I thanked Nina out of courtesy. She could feel the tension in the air. Then she said something from out of nowhere, perhaps attempting to ease it.

"So, Sands; is that any relation to Max Sands?" she inquired with a smile.

Neither Dianna nor the other FBI agents got the pun but I did, and laughed. You didn't really have to be of Native American heritage to get it; just an old movie buff or vintage reader. Max Sands was the lead character in the Harold Robbins novel 'Carpetbaggers' which was released as two movie films; the 'Carpetbaggers' and 'Nevada Smith'. Nina was referring to the later movie with Steve McQueen. Then I responded, "You know, not until recently have I wondered about it myself." Then we both laughed. The others remained oblivious to what we were talking about.

The reservation was huge and not at all what I expected it to be. The Navajo Nation extended from northwest New Mexico into northeast Arizona with most of it in the latter state. The land was untouched and beautiful. They had modern buildings and urban sections as well as rural locations like any other city, but instead of skyscrapers filling the cityscape, they had the incredible beauty of nature. They had the illustrious canyon cliffs and mountain ranges for their skyline!

We made our way to the Navajo Nation Council Chamber building, and introduced ourselves. They had been informed of our arrival in advance. Nina led the way as our liaison. She was versed in the Athabaskan language, in particular the Southern Athabaskan dialect spoken by the Native Americans of New Mexico, but she was of Cherokee heritage like I was. Not only was Nina beautiful, she was extremely intelligent. She made navigating the turbulent waters a little easier for all of us. The reservation police were at the meeting also. They would be included in the investigations conducted on the reservation.

We were escorted around like cattle being corralled before branding. They took us to all the places they wanted us to go and see. It was staged for our benefit. We interviewed some of the local miscreants, but didn't receive any of the answers we were looking for. Some were on our list of felons and persons of interest, but most weren't. We decided the best course of action was for us to head out on our own against the advice of the Council and Reservation Police.

There was much opposition met, even with Nina as a spokesperson. We weren't getting anywhere and spent most of the day running in circles until Dianna, who was the lead agent in our group, decided to go about our questioning in a different manner. She chose to look in the places where most notable criminals would be associated in one way or another; the casinos. The reservations weren't unlike any other place in regards to this; if you wanted to find the really bad guys, you followed the money, and around here the money makers were the casinos.

Home of the Brave

We split up and did recon at the bars and on the floors of the casino. The good thing about casinos was that there were a wide variety of activities, which meant they brought in a dichotomy of people. With a diverse crowd we had a good chance of getting some actual information. This would make our job a lot easier.

It was Friday night and like most casinos, it was packed. I could feel the excitement in the air, with people having fun in every corner. Everything was sparkling and illuminated. The employees made customers feel like a king or queen as soon as they stepped through the door, offering free refreshments and appetizers for the players. The only thing that wasn't invited to the party was the outer environment; night, day, the sky, the sun and the moon weren't allowed into the casino. It was a black hole in time and space. Once you entered, there was no way to determine how long you had stayed. They accomplished this by providing everything you needed right there.

There were night clubs, bars, gambling and restaurants all under one roof. The crowd was as diverse as we had thought it would be, with visitors, locals and people from all walks of life. We mixed and mingled for several hours. We engaged in a little gambling and nursed a small drink each. We were working a case, but needed to blend in as well.

After hours of enraptured conversation, Dianna and Nina were invited to a party in one of the hotel suites of the casino. It was a private party hosted by Will Hawthorne, one of the casino's owners and a major business investor. It seemed like a good place to start following the money. He wasn't a person of interest, but we were off the grid and putting our fishing poles out for whatever we could snag. I attempted to crash the party, but was met with resistance at the guarded door. Apparently you had to be invited or an attractive woman to gain access, so the other two male agents and I continued working the casino floor. Dianna kept us outsiders in the loop.

They reported seeing drugs and prostitutes in the suite. There was no immediate reaction to these illegal activities, but we would make a report to the Gaming Commission at an appropriate time.

We were there for a different reason and had more important things to investigate.

Nina cozied up to one of the local thugs at the party; Jay Horse. The Navajo thug who apparently worked for Hawthorne, who wasn't in attendance. Horse was a braggart who was drunk and eager to show he was a person of importance. Nina continued to engage Jay in conversation and entertained him and his narcissistic ego. Jay didn't fit our profile, and it was far-fetched to believe that the killer would be out mingling, as most serial killers displayed anti-social personality disorders, but we were searching for information.

We followed Jay as he left the party at around 0100 hours. Nina stated that her questions had begun to spook him, so he shunned her and warned her to stay out of Res (Reservation) Business before he departed. He led us to a secluded area about 10 miles from the casino. He was too drunk to be driving, and had no idea he was being followed.

There weren't any other residences or buildings around. This was a rural section of Farmington, like most of the county. Jay turned down a long dirt road off the main highway. It was pitch black, with no overhead streetlights to illuminate the darkness. We waited several minutes with our lights out before continuing behind him, and arrived at a huge barn near the end of the road. We stopped several yards away, where we couldn't be seen by anyone inside the barn. We didn't know where Jay's vehicle was parked, but there were lights on inside the structure. Getting out of our vehicle, we approached the barn stealthily and cautiously. Then the melee of gun fire ensued. Jay had led us into an ambush.

There were no lights; just the black of the night when the shooting began. This was one of those times I wished I had carried a gun. I had been to the firearms training because it was mandatory, but refused to arm myself. I didn't have a problem seeing. I had excellent night vision from spending so much time in the dark, isolating myself during dreamscape and on clinical sofas and lounge chairs. I stayed close to Dianna; not out of fear, but more to make sure she would

Home of the Brave 77

be safe. I acted as her eyes. She was a marksman who had instructor qualifications with a handgun. She had excellent vision also, but ask any sniper about the necessity of a spotter.

Nina stayed near Dianna and me. She was a good shot also, but nothing compared to Dianna. I believe Nina was attempting to protect me since I was unarmed. She didn't know how good Dianna was, but she soon found out. We called for backup and held it down until the cavalry arrived. This was definitely a message sent by Jay Horse. He had warned us to stay away from the business of the Res.

By morning we had the situation well in hand, with the other two members of our team shot and hospitalized, one ATF agent inured and two assailants dead. Jay wasn't amongst the remaining assailants who were apprehended. The barn had been a drug lab for meth and the cultivation of marijuana. The local newspapers blasted us for the effort. We were now harassing innocent Native Americans trying to make a living; forget about the illegal drugs and weapons confiscated. It was another notch on the belt for the FBI, but a blemish on the mission to capture the serial killer. Although it was a good bust and apprehension, the A.D. had some choice words for us at the morning briefing. We felt his wrath for our efforts.

"What the hell were you thinking? We're not here to start another damn war with the Indians! I don't want a Waco cluster fuck on my watch, you get it? I asked the Department of Interior / Bureau of Indian Affairs for liaisons, not some 'yippie ki-yay Die Hards running around shooting up the reservations. Now focus, and go catch this damn serial killer!" Then Steve took the lead, playing the good cop to the Assistant Director's bad cop.

"I know you're out there working hard, people, but let's not lose sight of the task. We are still racing the clock. Keep up the good work and remember to watch each other's back. Paul was shot by an elderly Native American yesterday who thought he was a trespasser, so stay vigilant." At our startled glances, he added, "He's in the hospital, and in stable condition."

We spent the better part of the morning and afternoon completing paperwork; filling out forms and writing reports on the shooting incident. It had been a long night and we had been up the whole time. We finished up late in the afternoon and our team was told to take the rest of the day off to regroup, so we went back to the Hilton to catch some much needed sleep.

I woke up a bit restless. Dianna felt the same way, so I decided to take her and Nina out for a beer in town. We needed to unwind. I felt like the luckiest man at the bar, as I was being escorted by two extremely attractive women. Not only were there a slew of men watching and wondering who I was, but several women were curious as well. We danced and had a good time. For a nerd, dancing was the one things that I did exceptionally well. I had actually taken dancing lessons when I was younger, as a way to relieve stress and to impress the women during my days of promiscuity.

A night out was exactly what the doctor ordered. We even got into a fight; well, Dianna and Nina had to kick some guys' asses. It really wasn't a fair fight. Either way, those guys had it coming. They were drunk and disrespectful. The ladies needed that stress relief. They were still feeling the adrenalin from yesterday's gun fight. We had a bit too much to drink, so we caught a cab back to the hotel. Nina was staying at the Hilton also. It was one big Federal Convention there. I'm not a drinker or a fighter, so I was literally punch drunk after the fight. When Dianna and Nina helped me to my suite, I passed out on the bed.

I woke during the dark of predawn after an unplanned foray into erotic dreamscaping with my lady. I was fully aroused, and Dianna jumped on top of me and we went at it like rabbits. We were horny as hell due to the foreplay of the previous dreamscape. Afterwards I had a lot of explaining to do. I had a dreamscape sex threesome with Dianna and Nina. This had turned us both on, but not without consequences. Dianna understood, because she knew how drunk we were. She was secure in our relationship, but how would we explain this to Nina? I had violated a co-worker and a partner.

Home of the Brave   79

Although it was a dream, it had all the reality of consciousness. We had seen and now knew every part of her body and her erotic fantasies. She knew ours as well. If we didn't hear from her again it would be merited. I could get thrown off the case and maybe suspended, or lose my job. I began freaking out, and then we heard a knock on the door. Panic just raced through my body. I just knew it was A.D. Pollin, who hated me anyway. Dianna went to the door quietly and looked through the peep hole.

"It's Nina," Dianna whispered, and then the stress really began to mount. "What do you want me to do?"

Nina knocked at the door again. "Christian, it's Nina. We need to talk." Dianna looked at me, as to inquire what to do.

"Christian," she called again, knocking to the door. Then Dianna turned from me and opened the door slightly.

"Yes, Nina," she answered lightly.

"Can we all talk," she inquired.

"I don't think Chris...," then before Dianna could complete her negative, I said, "Let her in, Dianna."

I had put on my lounge pants and a T-shirt before she entered. Dianna was sexy as hell in just one of my long T shirts, but when Nina entered she put on a hotel robe. Nina surprised us both. She was curious and excited about what had happened, rather than upset. She had a plethora of questions.

"My Grammy told me of people like you, Shamans and Medicine men with abilities to invade dreams, but I never thought I'd experience this. She used to place this talisman over my bed to prevent the invasion of my dreams; a dream catcher to keep bad dreams away," Nina said. She was like a kid in a candy store, excited, elated and filled with questions.

"So, did both of you experience the same thing I did?" she asked.

"Yes, everything you did and then some," Dianna answered with a grin as she prepared coffee for us.

It was truly amazing to see how well they were taking this. Then I became aroused and began thinking with my libido that something else was going to happen. Dianna knew me and gave me a look that I understood well.

"So, you're not upset?" I asked Nina, squashing my inappropriate feelings.

"No; I feel a little embarrassed, but I understand how drunk we were."

"So we can continue to work together in spite of it?" I inquired.

"I don't see why not, just don't do it again. As charmed and flattered as I am with the compliment. It could pose problems if it continues."

"I agree!" Dianna interjected quickly. We all laughed at it afterwards and met for breakfast in the hotel.

Wow; I just knew this was going to implode. Not only did we subconsciously share our bed with Nina, she was alright with it and flattered by the experience. She knew a little more than most at this point about Dianna and me. I had a feeling that too many people were finding out about our relationship. We needed to be a bit more careful just in case. Nina never inquired about my relationship with Dianna; there was no need, she already had all the information. On the flip side, we knew her intimately also.

The women didn't have a problem with it, so I just rolled with it. Nina, as was the case with many others, was just interested in my abilities and sharing or exchanging heritage information. Since Nina was of Cherokee heritage, I think the dreamscape helped Dianna deal with it all. It brought us all closer, since Dianna wasn't Native American. I guess the dreamscape was an excellent ice breaker and made us all better professional partners. This time it proved to be a gift instead of a curse, but it could have gone catastrophically wrong.

The morning briefing was a little less turbulent than yesterday's. The A.D. didn't have anything to say. He just sat in the back and listened to Steve and all the updates, which were minimal to say the least. What continued to bother and pose questions for Dianna and me was why Jay Horse had led us into an ambush. There must have been something more that spooked him. Perhaps he just gave us that

Home of the Brave

miner skirmish to satisfy us. Or perhaps he was hoping we'd be killed and our bothersome investigation would die with us. Either way, he was left up to the locals, ATF and DEA to sort out. We weren't assigned additional team members after the shooting, so it was just the three of us, which we didn't mind at all. We now had a closer bond than any. We had our own sub-meeting after the briefing to discuss our strategies for moving forward.

"I don't know about you guys, but that whole Jay Horse thing has really gotten under my skin," Nina stated as she handed us a cup of coffee from the cup tray she was holding. We smiled and thanked her in return.

"We were discussing the same thing earlier. He set us up big time," Dianna stated.

"Yeah; not only was he not drunk, but he knew we were following him," I added.

"And he led us right into an ambush," Nina followed up.

We were very in sync at this point and appeared to know each other's thoughts. "I guess there's no need to ask what you ladies want to do."

Then they both smiled and Dianna stated, "Yeah; let's find him."

"You both do realize that the A.D. will have our asses for this," I replied.

"Jay Horse is a part of this investigation, whether the A.D. likes it or not. Are you in?" Dianna inquired of both of us.

"Hell yes!" Nina responded. I nodded my head in agreement.

"I guess you didn't see anything last night that would assist?" Nina asked.

I looked at her with trepidation, because she still had hopes that Jessica was alive after I briefed everyone on her death. I responded solemnly, "He killed her," and left it at that.

We ventured back up to Shiprock and instructed Steve that we were going to remain up there for the next couple of days and would keep him briefed. After checking into the Holiday Inn in Farmington we paid another courtesy call to the Council Chambers. This time it wasn't going to be as pleasant as our first meeting. Our timing was impeccable; when we arrived at the chambers, Mr. Hawthorne was there also.

"Good morning, agents. I've been meaning to reach out to you. I received a call from the Gaming Commission this morning and the local authorities, in reference to some drugs that were at a party held in the casino Friday night. I wasn't present at the party, but I was giving it in honor of the Code Talkers; a celebration that ended Saturday. I was informed that some patrons got carried away and were in violation of the law. Well, you can rest assured that you have my full cooperation in this investigation."

Then he extended his hand to shake from the three of us. He had the smell of corruption all over him and we weren't buying it at all. We already knew that Jay Horse worked for him. Horse bragged about it himself!

"Well, I have to be going now. I hope you enjoy your day," he stated before departing.

After Hawthorne departed Dianna read the riot act to the council. She came down on them hard, informed them that we weren't going anywhere and that it was in their best interest for all to cooperate, if they wanted us to get off their lands. She also stated that the previous arrests and shootings were only the beginning. Dianna was taking a big chance with her approach. She could ostracize them and make them even more noncompliant. She was also taking a risk that they would take this over our heads and complain of harassment, which the local news would just love to hear. They summoned the local reservation police chief to assist us in finding Jay Horse.

We spent all day looking for Jay Horse, with no results. Once again we discovered numerous crimes unrelated to the case. We were exhausted, so we called it a day and went to dinner. We discussed the case over dinner and came to the conclusion that once again the Council was misleading us and had sent us on a wild goose chase. If we wanted to find Jay we would have to do it ourselves, without the help of the Council.

Home of the Brave 83

Dianna's speech hadn't gone over as well as we thought. The Council was famously stoic when it came to displaying their true feelings to the FBI.

The next day we began at the FBI Farmington Residence Office, a small satellite office which covered San Juan County only. We needed a base of operation while in Farmington, especially if we were going out on our own again. We needed to coordinate with Farmington local law enforcement and see what information they had about Jay Horse.

We came in contact with a real tough Farmington Sheriff by the name of Carroll Hughes, an ex-Ranger, who offered to assist in any way. Sheriff Hughes was a big burly man, but all muscle. He didn't look like the type to spend a lot of time in the gym lifting weights; he was just naturally that way. He was 6 feet 5 inches and weighed about 250 lbs. A man of honor and conviction, he wasn't wore an air of incorruptibility as sincere as the star on his belt buckle. He wore a black t-shirt displaying his large biceps and muscular physique, jeans, black cowboy boots and a black cowboy hat. He had one of those old western holsters with an old Colt revolver strapped to the right side. He looked like a throwback from one of those old Clint Eastwood movies, and definitely wasn't someone you would piss off or invite into a dark alley; unless he was on your side, of course.

We went to several bars, brothels and places of ill-repute inquiring about Jay Horse. Sheriff Hughes had a flair for getting what he requested from the degenerates that we were questioning. There were times when he just asked us to remain in the bar area as he went to the restroom with some hard case he was questioning. He would return with the answers we needed and the hard case would remain in the restroom. It would be a fair assessment to say the reprobate was attempting to recover from the questioning.

We had received valuable information that led us to a particular brothel on a ranch, located about 10 miles outside of New Mexico, in Durango, Colorado. Everything ever written about Durango was true. It was a place that lived up to its reputation. It was an infamous mainstay for bikers, smugglers and outlaws of all types.

The brothel was located on a dude ranch. These were plentiful in and around Durango. It was an old-style ranch house, flat-roofed, with just one story, but sprawling due to all the additions. It was retro in design; right down to the wooden log post fence surrounding it. There were several vehicles parked in a designated parking area for visitors. There were no CCTV cameras that we could see. We didn't see Jay's vehicle parked with the others. He was smarter than that; he parked in the rear of the house, near the back door.

We decided that I would be the one to go inside. Jay was clever and slippery. He had already led us into an ambush and eluded us once. We stationed ourselves around the brothel as best we could. Sheriff Hughes covered the back door where Jay's vehicle was parked. If he attempted to escape, he would most likely run for his vehicle.

When I went inside I was greeted by several women in the parlor, waiting for dates. I must admit, they were seductively dressed in sexy lingerie. They were like sirens, each with a provocative and alluring beauty. One of them approached me and took off my thick, black-rimmed 50s style glasses.

"You're a very handsome man. Why are you hiding those pretty green eyes behind glasses?" she inquired. She was close enough that I could smell the honey milk body cream she was wearing, and the cinnamon on her breath. These ladies were appealing in every aspect. The funny thing I kept thinking was why people assumed because a person is a nerd or a geek that they are unattractive. Some of the most attractive women I've ever met were gorgeous nerds.

I asked to speak to the madam of the house. They were reluctant at first, but they found their way to getting her. I asked the madam if we could discuss business in private, and she agreed. I had one of those trustworthy boyish faces and I seemed harmless to most. I was the exact opposite of Sheriff Hughes, waiting out back to take down Jay. I was just there to gather information and report. Everything about Sheriff Hughes said enforcer and he had a 'don't fuck with me' attitude to go with it. Once alone, I showed the madam my credentials and explained to her the reason for my presence.

Home of the Brave

"We have the place surrounded," I said, exaggerating. I had always wanted to say that. "We're not here to disrupt your business in any way. We're just here for Jay Horse, that's all."

Then she inquired, "Do you have a warrant?"

"Well, I can have several official police vehicles here with sirens to surround the place and scare off a full night's work while I wait for a warrant. It might even take a second day to get one. I have the manpower to put you out of business just by being present outside your ranch. Now, all I need is the room Horse is in. We don't want anything else."

She paused, then replied, "He's in room 13, down the hall to the left, near the back door."

Jay Horse wasn't a superstitious guy, that's for sure, because who in their right mind would check into room 13 on the left? How much bad luck is that? The Madam escorted me to the room and I let Sheriff Hughes in the back door when I arrived.

"He's in there with two of my girls. Nothing better happen to them," she said firmly.

"Can you get them to open the door," I asked her.

"And what is it you want me to say. Room service?" she drawled sarcastically.

Then Sheriff Hughes interjected, "You can either get them to open the door or I'll break it down!" She looked up at the giant sized man and rolled her eyes. She knew he wasn't kidding and had the power to back up his threat.

"Look, I don't want anything to happen to the women in there either, so we need you to get the door open without attracting suspicion." I stated.

"This isn't a hotel," she retorted, "I can't just knock on the door and..." before she could complete the statement, Sheriff Hughes kicked down the door with his shotgun in one hand and the other balled into a fist.

Jay was caught naked as a jay bird, excuse the pun, in a compromising position. The women jumped up naked and screaming, and Jay attempted to roll off the bed and make it to the table where his things were lying, but the sheriff was lightning-quick for a big man. He was standing over Jay before the man could make it across the room. He had zeroed in on him since he kicked down the door. He anticipated and checked his every move. You could see his military skills shining through. He didn't wait for Jay's next move, as he didn't want to give him the slightest opportunity to reach for his gun. He didn't want to kill him, since we needed to question him, and therefore hit him with the barrel of his shotgun, knocking him out cold.

During the scuffle the women remained naked and screaming with fear. They were in shock and couldn't move, even when the incident was over and Jay was unconscious. Then the Sheriff turned to them and yelled, "Shut the fuck up," and they stopped immediately. Dianna and Nina arrived just as the screaming stopped, to witness Jay Horse lying on the floor, naked and unconscious, with the two trembling naked women whimpering softly.

The madam then snapped out of it. She had been hiding outside the door to avoid any gun play that might have occurred. She must have known Jay had a gun and didn't warn us. I wanted to have her arrested, but the Sheriff was outside his jurisdiction. We were already in the hot seat with the A.D. and the arrests of prostitutes wouldn't go over well at this point.

Jay finally gained consciousness while handcuffed in the back seat of the Sheriff's SUV. We had the working girls dress Jay while he was unconscious. They probably assisted him in getting his clothes off, so why not place them back on him? Sheriff Hughes followed us back to the Farmington Satellite Office where we would question Mr. Horse. The Sheriff had been a great help in the apprehension of Jay, and I was going to make sure his supervisors knew of this.

"If you folks need any further assistance, here's my card," Sheriff Hughes stated. He was really making a play for Nina. He wanted to make sure she had his phone number. He just gave his card to me and Dianna out of courtesy. Then he turned and looked at Nina again, smiling, and said, "I mean anything at all, just give me a call." Nina

Home of the Brave

smiled and looked at us, blushing and waved the business card. It was clear she liked Sheriff Hughes also.

"Get a room already," I replied, making Dianna and Nina laughed. We all agreed that the sheriff had been a valuable team member. I would inquire from Steve in the morning if we could make him a temporary member of our team for this case. Next on the agenda was to interrogate Jay. We didn't know what, if anything, he knew that could contribute to this case, but scum usually sticks together, like the residue left in the tub.

It was already early in the morning of the next day, January 31st. We couldn't afford to worry about the time or sleep because the clock was ticking. Dianna was an expert interrogator. We always said she could pry water from a stone, so we let her do her thing with him. He began breaking down after about two hours.

"You people think you can just come here and do what you want? We've been here since the Long Walk and we're going to remain here long after you're gone," Jay stated.

"Well, they might be here, but you're not going to be. You see, that little ambush of yours killed an FBI agent. He was pronounced dead this morning, which means you're an accomplice to the murder of a Federal Agent. You will be sent to a Federal Penitentiary, not some Res jail, for the rest of your life. You might even be executed. I'm uncertain if they have the death penalty here in New Mexico," Dianna stated.

"You can't pin that on me, I wasn't even there," he sneered.

"Yes we can. You knowingly led us to that ambush to murder us. We have you on murder in the first and five counts of attempted murder," Dianna retorted.

She had made it all up in order to get some information, and her strategy worked.

For just a moment, Jay stared. His copper skin paled to the color of a rattler's underbelly. His chiseled lips turned downward, and was that a hint of a quiver? It was gone before I was sure what I had seen. He lifted a Styrofoam cup to his lips, attempting to cover his fear with a nonchalant sip, but the coffee in his cup wavered in his less-than steady hands. Defeated, he slammed the cup on the table, splashing its contents all over the wood and burst out. "You're looking in the wrong place. I heard some Hopis talking about death dealers coming back to right the wrongs of the white man. You should be looking at the Hopis," he insisted.

The Hopi Nation was within the center of the Navajo Nation. They were left alone by the Navajo because they feared the Hopis as great medicine men and guardians of the underworld. The Hopis weren't even on our radar. They were a part of the Pueblo Indian tribes and were considered a placid group. We didn't know if Jay was blowing smoke up our asses or what. He was already proving to be a great deceiver. We said our goodbyes to January the 30th and still weren't close to catching the serial killer.

Chapter 7

ꬰALL ꬰROM GRACE

When I woke the next morning I had received all the information I needed to know, through dreamscape, that Jay wasn't involved in these murders. He was a sexual deviant and a petty criminal, but not a serial murderer. The rest didn't really matter at this point since it didn't pertain to the investigation, and he was already in custody. Everyone had been called back to Albuquerque for an all hands mandatory meeting by the A.D. As usual, Steve didn't go into details. We left Jay Horse at the Residence Office in Farmington for questioning by the ATF and hit the road early that morning.

We knew the information given by Jay was 50/50 and whatever the A.D. had to say wouldn't be anything favorable for us, so we weren't in any rush. The A.D. probably received information by now of our questioning of Jay Horse at the Residence Office, or the Council made some calls in reference to our last meeting. I drove on the way back down to Albuquerque. I let the girls get a couple more hours of shut eye on the highway. I could function on four hours or less sleep by now; my body had gotten used to it.

Everyone was tight-lipped at the meeting, and curious to know why the A.D. called us back. It was the proverbial elephant in the room. We were all working diligently in the field and researching, but the clock had reset and was ticking down to another abductee. What

89

would happen after the countdown expired for the last victim? Would he retire never to be seen again? Would this become a cold case?

"It will be February 1st tomorrow, this killer threatens to strike again, and we still have nothing. We have all the best resources afforded to us and the assistance of several agencies, but we can't find one person. We can raid drug labs, brothels and make unwarranted threats, but we still have no results. We will be initiating road blocks and check points again. The standing curfew has been extended to start an hour early. Unless someone can offer me something outside of a crystal ball, we will have another murder on our hands," the A.D. stated. The A.D. was now feeling the pressure that we were used to working under. He was a bureaucrat and hadn't been investigating in the field in a long time, but his idle threats wouldn't make this situation any better.

"This is bullshit," Max stated after the meeting. He always had a habit of expressing what everyone was feeling. We left the meeting angry and wondering why he had wasted our time. As if we didn't know everything he'd spewed. We knew we were on a clock and that the time was ticking down. He just wanted to assert his authority more and act as if his insulting talks would make us do our jobs better. Everyone was out there, giving their all. We even had people sidelined for gunshot wounds.

Things went from bad to worse when the A.D. called our team in for a private pow-wow, with Steve present. Once again, he belittled our efforts pertaining to the investigation, but this time he sidelined us. He reassigned us to Homeland Security to assist with coordination, where he could keep an eye on us. It wasn't like anyone else was doing any better than us, but he disapproved of our methods; min in particular. This was no surprise as he'd let me know of his dislike for me on more than one occasion.

Then the unthinkable happened on February 1 at 0200 hours. Dianna's telephone rang and her face went blank as she listened in silence. I could tell that there was something wrong by her look. She continued to listen, and then responded, "We'll be right there."

Fall from Grace   91

"What's wrong?" I inquired as I looked at her with anticipation and concern. She seemed lifeless, then composed herself and briefed me on the situation.

"It was Steve; Gracie is missing. She left the office around 2100 hours yesterday and no one has been able to get in touch with her. She was supposed to meet Steve at the hotel, but didn't show up," she said solemnly.

"Yeah, I saw her leave. She was exhausted from pulling such long hours with Steve and Max," I replied. We paused for a very long time and then I broke the silence. "I'll drive; let's get going,"

Could this be the work of the serial killer? He wasn't supposed to attack until tonight; February 1 or the morning of February 2. What made him go early, if it was him? He had been so meticulous in the past with his countdown. At this juncture I was only hoping that it was all just a mistake.

We arrived at the RO around 0300 hours. The office was already packed. An FBI agent was missing in action, and the always stoic Steve was a wreck. It seemed the subject escalated as we had anticipated, after leaving the letter for us. He sent a clear message this time that he wasn't afraid of us, and that we could do nothing to stop him. The A.D. began the meeting, as he had taken over now. I drowned him out and judging by the look of every agent in that room, they did as well. It was personal now, more than ever. There was nothing this degrading A.D. had to say that we were interested in hearing. He had lost the respect of everyone in room.

We forged on in the investigation. There were no other victims taken on the night of February 1 thru the morning of February 2. That pretty much confirmed that Gracie was the intended victim. Our timeline for the abductions had been leaked or figured out by the Media News, which wasn't a hard thing to do. They were camped outside the RO. They didn't have any information on Gracie's abduction, but they have plenty of questions concerning the night of the 1st and early morning of the 2nd.

Their main questions were: has there been another abduction, and how close were we in catching the serial killer? They had a right to know; after all, we were public servants, but the FBI decided to keep this one closed to the media. It didn't involve a civilian; so we could keep the information as sensitive and because it pertained to an ongoing case. The A.D. explained all this in his press conference that afternoon.

Steve circumvented A.D. Pollin's orders and took my team off the bench. If Gracie had any chance of surviving this, it would be with me riding in the front seat. The A.D. was receiving too much heat to notice that we weren't in the office. He wanted the recognition and the limelight, and now it was time for the A.D. to feel what came with it; the stress, the pressure and the heat.

Dianna, Nina and I went to Gracie's apartment, where we conducted my dreamscape preliminaries as usual. Gracie's apartment was immaculate, she didn't spend a lot of time there. She was always working, like the rest of us. The bedroom wasn't as neat as the rest of the house. The bed wasn't made and there were clothes out, as if she'd been in a rush to leave and couldn't decide what to wear. Perhaps it was just clothes from the night before? I guess this was why Steve didn't want to come over with us. They probably spent nights together between here and the hotel.

There weren't a lot of people who knew of their relationship. They pretty much kept it a secret. There weren't a lot of framed pictures around, but she did have a photo album that I sat down on the sofa and perused. I grabbed a bottle of water from the refrigerator and attempted to mimic what she would do while at home. I turned on the television, but kept it mute and turned on the stereo. She had some nice jazz singers, to include Diana Krall, Norah Jones and Nina Simone. I put on the latest Norah Jones CD. Then I proceeded to water her plants, which were neglected due to the long hours we had been working.

While I was doing all this, Dianna was looking for clues around the apartment and Nina just followed me around and observed my

Fall from Grace

every move. It was her first time witnessing this. I would look at her from time to time and catch her gaze as she smiled at me in return. She didn't say anything, but had the look of approval for what I was doing. I treated Gracie's personal items like I was caring for her in person. When I completed my preliminary connection they took me back to the hotel, so I could conduct a dreamscape on Gracie. This was something I would have never conceived of doing; not in my wildest dreams.

After I prepped myself, Dianna gave Steve a call and informed him that I was about to go under. Nina asked if she could remain in the room when I went into dreamscape. It was usually a private affair that I only shared consciously with my doctors, until Dianna. I conferred with Dianna and we both agreed that it would be alright, since Nina had shared a dreamscape experience with us and was our partner.

I changed into a pair of sweat pants and a t-shirt; I was usually very active during my dreams. I grabbed my headphones and took two sleeping pills. I wanted to spend as much time as possible finding clues to assist the team in finding Gracie, no matter how messed up the pills made me. I lay down on the bed. "Now girls," I urged with mock severity, "promise you won't take advantage of me while I'm sleeping."

They both giggled, the inappropriate joking helping to break the terrible tension we all felt.

They had an iPad ready to record and a notepad for taking notes. I'd never felt so safe before going into dreamscape, as I was always concerned with the horrors that I might find. It'd never been this personal for me. I was sure I would make a connection. Thus far, the killer had kept the victims alive for about 16 days.

I woke up groggy with a headache, several hours after the dreamscape. That was the only problem with gathering the information. I was usually under for valuable time, but Steve always comforted me by saying that it was time worth spending in capturing the subject. Up until this case it always held true. Dianna had the bottled water waiting for me like an old pro and Nina was her apprentice, learning as she observed.

They were doing their best to be patient with me as they waited for me to brief them on what I'd discovered. They were observing my every move, from me unscrewing the cap off the water bottle to me putting it up to my lips and drinking. I didn't mean to prolong their anticipation or keep them in suspense, but I was parched and feeling a little dehydrated from sweating in the dream. Then I explained to them what I had observed.

"She was abducted at the liquor store parking area. She went inside to purchase a bottle of wine. The name of the liquor store is Kelly Liquors, at 6300 San Mateo Blvd. N.E., Albuquerque. Her car is still there also. She remembered how dark it was in the parking lot area and how she should have been more vigilant. She couldn't see the moon or a star in the sky, it was so dark. She did hear the howl of a coyote in the background, but it was too late once she recognized the sound. The perpetrator moved in quickly and grabbed her from behind, like the others, before she could enter her vehicle."

"Gracie was unconscious during the trip and woke up terrified on the dirt floor of the pitch black area she was being held, just like the rest of the women. She was already thinking that she was going to die because she heard this all before. She was bound like the rest, with plastic straps on her wrists and around her ankles. She had a gag in her mouth and a blindfold covering her eyes. He doesn't want her to see, like he didn't want the rest of them to see. His whole persona is built around being in the shadows. She is still fully clothed right now. She also experienced what Jessica did in reference to the changing temperatures while on the dirt floor. He hasn't approached her again since the abduction," I said in a very low and melancholy voice.

"Wow, that is amazing!" Nina stated in excitement. This was her first time experiencing what I could do. We understood her excitement, but it wasn't reciprocated. Dianna wanted to hear the information as Nina, but was subdued as I was about the demise of Gracie. After her initial stupefaction, Nina came back down to our reality

Fall from Grace
95

and was cognizant of the solemn mood in the room. She felt embarrassed, so I quickly moved on.

"Did you get anything from the session?" I inquired from the both of them.

"Yes, we received a lot, but it was once again her thoughts of fear and despair. She mentioned you and Steve. She hopes the both of you can find her. She also left a message to her parents because she knew you would enter her dreams. She asked if we could give it to them and stated that she would try to help you in any way possible."

Then Nina inquired, "Why can't you give us any insight on the subject?"

"I can only enter the dreams and experiences of a person I have a connection with. If she could see a face, I could give a description, but I still wouldn't be able to enter into his dreams. I need a personal connection to do so."

"You mean like a totem," Nina asked.

"Exactly," I replied. Nina was more knowledgeable about dreamscaping or vision quest, as the Native Americans call it, than I had realized.

"Can you take me with you, like when you pulled me into your dream the other night" she asked next.

"I've never attempted it while conducting investigations, because I need to concentrate all my focus on reading the dreams of the victim and making a connection with them," I explained.

"But it could be possible?" she inquired.

"Anything is possible, but there is something that I didn't divulge about that experience with the both of you."

"What is that," she asked as they both looked on with curious eyes.

"Well I didn't want to get into something so personal at the time, but to bring you in as I did without any prior experiences with you, it had to be a strong connection between us that night. I was as surprised as the both of you. Remember my reaction afterwards, Dianna?"

"Yes, I do. Vividly. You started freaking out."

"I began freaking out because I was surprised by what had occurred."

"So what are you saying," Dianna inquired?

"I know what he's saying," Nina interjected, "I was dreaming about him as well."

"This just became awkward," Dianna stated.

"We were all drunk, and I was just as horny as the two of you," Nina stated, attempting to deflect any further embarrassment. "So there's no way to recreate that?" She inquired.

"It was a first for me," I replied. "I'm not as close to Gracie as I am with the two of you. We were spending a lot of time both working and having fun together."

"Can we try it anyway?" Nina asked.

"Sure, but have to be later," I insisted. "I can't take another pill right now, and we have to brief Steve and the rest of the RO."

At the morning meeting, the A.D. spewed out his usual badgering, which no one was interested in hearing. Then it was time for me to brief everyone on my findings. The A.D. didn't have a problem with me speaking at the time, but his hard-eyed glare made me sure we'd have another private meeting after this one because I ventured off the reservation to acquire the information.

Everyone at the meeting was shocked by my findings. They immediately sent the local police to the liquor store to preserve the crime scene. When I finished briefing everyone, Ortega jumped out of his chair with tears in his eyes and attacked me. He was distraught and out of control.

"You saw him doing all this to her and you didn't stop it," he yelled, holding me down on the floor. Then Steve, who was the closest ViCAP team member, tackled Ortega, and the rest of the ViCAP team flew out of their seats as well. Steve hit him several times, rendering him incapacitated. He lay on the floor weeping.

"How dare you! He saw all of this after the fact! Don't you ever touch a member of my team," Steve yelled, enraged as he stood over the prostrate agent.

Fall from Grace

Amber went over to calm Steve, and Dianna accompanied me. No one from the Residence Office attempted to come to Ortega's defense; partially because he was wrong, but mostly because of Max, a former linebacker and Special Forces Marine, who was waiting to engage anyone who even thought about jumping in.

Max was our enforcer as he looked over the crowd between us and them. I've seen him on countless occasions take on up to four assailants at the same time without even breaking a sweat. He would never admit it, but he enjoyed engaging in physical confrontation. He would always psychoanalyze himself and his aggression as being a healthy way of relieving stress and that it was controlled and only brought out when necessary. Agent Max Maurice and Sheriff Carroll Hughes were from the same cloth. I wouldn't want to confront either man in a dark alley. They could have been brothers in a different life.

The A.D. seemed to take pleasure in what had happened. He'd had an unforgettable smirk on his face when I was attacked. I don't know what I ever did to the Assistant Director, but one thing was for sure; he despised me. The fight had been all he needed to break up the team.

Thus far we were down two ViCAP agents. Paul had been shot and was recovering from his injury and Steve had been suspended and relieved of duty. He was taken off the case due to personal involvement and the politics of bureaucracy. That left Max, Amber, Dianna and me; two African Americans, an Italian American and a half breed descendant of Freedmen. It didn't take a genius to surmise what would happen next. Yes racism still exists in the government. It didn't take long before the A.D. took total control of the investigation. It should have been passed down to Max, but apparently the team had fallen from grace in the eyes of Washington, with the abduction of Gracie.

The remaining team members continued to assist with the investigation. We currently had the most investigative history and knowledge on the case, but we were under close scrutiny. The A.D. threatened to fire me if I disobeyed him, and went out into the field investigating again. It was easier to fire me than the others, because I was only a consultant on contract. The others had civil servant positions and ratings.

Dianna and I were mandated to remain at the RO and assist with coordination. I immediately requested a medical leave of absence due to the pressure of the case. It was easy for me to request the leave since my contract had a medical clause. This infuriated the A.D. and he threatened to fire me again, but there was nothing he could do. My contract was drawn up by a very reputable lawyer. He also threatened to arrest me if he saw or heard of me getting involved in the case in any way. A.D. Pollin was self-destructing, slowly but surely. He vilified and put down the A-team, and we were the only chance he had of catching this killer.

I moved out of the Hilton where Pollin and the other agents were staying, and into the Ramada Inn. I wouldn't leave Gracie like that. I was invested in the case, but I knew I couldn't help her in my limited role at the RO. I informed Dianna of my intentions, and then called Steven. He was still in New Mexico also. We agreed to continue working the case together. The rest of the ViCAP team would assist us from the inside. Dianna's duties would be to shadow the A.D. After moving into the Ramada I received a call from Nina, who had also been sent packing.

"So I heard you're taking a leave of absence," she stated.

"Yeah, that prick just wanted to rub my nose in it. There was no need in me to stay there and take that abuse. I've never been a glutton for punishment," I stated.

"So, are you quitting or just needed to get away from the Anal Dude," she inquired?

"I like the abbreviated pun," I replied.

"I have my moments," she retorted.

"So, are you ready to go on a road trip with me?" she asked.

"Sure; where are we going?"

"We need to go back to North Carolina. I have someone I need you to meet," she stated.

Fall from Grace

"I don't know if this is a good time for it," I replied.

"This is the best time for it. We are running out of time and if you're going to find Agent Mullins, you need to utilize your abilities to the fullest. I know someone who can assist you with that. You are capable of doing so much more with your abilities than you are aware of," Nina stated.

"So, when do we leave?" I asked.

"I've already booked us a flight out in four hours," she replied.

"Well thank you very much, Ms. Confidence. I need to make a few phone calls then, can you pick me up?"

"Sure; I'll see you soon," she stated and hung up the phone.

Chapter 8

The Talisman

*"I circle around, I circle around, the boundaries of the earth
I circle around, I circle around, the boundaries of the earth
wearing my long winged feathers as I fly
wearing my long winged feathers as I fly
I circle around, I circle around, the boundaries of the earth"*
 – Shamanic Chant

Nina and I took the next flight out of Albuquerque; Delta flight 5098 to the Asheville Regional Airport, Swain County, North Carolina. She was certain that if I met with a medicine man there, he could teach me to target my abilities in order to find Gracie.

"So, how did Dianna take it?" Nina inquired.

"What do you mean?"

"You know; you going to North Carolina with me," she stated, grinning.

"She trusts us both to do the right thing," I replied, smiling in return.

"And what is the right thing," she asked, continuing to engage in the repartee to tease me.

"Not doing anything that would hurt her."

100

The Talisman

"You're funny, Chris, but I respect how much you care about each other. Besides, you both have already taken care of me ever cheating, haven't you? I guess she would feel safe and trust you after that," she stated, then exploded with a hearty laugh. "I'm just messing with you, Chris; don't take it personally. I love you both," she said with a Cheshire Cat grin.

I barely knew this side of Nina. This was an aspect of her nature I experienced in the dreamscape that night; the vixen. This was going to be an interesting trip, if she was starting out this way. Nina really did have feelings for me, but attempted to mask them around Dianna, which was appropriate since =the other woman was my girlfriend. The bad thing about it was that I was attracted to her as well, but I would never hurt Dianna by cheating on her again. Nina was extremely attractive, but my feelings for Dianna were more than just physical.

After landing, we rented a vehicle and drove about 60 miles to Cherokee, North Carolina. This was the setting I was used to, having grown up as a boy in North Carolina; the tall and dense trees of the forest, the running rivers, lakes, mountains and wilderness of the Carolinas. Nina and I enjoyed a scenic and pleasurable drive through the western county of Swain, NC. It was beautiful there in the Oconaluftee River Valley within the Smokey Mountains. This was the Nina's birthplace. She knew it well, and still had family here.

Nina currently lived in Washington, D.C., as I did, but traveled often between D.C. and Cherokee, which was the headquarters of Eastern Band of the Cherokee Indians. It was late when we checked into the Hilton in Cherokee. We used our government discounts at the hotel and Nina paid for the flights via her government credit card. She could justify paying for my ticket because I was an official consultant.

After getting settled we enjoyed a nice meal together in the Hilton's restaurant and called it a night. I telephoned Dianna before bed to see how she was doing, and for the latest FBI update on Gracie, but nothing had changed.

102   *The Talisman*

When I went to sleep that night I reached out to Dianna in my dreams. One great thing about dreamscape was that I could reach out to loved ones, no matter how far away. We made love that night in the other realm. I woke in the morning to the sound of my phone ringing. It was Dianna. She wanted to discuss our dream together last night. While talking to her I heard a knock on the door.

"Hey, someone's at the door. Can I call you back later?" I requested, hating to let the moment end.

"Sure, and be careful, alright?" Dianna urged.

"You bet," I replied. I was still in bed with my lounge pants on and a white fruit of the loom's V-neck shirt when I went to the door. It was Nina, already dressed with two cups of coffee in hand.

"Wow, young man; how long are you going to sleep," she inquired as I let her in the door.

"Good morning, Nina."

"I thought we'd get an early start since we're on the clock here." She placed the coffee on the table. "Can I open the curtains, Count Dracula?" she asked, opening them before I could even answer.

"Sure, go right ahead," I said sarcastically as the sun of the morning blinded me temporarily.

"I'm gonna jump in the shower real quick and get dressed."

"Go right ahead. I promise you, I won't peek, but it's not like you're going to show me something I haven't already seen," she stated laughing. "I'm only kidding you, go ahead and shower."

"You're not going to let me forget that night, are you," I asked and looked at her, grinning.

"Not a chance, buster," she replied and giggled. I must admit she was delightful and extremely charming. I could have thought of worse ways to wake up. Then she continued to talk to me while I was in the shower. "Did you visit Dianna last night?"

"Yes I did."

"That's sweet, but did you receive anything further on Gracie?"

"As a matter of fact, yes; I did. The subject fed and bathed her last night like he did Jessica. He is sticking to the same routine. He has

The Talisman
103

been meticulously careful, almost regimental, except he took Gracie earlier than scheduled."

"Do you think it could be someone with former military experience?" Nina suggested

"It could be. There are a lot of military traumas that would lead one to violent tendencies, but usually we see binge killing sprees, not meticulous serial murders associated with those disorders."

After I finished dressing, Nina drove us into town to a holistic healing shop. I was expecting us to go to a reservation or some old cabin in the woods and meet with a grumpy old guru type medicine man. I quickly discovered how far off my imagination had gotten me. The building we approached was a little store front shop. It even had a bell over the front door that rang when customers entered. The shop had solutions, herbs, potions and powders used for medical purposes. It was set up like a pharmacy, but for witches, warlocks and mystics, or as the letters stated on the large store front window: 'Earth Healers.'

They had a section of animal medicines: chicken feet, frog legs, powder of animal antlers, snake venom, animal gonads and other animal tissue cultures. There was a botany / ethno-botanical section filled with fresh and dry herbs, cactus buds, dream-inducing plant powders, extracts, resins, roots, bark, psychedelic seeds, magic mushrooms, assorted plants, oils and incense. The last section was dedicated to trinkets, books, crystals, talismans, totems and other assorted materials used in the practice of different Earth religions and arts. I was amazed at all the different eccentric items they had on display.

There was a beautiful young Native American girl at the counter. When she saw Nina, her face immediately lit up. They hugged and Nina spoke to her in Kituhwa, the middle dialect of Aniyawiya, the official language of Cherokees (Tsalagi) indigenous to North Carolina. I didn't understand a word. My grandmother would have understood it and spoken it fluently in return. My mother knew a little of the dialect but rarely spoke it, except on rare occasions with my grandmother, and even then it was mixed with American English.

Nina handed her the gift bag she had been keeping in the back seat of the vehicle. The young girl responded to her in Kituhwa. Nina introduced me to the young woman as her cousin, [1](#sdfootnote1sym)Kele.

"Kele, this is Christian Sands. He is a colleague of mine from work."

"Hello, Mr. Sands; how are you?" She extended her hand

"Very well, Kele, but call me Chris. Beauty must run in the family," I said out loud, grasping her warm palm in mine

I must have been tired because I'm never that forward and usually keep those types of thoughts and comments to myself. Kele began blushing as Nina looked at me with a huge smile, and nudged me with her shoulder.

"Look mister, don't be hitting on my cousin," she responded. Then Nina spoke to Kele again in their native tongue. They both laughed, and then Kele went to the back of the store into a private area separated by a door. When Kele returned she was with an older Native American gentleman who appeared to be in his sixties, but still had a vibrant, fit look about him. He was wearing a black cashmere sweater vest, blue oxford shirt, buttoned to the top, blue jeans and black Timberland boots. When he approached me he gazed into my eyes, as if to gaze into my soul. His intense concentration suggested the scrutiny I usually reserved for a favorite movie or novel He had the stare of a large cat, like a lion or a tiger. Then he greeted the both of us.

"Shi-yo," he said.

"Shi-yo, uncle," Nina replied, and hugged him.

Good morning, how are you?" he inquired, holding his hand out to shake.

"I'm very well, and you?" I replied while extending my.

Then he sandwiched my one hand between the both of his and replied, "Good; thank you for coming."

"Chris, this is my uncle Askuwheteau. Uncle, this is Chris, who I've been talking to you about," she stated.

The Talisman   105

He turned his attention towards Nina and they spoke in Kituhwa. Then he said "Good, good," ending their conversation in English.

"Daughter, I will be back later, look after the store," he said to Kele. Then we departed.

We drove to the outskirts of town, where Askuwheteau lived. It was a modern, two-story, single-family home like many others in Swain County. Once inside, I met his wife and oldest daughter with her three year old son. They were all elated to see Nina and vice versa. They spoke in English and kept the Kituhwa to a minimum around me, to be polite. I always wondered why most people who knew different languages didn't extend the same courtesy.

After the introductions I was offered some tea and homemade bread cake by Awenta, Asku's wife. After a couple of minutes, Asku returned from the basement with a backpack and two sitting rugs. Then he informed the rest of the family that he would be back shortly.

"Will you join me?" he asked me upon approach.

"Yes, sir," I responded and got up with the unfinished tea and bread cake in hand.

"Here, let me take that for you," Nina offered.

We got into Asku's truck and drove into the Smokey Mountain range, traveling up and down, for an extended period of time as if we were on a rollercoaster ride,. We finally arrived at a valley amongst the mountains, with a little stream running through it. It was so serene; I couldn't believe the beauty of it all. It was like something from a Norman Rockwell painting.

After hiking for about a mile, we came to one of the biggest trees there. It was an Eastern hemlock that appeared to be about 500 years old. It was about 150 feet tall and about 7 feet in diameter, with painted symbols on it. The tree provided a roof for a manmade altar and a fire pit, all made of stone, which had been erected beneath it. We stopped about ten yards from the area and Asku got on his knees. He asked me to do the same as he spoke several words in Kituhwa, as if praying. Then we stood and he explained to me, "This is a *Wakhan Waki*; it means 'sacred place' in English. It is called

Mahkah-Odahingum-Mahpee, or Earth-Water-Sky. The water meets the Earth and the Earth meets the sky." Then he showed me the spot in the valley where the river touched the land and the mountains touched the sky. "Everything leads back to the sacred number 3, which reminds us of the three realms," he intoned, his voice soft and far away, but supported by a sensation of power. His voice was like thunder over the mountains, or the rushing of a distant river. We paused a moment in respectful silence before we continued towards the giant tree and altar area. He laid the rugs out before the altar and took out several totems.

"My niece tells me that you have vision dreams. I, too, am a wanderer between the realms. We call it vision quest. Someone in your family was the same?" he inquired in his softly authoritative monotone

"Yes; my grandmother and her father," I replied.

"Not your mother?" he asked.

"No; but her sister, my aunt, has the gift," I stated.

"Your mother also has this gift, but has suppressed it for many years. She has suppressed it in you as well. You have never had anyone to guide you through, as my father had guided me, and his father and father's father back to the time when the gift was brought down from the Great Spirit. Will you let me instruct you through this journey?" Asku inquired.

"Yes," I replied.

"It will take many nights before you can achieve your full potential, but I will start by getting you in touch with your spirit guide. Your spirit guide is what directs you in your dreams. It is how you achieve what you do while in the spirit worlds; the Upper and Lower Realms, as well as what you achieve in this Middle Realm which represents consciousness. This is the one which you are connected. "Have you seen a constant animal while in your dreams," Asku inquired?

"No, never," I replied.

"This is why you can't continue past your one realm. You haven't made a connection with your spirit guide. You have been

The Talisman   107

taught to control your dreams by the [2](#sdfootnote2sym)Bilagaana
(Kachada), but it is not control that you need. You need guidance,
and to learn how to channel. Channeling is how Shamans direct their
efforts in the other realms."

"So how do you cross over?" I inquired.

"Most beginners enter through one or several senses; sight, smell,
touch, hearing or taste," he responded.

"I touch the personal objects of people when I want to make a
connection," I stated.

"You also look at the objects and probably listen to certain items
without even recognizing you are using your senses in conjunction,
but your main sense is touch, so let's begin channeling there."

Then Asku lit a fire in the pit and returned. He took out a pipe
and placed crushed peyote in it. "We will share this smoke together,
but first I will need you to repeat this chant in order for you to know
it and remember it. We will chant this after smoking. The peyote will
assist you in your awakening. It will release you from the bonds that
keep you bound to this realm, and show you enlightenment."

We began chanting in Kituhwa. He didn't tell me what the words
meant at the time, but I repeated what he was saying as best I could.

Hey
Oh o o We e
Hey
Oh o o We e
Hoo! Hoo! Hey ey
Ey ey ey O We
Hoo! Hoo! Hey ey
Ey ey ey O We

We repeated the verse several times until he felt confident I knew it.
I thought the verse was quite simple. It had a melodic ring to it that
made it easy for me, since I was a musician. I treated the verse like
chords. Then we shared the peyote pipe for enlightenment. It didn't
take long before I felt the effects of the cactus, as we began to chant
again. Now I saw why he wanted me to practice several times. The

world felt a bit different after smoking peyote. Things began slowing down for me, and appeared distorted. I watched the speeding wings of a humming bird appear to slow to the occasional flap of a soaring eagle. I also viewed the sinuous dance of a bumblebee as it sought a promising flower. I was amazed that I could even see its wings flight.

Then I made my wonderful journey. I could only imagine that this was how it was to take an acid trip. I constantly heard Asku in the background, chanting even after it felt like I had stopped. I appeared to be traveling over the skies and mountains, and then I came to rest in a rain forest. It was similar to the Amazon, where I had traveled while in college. Everything was so colorful and peaceful. Then *she* came to me; black and beautiful. I no longer heard Asku chanting in the background.

I wasn't frightened for some reason, and I should have been, but something inside me was telling me she wasn't here to harm me but to protect me. She seemed to peer into my soul with her ever staring green eyes. It looked like I was looking into my own eyes as she moved back and forth, pacing while checking me out. She finally came to a stop and lay down before me. I knelt beside her and rubbed her silky soft, jet black coat, as she purred and panted deeply. It felt like I could hear the rumble resonating deep inside my soul. It was as if we were one. I had never experienced such a delight in my life.

Then I lay beside her on the cool jungle floor, staring up at the sky, peeking through the flora of the jungle canopy. I hadn't a care in the world at that moment in time. I felt at one with nature and the universe. All the self-conscious feelings of doubt and insecurity had vanished. I finally felt like I belonged to some place. I felt so secure that I fell asleep lying beside her. Then, in the distance, I began to hear Asku chanting again. I suddenly understood every verse of the chant, as if I knew Kituhwa.

"I circle around, I circle around, the boundaries of the earth
I circle around, I circle around, the boundaries of the earth
wearing my long winged feathers as I fly

The Talisman   109

wearing my long winged feathers as I fly
I circle around, I circle around, the boundaries of the earth"

When I woke from my trance I was still sitting with my legs crossed
on the rug provided by Asku, who remained beside me, chanting. I
had stopped.

I turned to Asku like a little boy, wanting to give thanks to his
parents on Christmas Day. He fell silent. "I hope you found what you
seek," he stated.

"Yes, I did," I said with an enormous and enthusiastic smile. I
checked my watch and realized that I had been gone for several hours
in what had felt like just a few minutes.

"You saw her?" he inquired.

"Yes; it was the most beautiful black panther I've ever seen."

"She has always been with you," he explained, "but was waiting for
you to come to her when you were ready. She is the spirit of touch
and the guardian of the night. She is the ruler of the dark domain.
She is relentless and powerful. What she lacks in stamina, she makes
up for in cunning and agility. This means she is a fast learner. Due
to her quickness of mind and reactions she sometimes forgets to stop
and pay attention to details." I nodded. I could relate to what he
was saying.

Asku continued. "She is a natural climber which means she always seeks the higher ground; professionally, academically and in her
personal life. She is an overachiever who is extremely intelligent and
succeeds in most things she sets out to do. When she climbs, she feels
the need to be closer to the sky; the heavens or upper realm, but is
just as comfortable in the dark of the underworld or lower realm.

"Unlike the lion or tiger she is an excellent swimmer and just as
agile on land. It is this duality which enables her to transverses both
realms as fluidly as water in osmosis. She is the guardian of the realms
and holds the keys and knowledge of both worlds. This makes her an
invaluable ally, yet dangerous as well. Her knowledge holds the light

and the darkness. Sometimes her abilities can be a detriment to her, and others. It is a gift and a curse."

He met my eyes and I felt a cold chill creeping up my spine. *Be careful,* he seemed to be warning me. *We're not talking only about a cat.*

He spoke again. "Her power comes from the moon and the night, which makes her a lunar creature; an astral traveler. The night offers her a natural camouflage with her jet black coat. It's her security blanket. She feels the night and the moon as others baize in the sun. She is most active at night. While other animals hunt at sunset, she stalks her prey in the dark of night with the moon as her guide and only friend. She is a solitary creature, a loner who avoids the crowd at all costs.

She is beautiful, but doesn't know it. She has an insatiable sexual appetite and is naturally non-monogamous, passing from one partner to another without commitments or lasting ties."

This last made me want to squirm. *He's too close to the truth for comfort!*

It felt like Asku was reading my biography. I couldn't believe the things he was telling me about myself that were true of the Black Panther also. He described my affinity for the dark and my ability to see well at night. He also mentioned my sexual appetite and my love of running and swimming. He spoke about my need for solitude. He said things about my life that no one knew except for maybe my mother and two doctors; Dr. Banks and Dr. Green.

"So tell me more about yourself, Christian. What tribe is your family from?" Asku inquired.

I took a deep breath and began my own tale. "We are descendants of the Freedmen Cherokees of Sampson County, North Carolina. My paternal great-grandmother and great-grandfather were Cherokees. My grandmother was Cherokee and my Grandfather was a Freedman, half black and half Cherokee, who lived with the Cherokees. My mother is of African American and Cherokee bloodline. I never knew my father; he died when I was an infant. I am a half breed in

The Talisman   111

every aspect of the word. My family was shunned by the Dawes Rolls
Act and the emancipation."

"I am sorry about what happened to your family," Asku replied.
Mine voted against it. Greed and prejudice knows no boundaries.
Those whom you would expect to know of the pain of injustices are
some of the main culprits. The Cherokee's 'Trail of Tears' and the
Navajo 'Long Walk' are examples of these injustices, yet our people
chose to turn a blind eye towards the same injustices perpetrated
against Freedmen. It is this duality within you that gives you strength
and makes you strong in the Spirit Worlds."

I nodded, well aware of the cost and rewards to be gained from
suffering.

We continued our conversation under the huge hemlock tree for
several more hours.

"We don't have the time to go over everything as I stated before,
but now that you are in touch with your Spirit Guide, perhaps things
will get easier for you when you're crossing. This backpack is for you,"
Asku said and began pulling out its contents. "It contains a Dream
Catcher. I've created this one specifically for you, with the three
realms represented. Sometimes even dream travelers must get sleep
without the disturbances from beyond. This pipe is yours and I've
included some dream inducers and other ethno botanicals to assist
you as well. This Bowie knife has been infused Cherokee magic. The
handle is made from the horn of the sacred stag. It will save your life
when you need it. Keep the prayer rug also. Along with the experience
we shared together, it will allow you to reach out to me whenever
you need me," he explained.

"I have also taken the liberty of passing down to you this mystic
crystal. I have no sons of my own. Wear it and be proud of who
you are and your heritage. Your Tsalagi name is 'Cheveyo'. It means
Spirit Warrior," he further stated and placed the crystal around my
neck, and explained the rest of the contents of the backpack and
their purpose.

"When you complete your journey you must return, so we can continue your teachings. There is great power in you, Cheveyo. I felt it as soon as I stepped into your aura. I confirmed it when I shook your hand, and now I've seen it after this session. You have the power to be a great healer as well, but this path I must show you at a later time." Then he said, "Chankoowashtay," which means 'go on the good road'.

The sun had gone down before we departed from the mountains. We doused the fire and left under the starry skies of the Smokies. I was energized with new confidence in myself and in my abilities. I didn't feel like a weirdo any longer, after bonding with Asku.

Awenta, Nina and Kele had dinner prepared and waiting for us when we returned from the mountains. It had been a long time since I'd sat down and had a family dinner. I learned a lot about my abilities, the Cherokee heritage and the Kituhwa language. It was a pleasure spending time with Nina's family. I conversed with her family after dinner then we drove back to the hotel late that night.

"So, was the trip worth it?" Nina inquired in the vehicle.

"We'll see," I replied. "I need to make contact with Gracie tonight, but thus far it has been worth it. Thank you very much, I really appreciate what you've done for me."

"Don't mention it. Have you spoken to Dianna today?"

"I did this morning. I haven't had time to call this evening."

"I'm sure you can't wait to call her."

"I had an interesting conversation with Asku about you on the mountain."

"Really? How embarrassing is this going to be?" she inquired, laughing.

"Oh; he wanted to know if we were seeing each other. I told him that we were just colleagues. Then he stated that I was the first male friend you've ever brought home."

She began to blush. "Oh, he did,"

"Yes; he did," I responded.

The Talisman 113

"Well, you got it easy. Awenta telephoned my parents and told them about you also. They started to come over for dinner until I talked them out of it," she informed me.

"I guess they're waiting for you to bring that special someone home," I replied.

"I guess," she said with a smile, looking at me.

"I'm sorry you didn't get a chance to see them," I added.

"Oh, I did; I went over there when you were at the mountain. I wouldn't have been able to come back down here if I didn't," she replied.

"It's good to see how close you are with your family," I said.

"You're not," she asked?

"Not really."

"Well, consider yourself family. They really liked you," she said.

"I like them as well. I told Asku I would be back down after this case is over," I informed her. She attempted to hold back the smile I saw written on her face. Nina was infatuated with me and it was very clear to see.

When we arrived back to the hotel, Nina asked, "Are you going to Dreamscape tonight?" There was something pointed in her tone, which I couldn't quite put a finger on.

"Yes," I replied. "Of course. It's critical I make a connection with Gracie. We're running out of time.

"Can you try and take me there when you go?" she asked.

"We discussed this earlier, Nina. I don't think it would be a good idea."

"Why not; four eyes are better than two. You and Dianna have already admitted that I'm a part of this." She stuck out her lower jaw and compressed her lips into an expression of absolute stubbornness, daring me to defy her.

I sighed. "Alright; we'll see if it works. Your spirit is strong, Nina; that's how we connected so easily," I stated. "Your uncle told me you are the daughter of the Chieftain. Why didn't you tell me you were a princess," I inquired?

"We don't consider it in those terms," she replied.

"Your family bloodline has been great in the Eastern Band Cherokee Assembly," I stated.

"Thank you, but I like to consider myself independent," she replied.

"Well, you definitely are that," I responded with a smile, then continued, "Hey, I need a few minutes to talk to Dianna first, then we can get started. OK?"

"Alright; come and get me from my suite when you're finished," she replied.

"Alright," I responded.

I wasn't sure how Dianna was going to accept this news of dreamscaping with Nina, especially after our last sexual encounter in dreamscape. Nina had already admitted to the both of us that she had been aroused and thinking about me that same night, which opened the door for the experience.

I spoke briefly to Dianna and told her all about my day and she briefed me on the proceedings of the investigation, which wasn't that good. I told her about Nina's idea and she didn't mind, as long as we kept it civil. I knew what she meant, but how civil can I be entering the lair of a psychotic killer? When I finished my phone call with Dianna, I went next door to get Nina. She had showered and changed by the time I arrived.

She had pulled on a pair of stretchy spandex gym pants and an athletic bra top that only covered her breasts and left her stomach and mid-section exposed. She changed into a pair of running shoes and some ankle socks. You would think she was going to work out or for a run or something. She was looking sexy and distracting as she showed her body's every curve and accentuation. I knew she wasn't going to make this trip an easy excursion, and sooner or later I would have to deal with the consequences of my actions; the dreamscape and its sexuality.

She grinned, following my eyes as I gave her the once over. She then threw on a long t-shirt that covered it all up, but made sure I

The Talisman   115

saw her physique first. Nina was a tease, so I attempted to distract
her. I was really trying to be good.

"Did you ever call Sheriff Hughes back?"

"No, not yet. I don't know about those long distance relationships.
They never work out. Commuting back and forth from D.C. to New
Mexico would be hell," she replied.

"I guess it would be."

"Where do you live in D.C?" she inquired, hitting the proverbial
ball back into my side of the court.

We volleyed back and forth like a tennis match with the questions
and distractions for a couple of minutes, until I finally put an end to
it by bringing up Gracie. Nina knew immediately that it was time
to get serious.

"We're going to do this differently than what you witnessed with
Dianna. Your uncle gave me some instructions." I laid down the
prayer rug on the floor and took out the dream catcher totem and
the pipe.

"Do you have a particular herb or inducer that you would like to
indulge in," I asked Nina.

"No; this is your show. I know nothing about it. The skill of being
a Medicine Man or Shaman is only taught to those who already
have the gift. My spirit is strong –the name Nina means *Strong* in
Cherokee – but this is not my path."

"Your uncle taught me well in the short time we spent on the
mountain. He's a great teacher," I said.

We sat down on the rug together and I instructed Nina to repeat
everything I said and did. We began with the learned chant, then
smoked from the pipe and began chanting again. After repeating
the chant and smoking the drug several times I placed the pipe in
the ash tray. I could feel the transcendental state coming on as we
continued to chant. Then I found myself in the rainforest again with
the panther. I concentrated all my thoughts and willpower on Nina
and she appeared next to me.

"What is this place?" she inquired, looking all around and amazed at its beauty. There were so many different brilliant colors and the jet Black Panther stood out and seemed to absorb them all. I was kneeling next to her, petting her. Nina was in total shock and fear of the animal.

"Come on over. She won't harm you. She is a part of me," I said. Asku didn't have to tell me that. I felt it from my first experience with her and knew it even more after he explained to me the Spirit of the Panther. Then Nina approached slowly and with trepidation.

"Here, pet her," I instructed. She knelt beside me in awe at the wonders of my totem's beauty.

"This wasn't a part of the dream that I shared with Dianna and you."

"No." I agreed. "I told you this was going to be different. Your uncle unlocked it for me."

"I thought we were going to see Gracie," she commented.

We are, and the panther will guide us." I said, petting the large cat. I instructed her to lie down on the jungle floor with me as we transcended into another dream state. Asku had instructed me of the many doors and realms in the spirit world and how the panther would guide me through them.

Then we were in the cool dark room where Gracie was lying on the dirt floor. He hadn't been taking such good care of Gracie as he had with the other girls. She was naked on the dirt floor, tied up and gagged. She didn't have on an adult diaper as the other girls. She was wallowing in her excrement. She didn't have on a blindfold, at least not yet. It was apparent that he had only taken her out of spite. She fit his profile; young and beautiful, but he had also known this would up the ante tremendously. The place was completely dark, except for the light coming in from the silhouette of the door. At least Jessica had had a candle at one point or another. Nina reached out a hand to Gracie, but couldn't connect. She started at the surreal restriction.

"You can't touch her, Nina. We are in her mind right now. We only see what she does, but look around. We might notice clues she missed.

The Talisman   117

Usually I see clearer than the victims because I'm not under the stress and fear of being abducted." Nina walked around and observed everything within the parameters of what Gracie observed.

Gracie had taken in a lot because she knew of my talents, expecting me to come, and attempted to curb her fears and concentrate, but the subject hadn't left her much to go on. We moved in her mind to when he fed her, but she was blindfolded. He didn't want her to see him at all. He hid in the shadows, but was unable to prevent her from smelling something peculiar. It was something that she hadn't smelled in a long time. She had definitely smelled it before, but couldn't think of where.

"Yes, Nina; we are sharing the same thoughts. That's what happens when you're in dreamscape with another."

"It's like telepathy," she said without moving her mouth.

"It's pretty cool, right," I said.

"I'll say," Nina replied. After gathering whatever information we could, we departed.

I wasn't suffering from any side effects like when I took those sleeping pills. I didn't feel drowsy or depressed; I felt great physically. My emotional state was still a mess though, because of Gracie's situation. Now was when things got tricky. After sharing such a personal thing with someone, their reaction usually tended to lean towards sex. You have just mind-fucked them even if it wasn't a sexual dream, due to the personal nature of sharing one's psyche. You become one with that person. This was no exception. When we woke up from the trance, I was aroused and peaking on all cylinders, and so was Nina.

We were sweating, excited and filled with unspent adrenalin and a release of the hormones our minds had been tricked into experiencing while stationary. I jumped up and grabbed two bottles of water from the small fridge. I handed one to Nina and went into the bathroom to compose myself. She knocked on the door a couple of minutes later.

"Are you alright?" she asked.

"Yeah, sure. I'll be out in a minute," I responded.

I had to calm down mentally and physically. My libido was aroused and standing at full attention. After I calmed down I exited the rest room. Nina appeared to be in full control.

"What happened to you?" she inquired.

"I had a panic attack," I told her, but she knew I was lying. She felt exactly what I did, and was attempting to play off.

"Look, we can't do that again. It is too risky," I said.

"Too risky for whom? We accomplished a lot and gathered a great deal of useful information," she said.

"What do you mean? I saw the same things as briefed everyone on before!" I protested.

"That's why it's good to have a second opinion. Maybe it was the way you explained it before, but I saw more," she replied. "You see, the dirt floor is actually the ground," she said.

"And how does that help? There are lots of unfinished basements with dirt floors," I countered.

"Perhaps there are, but the rest of the layout gave me further insight into what type of enclosure it is. It has no windows and a floor. Did you notice the walls? They were dirt also. There aren't many unfinished basements with dirt walls," she stated.

"So you're saying it's a cave?" My jaw dropped. *Why didn't I notice that?*

"It could be, but there are other elements that she would have come in contact with, and caves don't have doors."

I could see she was trying to steer me towards a conclusion. "So what are we looking for?"

"Most of the Southwestern Indian tribes built Kivas for worship. They are underground chambers, usually one room structures built below ground," she stated.

"So we need to narrow down which tribes utilized the Kivas in the Southwest," I said with enthusiasm, the significance of the find suddenly dawning on me.

Absolutely," she replied.

This is a big break! Let me inform Steve and Dianna and see how they want to approach giving this information to the FBI, since we are both officially off the case. The A.D. said he would arrest me if I was found anywhere near the investigation," I said.

"But you're thousands of miles away," she replied, smiling.

"You know what I mean," I retorted.

"Alright; I need to go take a long cold shower after that," she said, grinning at me again as she departed. Whew; that woman really knew how to make me squirm.

After speaking to Steve my mood had dropped a notch. He was optimistic, but still depressed. I called Dianna for some comfort, and we spoke for about an hour. I informed her of our progress. She could tell that I was a bit melancholy after hearing about the team's limited involvement in the case. Gracie deserved better, she deserved the best people handling this. She was one of our own, and a friend.

"Are you going to be alright" Dianna inquired?

"Sure; it's not me that I'm concerned about," I replied.

"I know. I hate it as well, but we do have an army out there investigating this now," she replied.

"Yeah, but are they good enough?" I replied.

"Hey, I have to go. The AD is here for the morning briefing. I'll call you later and keep you updated," she said and hung up the phone.

After the phone call with Dianna I took a long hot shower. It was funny because now I could feel Gracie while I was awake. I could feel her distress deep down inside. My newly acquired abilities placed me in even closer contact with her emotions while I was conscious. At first I was just experiencing them subconsciously while in the dreamscape. I never even noticed it until Dianna witnessed me talking in my sleep and wrote it down. I wondered if she could feel me consciously as well.

After showering I sat down in my bathrobe in the dark and contemplated all that I needed to do to save her. I would have to risk imprisonment, because I never doubted for a second that the A.D. would carry out his threat. He hated me and my methods vehemently. He was old school and was opposed to everything I stood for. I infuriated him even more when I wouldn't play ball with him. I had often seen his scowling disapproval and heard the rage in his voice. That was one of the good things about being a consultant on contract; I didn't have to play by all their rules. I only had to adhere to just enough to remain employed, and since I was good at what I did and valuable, I could even bend the few rules I was expected to follow.

The A.D. had considered it a pleasure to disband our group. He was a power freaks who would shoot himself before giving in to compromise. He was the type who got in his own way and couldn't get pass his prejudices.

I couldn't get to sleep thinking about Gracie. Nina was probably out for the count by now. We had been up all night. I ordered some breakfast and listened to some Coltrane on my iPhone. It was raining outside, so I opened the curtains. I hadn't even noticed how dark it was in the room until I opened them. So much was true about what Asku said about me; my affinity for the dark. I loved rainy days in particular. I don't know how that fit into the Spirit Guide equation, but I had always felt a sense of calmness and comfort during the rain. I enjoyed the cleansing effect that it had, same with the snow. Things appeared to slow down during the rain. There were fewer people outside, and I enjoyed that also.

I ate my breakfast and enjoyed a cup of coffee while looking out the window at the beauty of the rain and nature. North Carolina is a beautiful state, especially in the mountains. This place was special. I was thankful Nina had brought me here, but soon I had to leave. I had to go back to New Mexico and catch a killer. I was even more confident now that I could catch him with my new arsenal of abilities.

Nina knocked at the door around noon. She had been asleep for about five hours. When I opened the door to let her in, she immediately noticed the lighting in the suite. "Wow, someone opened the curtains for a change. It only took a rainy day to do it, but it's still dark in here," she stated, turning on the interior lights.

"Did you enjoy your rest?" I asked her. "No. not really. I kept tossing and turning. You didn't get any sleep either, did you?" she inquired.

The Talisman 121

"No. I've got too many things on my mind," I replied.

"I know, but you need to rest before you fall over," she said.

I changed the subject. The case, not my personal state, needed to be our focus now. "I informed Steve of our progress, but he had some bad news. He told me he was called backed to Washington since he was suspended and taken off the case. He left on the ViCAP jet at 1000 this morning. Dianna, Max and Amber are remaining in New Mexico to assist the A.D., but they've been taken out of the field and assigned as Special Assistants to the A.D. He wants to keep them close. He needs to cover his deficiencies with them by his side to make any necessary corrections. That just leaves me to find Gracie. The A.D. is too anal and closed-minded to find her with his methods," I stated.

"What do you mean only you, mister? What about me?" she inquired.

"I figured your superiors would need you back by now," I replied.

"No. as far as they are concerned, I'm still on the case. My bureau is a little more flexible than the FBI. I'm on a very long leash. Besides; you guys aren't the only ones who are doing good things out there. I've got carte blanche with my cases," she said.

"I know. You came highly recommended by the A.D. He gave us a background on your accomplishments," I stated.

"Well, that's not saying much coming from him, now is it," she replied as we both laughed.

"Well, the first thing we have to do is research the Southwestern Indians with Kivas in New Mexico, unless you already know the information," I stated.

"No, it differs per tribe and sect in the Southwest. Our people the Tsalagi, are mountain people. We don't have Kivas," she said.

"Tsalagi means Cherokee," I responded.

"Yes, but our original name is Aniyawiya," she replied, then paused for a few seconds and asked, "Why haven't you ever attempted to get back in touch with your Tsalagi heritage?"

"It's complicated," I replied.

"I can keep up," she responded as if to say she wasn't giving up on this particular conversation that easily.

"It's like I told your uncle. My people were excluded from the Dawes Rolls. It felt like they didn't want to have anything to do with me, so I felt the same way about them. I am a half-breed in every sense of the word, Nina, and I really don't know where I belong," I replied.

"You're confused, Chris, but know this: not everyone agreed with the Dawes Rolls Act. My tribe didn't agree with it. The gifts you possess have been passed down through your Cherokee heritage. Your bloodline is strong in Tsalagi, so put your mind at ease and consider yourself family. It doesn't matter what percentage of Tsalagi you are with us." Then she held her hand to my face to caress it.

"Thank you, Nina," I replied as we buried the subject and went back to the case.

"I have access to the database of the Bureau of Indian Affairs library. It's the best library in the country on Indian Affairs, history and heritage. We can use my laptop, but first I need to get you out of this doom and gloom, Count Dracula. It's raining outside, but that doesn't mean we need to be down about it," she stated.

"But I enjoy the rain," I responded.

"Good; then you'll love this place. We're going to find this psycho, so get dressed," she commanded.

Nina took me to a cabin in the mountains. It was located in a secluded area, high in the mountains, surrounded by the forest. The building had high ceilings and an enormous glass skylight that allowed us to view the rain flooding the glass, like a waterfall. It felt like being on top of the world as we looked out over the tree tops below.

"Whose place is this?" I inquired.

"It's mine. This is where I stay when I'm in town," she replied.

"Why didn't we just come here instead of the hotel," I asked?

"I didn't want you to get any false ideas of why we were here or distract you in any way. Most people feel more comfortable when they are on neutral ground," she replied.

"This place is gorgeous," I said in amazement.

The Talisman
123

"Before you get any bright ideas; it didn't cost as much as you might expect. The land was already ours and it's cheap to build cabins out here. Also, my family is old fashioned; as soon as I told them I was in town with a friend, they wanted to know the details. If we had stayed here I would never have heard the end of it. Make yourself at home while I get some firewood from storage. There's Wi-Fi installed, so we can just stay here in the living area near the fireplace. The lighting is better in here," she said.

Judging by the architecture of this place, Nina was the exact opposite of me when it came to lighting. There was light coming in from everywhere in the cabin. At least we did share a love for the outdoors, but I could never stay in a place like this. It was obvious her astrological guide was the sun, whereas mine was the moon. That's why she constantly wanted the curtains opened and attempted to illuminate whatever area she was in. Asku really enlightened me about some fundamental things that I would normally have missed. They are minute things, but lent great knowledge into someone's psyche. This would assist me in catching this killer as well.

We settled down with a bottle of wine in front of a crackling fire and went to work. It was peaceful here, with no distractions. Nina was on her best behavior. She knew when to get serious and this was that time. She displayed the seriousness I saw back in New Mexico. I think she just liked teasing me because of what happened in the shared dreamscape with Dianna. Now that she was concentrating Nina was a very intelligent, focused, career-driven and accomplished agent. We conducted research with our laptops until sundown. I hadn't thought I would still be in Cherokee for another day, but there I was.

"I'm hungry, what about you?" Nina inquired.

"I could go for something," I replied.

"Alright; I'm not much of a cook, but my father keeps food in the cabinets and fridge for me. Let me see what I have." She returned in a couple of minutes. "I have some venison tenderloins I can fix with some rice and vegetables," she said.

"Sounds great. Do you need some help?" I asked.

"No. You continue with the research. I'll get started in the kitchen and be with you in a little while."

After prepping the food and placing the tenderloins in the oven, Nina returned with some cheese, marmalade and crackers to hold us until the dinner was ready. We continue with our research, and discovered everything we needed. The Bureau of Indian Affairs' library was very extensive.

We ate dinner by the fireplace a few hours later. It was dark outside now, and time seemed to escape us while researching. Nina didn't give herself enough credit.

"Dinner was marvelous, Nina. Thank you very much, you're an excellent cook."

"I'm glad somebody think so," she responded and laughed. "So, how do we proceed from here, Mr. FBI?"

"Please don't start calling me that. You've progressed from calling Mister to Count Dracula to Mr. FBI. Whatever you call me, just don't call me that."

"Why not?" she asked, smiling.

"It reminds me of the A.D.," I replied.

Her smile faded. "I'm sorry. I definitely will drop that one. You're nothing like him. If it makes you feel any better, the names were all given affectionately."

"No, it doesn't, but I'll live with it," I retorted.

"You know, your uncle gave me a Tsalagi name," I said to Nina.

"Wow, I don't know what you've done to him, but he really does like you. For him to give you a Tsalagi name means he has accepted you into our clan. It is a high and noble honor," she stated.

"Thank you, and I am honored," I replied.

"What is your Tsalagi name" she inquired?

"Cheveyo."

"Welcome to my family, Spirit Warrior," she replied.

"He also gave me this crystal," I said, showing her the stone I was wearing around my neck.

The Talisman 125

"It's our family crystal. Christian, now you belong to the great and noble clan of the Aniyawiya Tribe; wear it with pride." she said. Then she showed me her own.

"I didn't see the crystal before while we were in our dreams," I commented.

"No; it can't be seen then. This is your anchor. It makes itself known when you need it, such as when you're in trouble and need to find your way home. It has its own magic which isn't rooted in the spirit realms. This is the magic, or energy, from Mother Earth. Every realm has its own powers. My uncle will teach you this later, and explain it better," she said.

After dinner we continued conversing about the heritage of the Tsalagi until it was quite late. We agreed to spend the night at the cabin. I informed her that I needed to dreamscape alone tonight, and that I wanted to visit Dianna alone. Nina didn't put up a fight, as she had a lot to absorb. It was apparent that her family had accepted me fully into their clan, but to what extent? I think they still had ideas of her and me being together, but my heart was somewhere else. I called Dianna after assisting Nina with the cleaning. I assured Dianna that Gracie was still alive and that I was leaving in the morning for New Mexico.

I was fresh and invigorated the next morning. I slept like I never had before. This place was good for me; my home State. Nina and her family were good to me as well. I wished we had met under different circumstance. I could see myself being happy with her.

"Shi-yo," I greeted Nina with a big smile when I saw her.

"Shi-yo, Christian. You're a fast learner. You've picked up all of this without a problem, including the language," she responded.

"Thank you, but I had some excellent teachers."

She smiled." Do you want some breakfast before we leave?"

"Sure; I could eat a horse."

"We no longer eat those, but I do have rabbit, deer, goat and the occasional road kill possum," she replied. We both laughed and sat down to a nice bacon and eggs breakfast with coffee, juice and toast. Nina had risen before me and already had the food prepared.

"I scheduled our flights out this morning. The earliest we can leave is at noon. That gives us plenty of time to prepare," Nina said.

"Nina, I don't know where to begin thanking or repaying you and your family for all you've done for me."

"You don't have to. You are a part of my family now. This is what family does for each other, but the main objective here was to help Gracie. Hopefully by assisting you, we can catch this psychopath."

"Thanks again," I replied.

Before departing we stopped by the Earth Healer's Shop and said good bye to Asku and Kele. I promised Asku that I would return and meet the rest of the family, namely Nina's parents. Then he warned me that I would become lost during my journey, so I should always wear the crystal.

I had spent three days which seemed like an eternity in Cherokee, NC. It felt like I had been caught in a time warp in this serene place, or like I just completed R&R at a spa retreat. Now it was time to get back to the hustle and bustle of the bureaucratic society that we both called home and work. I wasn't looking forward to the complications ahead of me with the A.D., but if I stayed out of his way and channeled my progress through Dianna, I could remain out of jail.

The connecting flight out of Atlanta, Georgia was crowded. Hartsfield International is one of the busiest airports in the Southeast. The plane was packed on the way back to Albuquerque. We sat next to an elderly woman, Mrs. Julia Jerrells, in the three center seats. She was a retiree living in New Mexico and was returning from visiting her son and family in Atlanta, which was the stop over from Asheville, N.C. to Albuquerque. She thought Nina and I was married and made a nice couple. Nina corrected her, but Mrs. Jerrells was persistent and continued her quest in pairing us.

The Talisman   127

"Marriage is a wonderful thing. I was married for 40 years until my Josh passed away. Don't wait too long, young man. You make such a gorgeous couple. I can see the connection between you."

We smiled, attempting not to laugh, because she was a sweet elderly lady and a grandmother. She continued to talk about the serial killer and how afraid she and her neighbors were. She didn't have anything to worry about though. The serial killer only abducted young women in their twenties. The partial media attention had most residents in the vicinity of Albuquerque on edge.

I received a text from Steve while in flight: *Chris; I've been reinstated on the case. C u in New Mexico and explain the details. Don't go 2 HQ till we speak.*

When we landed at the ABQ International Sunport we assisted Mrs. Jerrells with retrieving her luggage and noticed that there was no one at the airport to meet her. We inquired if she needed a ride. We were on a schedule to catch a killer, but we felt like it was our duty to be sure she arrived home safely

Mrs. Jerrells carefully accepted our offer after examining my face. Our conversation had been very pleasant, but her scrutiny of my face was to confirm my intentions. She was reading it like a map. I guess seniors have seen it all. She probably would make a good profiler with all her knowledge and wisdom. She agreed to wait until Nina rented a vehicle on the GSA Card, then we drove her home. She lived in Los Lunas, a couple of miles south of Albuquerque off Highway 25. Steve texted me again while we were driving Ms. Jerrells home.

Steve: Im in abq r u here?

Chris: Yes, but had 2 driv 2 Los Lunas.

Steve: Let me no wen Ur bck n abq 2 meet.

Chris: ok.

Most people love to text these days like Steve, but I prefer the good old fashioned phone call where you can have a conversation with the person.

"Thank you both so very much for helping an old lady in need. Can I give you something or get you anything for your troubles? I'm in the house alone nowadays and wouldn't be ungrateful for some company." This was her way of asking if we would check out the house for her, which we did.

Once inside, inspecting the house for intruders; Mrs. Jerrells asked if we would sit with her for a little while. We didn't have the heart to say no. We sat down and drank some tea and watched Jeopardy on the television. It had been a long time since I'd actually sat down and watched T.V. The Tournament of Champions was on with Alex Tribeck. I always wondered if he already knew the answers to the questions – or is it questions to the answers –since contestants have to state the answers in the form of a question. Does the host have to look at the answers on the cards or what? He appeared to be very intelligent.

I managed to sneak in another text to Steve while asking to be excused to the restroom. He agreed to meet us at the Sheraton where we would be staying. After Jeopardy we gave Ms. Jerrells our telephone numbers and departed. We knew that we wouldn't see her again, but it would be nice to check in on her every now and then. Sometimes seniors her age just needed someone to talk to. We were only in New Mexico to catch the serial killer, but she didn't need to know that. Then Mrs. Jerrells said something quite strange to us just before we departed.

"Christian, you should always follow your heart. Have faith in it and it will always guide you in the right direction." Then she placed Nina's hand within mine. "I need you to journey safely together."

We talked about what Mrs. Jerrells said to us the whole trip back to Albuquerque. The wisdom of seniors never ceased to amaze me. It was like they have a third eye or something. We met Steve at the bar of the Sheraton.

"Hey Chris."

"Hello, Steve."

"Agent Blackwater, how are you?" Steve inquired with a nod of his head.

"Doing well, and you?" Nina replied.

The Talisman   129

"I'm making it, Nina. I appreciate your continual assistance to our bureau. I'll make sure your superiors know of your vital support. I can assure you a commendation out of this regardless of the outcome. I could use a drink. What are you guys drinking?"

Nina ordered a Grand Mariner, neat, I had a Dos XXX dark and Steve ordered cognac.

"Here's the deal; I've been reinstated and given the case back, but I can't pull you back in with the A.D. over my shoulder. He caused a bit of a rift in D.C. when you walked out on him on medical leave, but I need both of you if we're going to find Gracie and catch this killer. I want you to continue with the investigative work you're doing, but only report to me. I will provide you with whatever you need from the Bureau. I need you to step lightly though. I can't have the Indian Council or others calling the A.D. about anything that you're doing," Steve stated, then took a sip of his cognac and continued. "So where will you be starting?'

Nina interjected, "We received some collaborating information from Jay Horse that some Hopis in the Navajo Nation had been talking about killings and violence while on Nation Land. This is so irregular for the Hopis, we thought we'd shake some feathers there."

"Interesting choice of words, Agent Blackwater," Steve replied.

"Yeah, she does that," I replied, smiling.

"Oh, please just call me Nina, Steve," she stated and raised her glass.

"Will do," Steve responded.

"They also are the builders of Kivas. In fact they are considered the people of the lower world," she further stated.

"You guys seem to already have your strategy well planned. Can I interest you in another round?"

"Sure," Nina replied as I dipped my head in affirmation.

"You never said how you reacquired the case," I pointed out to Steve.

"Wow; you really don't watch TV. It's been plastered all over the news. The story was leaked to the press about Gracie's abduction from an unknown source," he stated and smiled with a Cheshire Cat grin.

"And of course you don't know where or how they received that information," I replied.

"I haven't the foggiest idea, but the A.D. caught the heat for it," Steve stated, smiling from ear to ear.

"Well, gentlemen, in that case I propose a toast to the lucky person who got a chance to stick it to Pollin. Normally I'd say we have reason to celebrate, but under the circumstances," Nina stated and raised her glass in a toast.

"Steve, you know Ortega is investigating the Pueblos. What if we run into him or someone says something to him?" I asked.

"You know, that's the last thing I'm afraid of," he replied.

"What's the first thing?" I asked.

"Why hasn't he discovered or reported the information that you found? He's the resident official here. Could he be involved, or is he just that inept? Either way, it's a problem," Steve stated.

After leaving the bar I settled into my suite and telephoned Dianna. I couldn't wait to see her again, but it was getting late and I had to work again tonight in dreamscape. We talked for about an hour, after which I said good night. She had to get up early to work at the RO, and I had to get to sleep.

Chapter 9

Kachina

Gracie was still alive and tied up in what we now believed to be a Kiva. She had given up hope by now, of me finding her. I sensed her despair even when I wasn't in dreamscape. I still had no further clues in reference to the killer, or where he was holding her. It was as if he knew how to shield himself from me, but how likely was that? Perhaps our investigations of the Hopis could shed some light on what was starting to become a futile search and rescue, like the rest.

When I woke up I gave Steve a call to assure him that Gracie was alive, and then called Dianna. It was good to be within miles of her now. I looked forward to seeing her, but I was heading out of town again this morning. It seemed like I was spending more time away from her than with her these days. It also seemed like I was spending more time with Nina, who had been a good friend during all of this.

Dianna and I discussed Steve's return to the ViCAP and my eventual return. She pondered about the media leak with me. We both suspected Steve of being the source of the leak, and if we suspected him, I'm sure the A.D. suspected it as well. Steve needed to tread lightly around Pollin and he wasn't getting off to a good start with Nina and me working as his rogue agents. Nina was up early, as usual, and knocking on the door while I was on the phone. She had coffee and bagels with her.

"Come in, Nina. Dianna says hello," I stated while allowing her to enter the room. I had on my sleeping attire, which consisted of my favorite lounge pants with Felix the Cat on them, and no shirt, just the crystal her uncle gave me around my neck.

"Tell her I said hello," Nina said as she walked towards the window and opened the curtains in her usual manner, but now I understood her need for the light.

I said goodbye to Dianna and hung up the phone. We didn't have time to waste on a formal sit-down-and-eat breakfast. We were chasing the clock again, and the 16th was approaching. By now I was used to getting dressed in her company, as she would put it - *'she has seen it all by now'*. I wouldn't get naked in front of her, of course, but she definitely wasn't one who respected my personal space, I owed all this to that one drunken night and now I had to live with the consequences. It wasn't much of a tradeoff, and it could have been worse. This was the gift and the curse.

The one thing I enjoyed the most about Nina was her patience. She never came in and attempted to rush me, but allowed me to move at my own pace. She knew I was a creature of the night by now, and she was a creature of the day, which made her an early riser. She always had confidence in my ability to recognize the urgency of the situation. Besides, I only woke up late because I would be up half the night. She recognized that as well by bringing the coffee to give me a jump start. She also knew how fast I moved once awakened.

I had showered and dressed in no time and we were out the door. Steve had arranged for the ViCAP jet to take us to the Hopi Nation. There was a private airport in Kykotsmovi Village, the third mesa, where the Hopi Tribal Council was headquartered. It would have taken us a four and a half hour drive otherwise, and the only closest commercial airport was in Flagstaff, Arizona, which was two extra hours in the opposite direction.

"So this is how the famous ViCAP team travels. It must be nice to have your own jet," Nina stated as we entered the jet.

Kachina

"It's not mine, but it does save on time. Can I get you something to drink?"

"You mean you don't have a pretty young steward to serve us?"

"That would be me, madam," I stated and laughed. The jet was stocked with beverages, including alcoholic ones. I served us both iced mocha lattes. The team and I loved our coffee, and we had an espresso machine on the jet.

It only took us 40 minutes to reach the Rocky Ridge Airport in the Kykotsmovi Village. The Hopi Nation consists of a total of 12 villages situated on three mesas, picturesquely set high in the cliffs and plateaus of what is called the Black Mesas.

The Hopi Nation was located exactly in the center of the Navajo Nation. They had been disputing over land boundaries for centuries, and it hadn't been until the middle to late 1900s that the Navajos had actually begun encroaching and attempting to settle on Hopi land. In 1974 the U.S. Government had passed the Navajo-Hopi Land Settlement Act, which had forced Navajos off Hopi lands and established true borders thereafter. Before these encroachment issues in the 1900s, the Navajos had been too afraid of upsetting the descendants of the Anasazi or 'Ancient People.'

The Hopi were believed to be the descendants of the original inhabitants the people of the other world, the Chacoans, who were considered to have great mystical and magical powers, since they came from the other world. Their lands were revered and sacred amongst the Pueblo and other Indian Tribes of the Southwest, including the Navajo and Apache.

This time we didn't inform the council in advance of our arrival. I'm sure they had already been approached by another team of FBI agents before us. Ortega should have reached out to them by now during his investigation. Ortega, like the rest of FBI teams, didn't seem to have anything concrete or useful to assist in the investigation.

"So I'll meet you at the Cultural Center. There is a restaurant and inn located there," I said to Nina before going into the Tribal Council Building.

"Good luck," she replied.

"Yeah. We'll have to give them the benefit of doubt," I stated, then Nina took the vehicle and drove off.

The council was surprised to see me, as expected. I introduced myself and the Hopis were as reluctant as the other tribes to assist; perhaps even more. I informed them of the purpose of my visit, which they had been made aware of by the Navajo Tribal Council and the media. They also stated they had already spoken with Agent Ortega and given him all the information that I would require. This immediately raised my curiosity. How did they know what I required or was going to ask? I didn't question them about that at this point, but it definitely roused suspicion.

I didn't want to upset the council, so I played along and concocted a story about us all working on different aspects of the same case. I also tried to ease their mind by telling them I had been at the Navajo Tribal Council Headquarters. I had to continue to fly under the radar on this case. I questioned them on any unusual behavior or recent crimes on the Reservation. They didn't contribute anything substantial. They, like their Navajo counterparts, had the Reservation Chief of Police assist and escort me around. This appeared to be protocol on the Res. The Police Chief inquired if I had spoken to Ortega also.

I had the police chief escort me to the hotel, but instead of taking me to the local Hopi Cultural Center in Kykotsmovi, he took me to the Moenkopi Legacy Inn and Suites. The Moenkopi Legacy was located in the Moenkopi Village, which was further out toward the Western Gate of the reservation, near Tuba City. It was the newer hotel, just built on the edge of the reservation. I didn't know if he did this to impress me, and get me to spend more money or just get me out of the way. I didn't question him and once again went along with it. I could see that staying under the radar would be a hard task with the Hopis. The police chief was clearly sending me a message by escorting me to the western gate. They wanted me off the Reservation.

Kachina   135

Out of all the Indian Tribes in the Southwest, the Hopis had best managed to preserve their ancient culture. They refused to give into the pressures of gambling casinos and the negative baggage of greed that issued from it. The secured borders of the Hopi Nation, being situated within the secured borders of the Navajo Nation, assisted tremendously in the preservation of their culture and isolation from outsiders and their influences.

The Hopi borders were practically closed to the public and only guided tours were permitted in most villages of the mesas. The villages of the second mesa were precluded from visitors. These tours were conducted under the strict supervision of the Hopi Nation, with Hopi guides. The Hopis had built lucrative businesses in coal mining, tourism, artistic handcrafted merchandise and other capital ventures, while maintaining true to their culture and beliefs.

The Hopis remained one of the most secretive tribes in the Pueblo Indian Nation, with several clandestine societies that were off limits and never seen by non-Hopi members. These societies weren't even open to all Hopis. The members were carefully selected, and had to endure an initiation period or rite of passage before being inducted. These secret societies would be the center of our focus. Jay Horse implicated a particular society dedicated to the extinction of outsiders, non-Indian people. This seemed like a good place to start.

My interrogations turned out exactly as we'd thought it would. The Hopi Council reacted just as the Navajos had. They were polite and very direct in their approach when they escorted me to the door, but the results were the same. Fool me once, as the saying goes. I telephoned Nina after being dropped off in Moenkopi, she had already reserved two rooms at the Cultural Center Inn and checked in.

"Hey Nina, I'm in the Moenkopi Village at the Legacy Inn."

"What are you doing there?" she inquired.

"The Police Chief brought me here. Instead of asking me to leave, he politely showed me to the door. He stated that this was their new hotel and better than the Cultural Center. I had to agree with him on that. It looks great here, but also expensive," I stated.

"I guess they will refund me for the reservation here at the Cultural Center. I'll come up with some elaborate excuse. You know I'll be making a budget transfer to the FBI when this is all over," she said and laughed.

"Please do. They seem to have a ballooned budget," I replied, laughing in return.

"Alright; I'll see you in a little while," Nina responded and hung up the phone.

Our plan was to have Nina go undercover on the reservation and attempt to blend in with the Pueblos. She knew the Uto-Aztecan language well, and could assimilate. This was the only way of getting any information from the Hopis. They weren't like the Navajo, it would be even harder to get information from them since they were so secretive and isolated. Nina would be gathering viable information while I was being escorted around by the Reservation Police Chief. My wild goose chase with the police chief would actually be a distraction for getting him out of Nina's way.

After we checked into the hotel, we went to the lobby concierge to question her and explore for local information if possible. This hotel was set up just for the outsiders; that's why it was located at the border of the Western Gate. We interacted with some of the visitors and hotel workers, and Nina scheduled several tours of the villages to meet and talk with the Hopi people. Then we ventured outside the hotel to the Tuuvi Café for a meal and conversation. Nina did most of the talking with the staff, which consisted of Hopis and Navajos. I spent my time listening and talking with visitors on the reservation. After leaving the Café, I called the police chief for my escort and tour.

Chief Tohannie escorted me around the villages of Hotevilla and Kykotsmovi. He took me to all the designated places where I couldn't disturb villagers. We visited about three malcontents, but no one worth attention or fitting the profile we were looking for. It was basically a sightseeing tour and a waste of time in reference to finding the killer. I did obtain much knowledge about the villagers, and enjoyed

Kachina

the cultural experience. I didn't mind the distraction, because it gave Nina the time she needed to conduct the real investigation.

The Hopituh (People of Hopi) were expert craftsmen and renowned artisans. I saw the most exquisite pottery, basket weaving and silversmithing I have ever encountered. I was also amazed by the other contemporary arts; paintings, sculpted glass and of course the Kachina dolls. I attempted to purchase a necklace for Dianna, but the young woman insisted on giving it to me for free. The Hopituh were extremely kind and peaceful people. They refer to themselves as Hopituh Shin-nu-ma (Peaceful People of Hopi) and they truly were, as far as I could tell. They welcomed me into their homes as you would treat a guest you have known for a long time. After visiting the two villages for the day, the Chief took me back to the Legacy.

"Thank you for the sightseeing tour, Chief Tohannie," I said sarcastically smiling.

"Any time, Mr. Sands. I'll show you the rest of the villages of the third mesa tomorrow," he stated with a fake smile of his own. We were like two men playing a game of poker or chess; each bluffing or making moves to distract the other, In this case, the Chief believed he was fooling me, but he was the one being manipulated.

There was a crescent moon out that evening. It felt as if the night was calling to me. I was restless and full of life's energy, as I stared at the night clouds passing through the sky. Most people don't even notice them. It is as if they disappear at night, but they can be just as beautiful and wonderful as those of the daylight. I decided to go for a swim to wear off some of the energy and restlessness I was feeling. It was late and the pool was closed. I swung over the five feet high gate like a pole vaulter, with grace and ease. I didn't make a sound hurtling over the metal gate and letting myself in. I didn't break a sweat, nor did my heart rate elevate.

I surprised myself with my agility. It was something I had never experienced before. I suddenly had cat-like reflexes and I had no idea where they had come from, but something inside me told me I could do it. It was as if the panther had imprinted its physical abilities upon me.

I looked around for a second to see if anyone noticed me entering the closed area, but there was no one around. I placed my towel on one of the lounge chairs, then dove into the deep end with the same grace I displayed hurtling the fence. The sound of the dive was light and effortless as well. I was an excellent swimmer and often thought about competing as a boy, but I had too many other issues going on.

I had completed several laps to burn off the built-up energy when I heard a voice on the other side of the fence. I didn't recognize it at first because I was partially under the water, but then I felt her presence. It was Nina. How could she have known where I was? She spoke again from the other side of the fence.

"You do know the pool is closed, right?"

"Yeah, I know, but I needed to burn off some energy," I responded.

"Yeah; I couldn't sleep either. It's a shame they don't have a bar at the hotel," she replied.

"Do the other reservations have bars?" I inquired.

"Yes, some do. It all depends on the tribal council."

"How did you know where I was?" I asked.

"I didn't, I was just out for a walk," she stated.

"Want to join me" I inquired?

"Sure, but I don't have my swimsuit with me," she replied.

"What's wrong with what you have on? I don't think anyone will mind," I stated, then gestured, looking around at the empty poolside.

"I see your point," she responded. She was wearing white spandex running shorts and one of those athletic spandex type bra shirts, which showed her midsection, with white Nike running shoes.

"Do you need help getting over the fence?" I asked.

"I grew up in Cherokee County, remember," she replied and climbed over the five foot fence with almost as much ease at which I swung over it.

Nina was a very athletic woman. She wasn't as quiet as I was when she scaled the fence, but she did it effortlessly. She took off her shoes

Kachina   *139*

and ankle socks and dove in. She was looking sexy as hell. When the water wet her outfit you could see the contour of her breasts, and the shorts clung skin-tight to her perfectly round hips and butt. This is when I knew I had made a grave mistake.

She immediately swam over to me and pulled me under the water. Then she tried to escape. She was a good swimmer, but not as fast as I was in the water. I caught her and returned the favor of pulling her under. We wrestled and played for a little while, until I became tired. I had already completed several laps before she arrived. I waded in the pool while she did a couple of laps, then she joined me at the poolside.

"This place is incredible, Nina. I can feel the energy from its spirit. I've never felt like this before, until your uncle woke me up to it."

"And I thought it was me making you feel like that," she replied, smiling. "But seriously, that's good. This place is mystical. It's called the Four Corners because it is where the four states meet, and mystics believe this is where all worlds meet; the intersection in spiritual and astral planes. This is why the ancients built astrological signs and symbols to the heavens in places like Fajada Butte. Can you use this spiritual energy it to assist you?"

"I'll find out tonight," I replied.

"I visited several places today, but didn't pick up any negative or familiar sensations. I'll attempt to channel the energy from this place and revisit the places and people I saw today with the police chief," I stated.

"Can you visit the places I've seen today as well?" she inquired.

"I'm sure I can. Why, was there anything suspicious that you encountered?" I asked.

"No, but there were some very interesting people," she stated.

"I would have to enter your dreams again to do that, Nina, and I don't think it's a good idea."

"I thought we agreed this is all for Gracie, and we are running out of time! I need you to stop trying to protect me and forget about what's going on between us, and concentrate on saving Agent Mullins," Nina firmly stated.

I was speechless and quiet after that scolding. I paused for several minutes, but she wasn't one to beat around the bush. She went straight to the point and was right about all of it.

"Look, Chris, I'm sorry for snapping at you. It's obvious that there is something between us. I know you're with Dianna and I don't want to come between the both of you, but it's about time we just put it on the table. Since that night when we were all in the dream together, there has been this connection between us. I know you're attracted to me and I'm attracted to you, but I won't push you into anything you're not ready to do."

I was still quietly thinking, examining every word as they captured my attention and held me in a stasis.

"Well, are you going to say anything?" she inquired.

I moved in closer to her and put my arms around her. We were still in the water with no one around. She gave in to her feelings and her expression reflected her vulnerability. I could see the tears beginning to well in her eyes from baring her soul. She knew we couldn't be together and everything she said was true about us. I held her quietly for a while, and then spoke.

"Yes, Nina, I do have strong feelings for you. You're right about all of it, but like you said, I am with Dianna. I'm sorry for that night. I didn't mean to lead you on or hurt you in any way."

"I know it was in the moment, Chris, if I can say that about a dream, and you don't have to be sorry. I enjoyed the experience and wouldn't trade it for the world. I can only imagine you as being that passionate lover outside of dreams. You really know how to care for a woman and her needs, you were gentle, yet strong that night. Don't be sorry, because it wouldn't have happened if I wasn't feeling the same way you were that night," she stated. Then she looked me in the eyes and kissed me, as I kissed her return. Then I abruptly broke the connection.

Kachina   141

"Nina, as much as I would like to continue, neither of us would respect the other afterwards. You were correct with what you said in the beginning - *As charmed and flattered as I am with the compliment, it could pose problems if it continues.* You were very prophetic."

"Wow, you remember that? See, it is those kinds of things that make you special, Chris. You actually listen and care."

"Thanks, Nina, but let's go back inside, the water is starting to get cold."

"You don't appear to be affected by the cold," she smiled, gesturing at how excited my libido had become. She was still in a good place emotionally, as he joking demonstrated; we both were as we departed the pool area.

As much as I wanted to just take her in my arms and make love to her right there in the pool, I couldn't. It wouldn't be fair to her, or to Dianna. She could see and feel how aroused I was and how I was fighting my natural instincts. I was definitely getting stronger since leaving Cherokee Country.

That night when I lay down for bed, I could still feel the energy of the night calling me. I laid out the prayer rug and began chanting and smoking the peyote pipe. Luckily they had smoking suites at the Legacy. The peyote would help induce my dream state.

It didn't take long. The Panther was waiting for me as I crossed to the other side. She was upset and pacing back and forth, like large cats do, but this time it was faster than usual. The tip of her elegant black tail twitched in obvious irritation. Her purrs weren't soothing like before, they were more like growls. Then she spoke to me. It wasn't like you or I would speak. Her mouth didn't move, it was more like mental telepathy.

"The path you have chosen has no longevity. It will not sustain this journey. This is not your destiny. You must live in the moment and accept all that it has to give you. Don't neglect the now for the future."

Then she roared and pounced on me. I refused to accept what she was telling me, and I argued it over and over as we wrestled, rolling back and forth on the ethereal jungle floor until I gave in to her strength and power.

I was amazed at my own strength while fighting her, and my stamina also surprised me. But at last I found myself pinned down on the colorful jungle flora. She growled at me, starring deeply into my eyes as if hypnotizing me. I was taken into a deeper transcendental state. There I met an elderly woman. "Loloma," she said, greeting me and I knew exactly what it meant even though I had never heard it before. It meant hello and welcome in Uto-Aztecan. I had never learned the language, but could now understand it and speak it fluently, as if it was being translated in English.

"Sit down next to me. I would like to show you something," she stated, patting the rug next to her. Then she began drawing on the wall. She drew a picture of a man in a mask, with feathers protruding from it. He appeared to be wearing ceremonial clothing. "This is Kachina," she said after completing the drawing. Then the figure on the wall became animated and began dancing as he would in an Indian ceremony.

She drew another and another; three in all. Each had a different mask and clothing. They danced around the fire she drew. I could feel their spirits. They were warriors who protected the village. They were also priests who blessed it and kept away bad omens. I blinked, feeling dizzied by the swirling colors and the non-corporeal chaneling. When I opened my eyes, I was among them, I sat down with them and smoked from a pipe we shared. There was no conversation, just the passing of peace. Afterwards they wrote the number 5/5 in the dirt near the fire. I had no idea what it meant or represented.

The panther roared again, waking me from my communion with the elderly lady. The panther was still on top of me and staring into my eyes. She had calmed, and stepped off me. She lay down beside me, purring calmingly once again as I just lay there, astonished at what had occurred.

When I woke, it was morning and like the other dreams, what appeared like minutes in the dream state was hours in the middle

Kachina   *143*

realm, which was what Nina's uncle had called our realm, conscious reality. Before I could even yawn, Nina was knocking at my door. She didn't have coffee and bagels this time. It appeared that she had just wakened. She must have slept in, she still had on her Batman pajamas when she entered my suite. That had been my favorite superhero as a kid.

"Wow, I would have taken you for a Superman kind of girl."

"No; I have Supergirl pajamas, but I have this thing for Dark Knights." Sudden understanding clicked. She was a sun woman, like Supergirl, but was attracted to the bad boy or, in my case, the odd man out. I knew immediately there was something wrong for her to have slept in late and arrived in her pajamas, but I would wait for her to inform me instead of prying.

"Wow, you look like something that cat dragged in," she said, laughing. If only she knew; it was more like something that the cat dragged, tossed and pounced on. "Another fun thrilling night with the leopard, huh?" she inquired.

"You can say that," I replied, then went over towards the window. This time I opened the curtains without waiting for her to ask.

She said thank you without even blinking, and kept right on talking. "I had the wildest dream, Chris. This old lady came to me and asked me to bring you to her."

"She came to me also," I replied.

"But I didn't see you," Nina stated.

"I know. She came to us separately, but wants us to make the journey together," I responded.

"What does that mean?" Nina inquired.

"She's saying that you were right last night. I need to do this with you in every aspect," I stated, but didn't go into full details about how far she needed to assist me for now.

"So she's a Seer also?" Nina inquired.

"Apparently she is, one with great powers. She's the one who's been calling for me," I said.

Then Nina looked at me curiously and asked, "Do you know where she's located?"

"No, she said you would bring me to her."

"In a dream or what?" Nina asked.

"No. I've already seen her there," I replied.

"Duh, I'm sorry. I'm just so excited to have experienced this," Nina replied. She had been raised around mystics who had helped her cope with the supernatural occurrences that we were experiencing. Most people would have been freaking out by now, but Nina welcomed it!

"OK, so where do we start?" Nina inquired.

"Well, that's up to you. What were you going to do today?" I inquired.

"I was going to explore the villages again."

"Well, there's the answer. The Seer already knew this. She just wants me to come with you. I'll cancel my ride-in with the police chief," I stated.

"Won't he become suspicious?"

"You're right, I'll tell him to come later. That way we'll have a couple hours start on him attempting to follow us," I replied.

Then my cell phone rang. It was Steve on the other end. "Good morning, Chris. How's everything."

"Things are going well, and you?"

"I'm doing the same. How's the investigation going?" he inquired.

"The council was pretty much the same, but we managed to secure some leads on our own through dreamscape," I said.

"Really? That's excellent!" he stated.

"Yeah, I know," I said excitingly, "As I told you before; I've acquired some new gifts from my Cherokee visit."

"OK, just remain under the radar. The A.D. is scrutinizing our every move here," he replied.

Then Nina whispered in the background, "I'll go get ready."

She departed for her suite and returned fresh, dressed and smelling like apple blossoms.

Kachina   145

"Steve said hello and thanks again, so did Dianna," I said, feeling a twinge of guilt when I thought of my girlfriend, far away out of sight while I ogled the beautiful woman before me. She had coffee and my favorite bagel this time; Cinnamon Raisin. "I don't know how you managed to dress and get breakfast so quickly, but thanks. I already telephoned the police chief and told him to meet me at 1300 hours. That gives us more than enough time of separation. I'll call him around noon and cancel my ride.

We wanted to get as far away as we could from the villages of the Third Mesa, as quickly as possible. Yesterday Nina had toured the villages of Old Oraibi and Bacavi on the Third Mesa and I visited Hotevilla and Kykotsmovi with the police chief. That left only the village of Moenkopi, where we were located. We both felt that Moenkopi wasn't the place. We trusted our instincts and traveled all the way to the First Mesa to avoid interference from the police chief.

It took us most of the day driving and touring the villages of Sichomovi, Polacca and Tewa. We were sightseeing and attempting to find signs or symbols that would lead us to the Seer. It was quite an experience, filled with knowledge and history. We ate at a quaint, family-owned diner in the village of Polacca. It was sunset when we reached the village of Walpi; I knew immediately we were in the right village.

"She's here," I said aloud, "I can feel her presence, and I'm sure she can feel mine as well!"

We were lucky because there were no street lights here and the sun was going down. The Walpi Village didn't have electricity or running water, it was one of the oldest of all the communities.

"Follow me," I said, jumping out of the car. "I know where we're going."

We came to a dwelling that was situated overlooking the rest of the villagers. The structure hadn't changed since it was built, like most of the dwellings here. There were feathers and chimes hanging outside, and an ancient buffalo skull on a totem near the entrance. Not only was this dwelling higher than the rest, but it was larger.

146   *Kachina*

One would expect someone of importance to have lived here long ago, perhaps even to the present day.

She was waiting for us in front of a burning fire and the ancient symbol of the compass was drawn in a large circle, covering the floor before us. "Loloma," she said to both of us, as she had the previous night in the dream.

"Loloma," we responded together. Then she continued to speak in Uto-Aztecan. Nina attempted to translate for me, but I quickly realized it wasn't necessary. I told her, "I understood what she was saying. She asked us to sit down beside her in front of the fire."

Nina's eyes almost popped out of her head and her jaw appeared to drop. She stood there, frozen with her mouth open until the elderly woman urged us to a seat.

Nina finally composed herself to speak. "You know Uto-Aztecan?"

"I do now. She taught me last night," I replied.

"You learned Uto-Aztecan in one night?" Nina inquired in amazement.

"No, it more or less just came to me. There was no formal teaching. She just started speaking to me in my dreams, and I knew what she was saying in Aztec."

Then I spoke to Nina in Aztec. She was still in awe of what was taking place, as she had heard and seen Shamans speaking in different, unrecognizable tongues, but had never actually witnessed it to this degree outside of a ceremony, and in a tongue that she recognized. Up to now the only other language that I knew was Spanish, and that was extremely marginal; it was a school prerequisite. Then I spoke to the elderly woman in Aztecan.

"Thank you for having us, Great Mother, and for showing us the path."

"You are welcome in here, Toquer Shoo-coots." With my new knowledge I recognized the name she gave me to mean Black Cat. "I am Kayah, Kiva Priestess."

I responded, "I have been given the Cherokee name Cheveyo in preparation for you."

"I know, Spirit Warrior and this is Nina. I don't need to tell you your destiny. You already know this, but *I need you to journey safely together.*"

This was the exact thing Mrs. Jerrells had said to us in New Mexico. *This has to be more than a coincidence.* Nina, are you ready?" Kayah inquired.

"Yes, Great Mother," Nina responded.

Kayah escorted us to the village Kiva, which was located at the highest point on the mesa. When the sun went down she began to chant aloud, so the whole village could hear her say the nightly prayers. It was beautiful listening to her voice echo over the village as she blessed it. When it was over she went up the ladder to the Kiva, then down into the aerial opening of the structure. It was amazing how agile she was for her age. She asked us to join her inside.

There were Ancient Aztecan writings, signs and symbols decorating the walls of the Kiva. In the middle there was a huge circle sunken into the floor, about two feet down from the surrounding surface. There were signs and symbols going around the circle with four different colored arrows emanating from outside the circumference. There was a white arrow pointing north, a red arrow pointing south, a yellow one pointing east and a black one pointing to the west.

There was a stone altar on the West side of the Kiva, with an elaborately adorned black pottery vessel in the center. The vessel contained water. Kaya lit a fire in the circular sunken floor, and then the Great Mother asked that we emulate her actions and repeat her words. First she knelt in front of the altar and paid homage to the Great Spirit Massauu and other spirits with a chant. Afterwards she turned towards the circle with what appeared to be a thurible, and threw some smoke to the north while chanting. Then she turned, faced south and threw smoke, repeating the chant. She did the same to the east and the west.

Then the Great Mother took out the feather of a large bird, perhaps an Eagle. She made hand and arm gestures towards the fire with the

148   *Kachina*

feather, and then handed it to Nina. She asked us to hold hands in front of the circle as she began speaking to the spirits, and then to us. "You are strong, Nina, like most who bear the mark of the Eagle. Like her, you are incredibly patient and courageous. The Eagle peers down from the highest of trees, waiting patiently for hours to strike. You are a relentless tracker, you won't give up on anything or anyone. Once something or someone is in your sight, you will pursue it until caught. The Eagle is extremely dedicated and loyal. Once its powerful talons grasp a hold of something, it won't let go. This is why you chose the work you do.

You are very emotional like the Eagle, but being very powerful and emotional leads to extremes. This is why the eagle flies erratically at times, like when it does the death drop. It falls out of the sky at extreme speeds; racing down, coming so close to the ground, and pulling up at the last minute.

The powerful beak and jaws of the Eagle makes you talkative. You are straight to the point and your words are strong; direct and blunt. Sometimes you speak without thinking of the consequences and end up hurting others when you had good intentions in mind. Your words also hold the power of your emotions. You can say what's in your heart that others can't convey. The Eagle has extraordinary hearing. People can hear what is in your heart as well as you can hear what is in theirs. The Eagle also has great vision and insight. It will help you illuminate what is hidden. You are able to see and hear what others can't or refuse to see or hear.

The Eagle lives in the Upper Realm of Heaven and Middle Realm. You are attracted to the light and the sun, yet you also look for the shade for comfort to build your nest for your family. You often fly too close to the sun because you are fearless, and need the cool that the shadows have to offer.

You both live in trees, you see. Just as the panther climbs to be closer to the heavens, yet lives in the dark, the Eagle soars in the sky yet seeks the shadows to be closer to the dark. This is why you are here together. It has been destined. Nina's wings will help you

Kachina   149

acquire the aerial perspective that you need to continue, Cheveyo.
She will be the one who rescues you when you can no longer see past
the darkness."

Then she got up and began chanting in front of the fire. She took
the thurible and threw smoke to the four corners, again. Then she
gave us each a pipe with peyote and sat back down. We lit up
the pipes and began chanting again. I guess the peyote ceremony
was pretty much universal, but the languages and chants differ. She
chanted to Massauu to assist us in our travels. She guided us into the
vision quest. We visited the Great Havi in the Spirit World, where
she showed us the Hopi's history from the Ancient People to now.

We stayed with the Great Mother for three days straight. She fed
us and provided a place for us to rest, but we didn't get much sleep
while we journeyed in vision quest with her. We took the batteries
out of our cell phones and I contacted Steve via dreamscape. I let him
know that we were safe and what we were doing. I'm just glad he was
open-minded and intelligent enough to accept the dream implant.

When we completed our journey with the Great Mother, we were
arrested and taken to see the Tribal Council. They wanted to bring
me up on charges of trespassing on reservation property and get Nina
fired from her job. Ortega and Steve were present, but the A.D.
wasn't aware of what was going on. Steve intercepted the phone call
from the council members and flew down. The Great Mother inter-
vened on our behalf and informed the council that she had invited us
to her dwelling, and to stay with her. The Great Mother was revered
throughout the Hopi Nation, including the Tribal Council. She was
a descendant of the first Hopi Snake Priest. I spoke to the Tribal
Council in Uto-Aztecan with Steve and Agent Ortega looking on in
astonishment.

"The Great Mother has enlightened me about the past, current
and future of the Hopi People. She has shown me the injustices and
wars brought about by the Spanish invaders, other tribes, missionaries and priests past and current. She has alluded to cover ups involving missing priests and the Order of Jemez. We were shown the

secret societies of the Hopi, in particular the Coyote Society which Agent Ortega, with his Hopi heritage, is aware of. When the killer identified himself as the Coyote, Agent Ortega felt the need to hide this information. The Coyote Society are the protectors of the Hopi Tribe, security guards and warriors. Since the days of the Anasazi, the Ancient People, they, along with the Kachinas or Great Spirits have been the hunters and guardians of the Hopi. They have been in conflict with outsiders and missionary priests for centuries."

"The Great Mother has summoned me on this quest for the truth. I will get to the bottom of this. There are some missing priests involved, and I hope the investigation doesn't lead me back here because I will come with the full force of the U.S. Government. The Great Mother has placed a lot of trust and faith in me. Your land is sacred and if I do return, I hope it is to be welcomed as a brother. One who fights righteously for Hopis, not one who covers up injustices or wrong doings." I looked directly at Ortega when I said the last.

The entire assembly was in awe, including Steve and Agent Ortega. They were astonished by my command of their language. The entire Tribal Council shook my hand afterwards and accepted me into their Nation. Agent Ortega just looked at me like the A.D. always did, and departed.

"I had no idea you knew the Hopi language," Steve stated.

"I didn't, Steve. I acquired it during a dream with the Great Mother."

"What did you say to them?" he inquired.

"I told them what I learned while with the Great Mother," I replied, and then inquired, "Can you take Nina and me to Jemez?"

"I can make that happen," he stated.

"Good. We'll meet you at Polacca and give you a full briefing on the jet. We are finally getting somewhere, Steve," I responded.

Ortega was waiting in the lobby for me after Nina and I checked out of the hotel." Mr. Sands, can I speak with you?"

"Sure. It's alright, Nina, I'll see you outside."

Kachina   *151*

She was hesitant and didn't want to leave. Nina was becoming more and more protective of me, especially around Ortega. The Watchful Eye of the Eagle, hovering from above and waiting to protect. I understood her feelings after finding out what we knew about him and his attack on me at the Residence Office.

"I never apologized for my actions at the Residence Office. I just want to say I'm sorry. I was beside myself after hearing the information about Gracie. She's the youngest of my agents and I feel personally responsible for her. She is the first neo I received directly from Virginia, since I've been the SAC," he stated.

"I understand that, Agent Ortega. I didn't think twice about it. Most people do irrational things when faced with adversity, but we are in the business of facing those adversities head on and with rational judgment. If we don't keep our heads, who will? What I don't understand is why you hid the fact that you're Hopi?"

"I'm not Hopi. My mother is Navajo and my wife is Hopi. Aren't you hiding something as well?", he asked.

"What do you mean?" I inquired.

"What tribe are you from?" he asked, raising his right eyebrow inquisitively.

"I am the descendant of Cherokee Freeman from North Carolina, but it's not a secret. The FBI hired me with full knowledge of who I am."

"I just want to say again I'm truly sorry for the way I treated you. I thought you were just some kind of con man or mentalist, to say the least, until I saw what you did in the Council Chambers. The Great Mother could have told you verbally everything you know about us, but you could not have hidden the fact that you speak Aztecan and waited for this precise moment in the case to begin speaking it. Besides, you must be authentic if the Great Mother shared all the Hopi ancient secrets with you," he stated.

"Thank you. She is quite a remarkable woman," I replied.

"Sands, I don't know anything about any missing priests, but I heard the rumors. You see, the Hopis don't share all their information and secrets, even amongst each other. There has never been any documented proof that they went missing. No one ever filed a missing persons report in reference to the rumors. There are no signs that these priests ever existed. Can we call a truce between us?" Then he extended his hand.

"Sure," I replied and shook his hand.

"Is she really still alive?" Ortega inquired as I was leaving.

"Yes; she really is," I stated, dipping my chin in confirmation.

While on the flight to Jemez, New Mexico, I gave Steve a full briefing.

"But how do these presumed missing priests have anything to do with the abduction of Gracie and the others? It doesn't fit our serial killer's profile of abducting young women in their twenties," Steve inquired.

"That question I can't answer yet, but there has to be a connection or I would not have received it. It is all connected," I replied.

Nina fell asleep on the jet while Steve and I talked. "How long has it been since the both of you slept," Steve asked?

"I don't know; about three days," I replied.

"It looks like it. You look like..."

Then I cut him off before he completed the sentence, "Yeah, I know."

"Have you been eating? Looks like you've lost some weight," Steve commented.

"I'll grab something from the kitchen before we land," I replied.

Nina was wiped out. The Great Mother had used her as a conduit. Kayah was old and didn't have the strength that she once had. She needed Nina's assistance to continue. I guess the best way to describe it was that Nina was used as a vessel by the Great Mother, who channeled through her. There were times when Kayah would speak through Nina, as though she were possessing her, except Nina was still present as well. Nina knew everything that was going on. Kayah stated that it was Nina's strong spirit which allowed her to remain

Kachina

present. She also stated that she wouldn't have been able to enter Nina if she didn't want her to.

Nina was specially gifted, like others who bear the sign of the Eagle; their dreams can't be entered unless they invite you. Observing the Great Mother channeling through Nina was like watching someone with Dissociative Identity Disorder vacillating between personalities. I could see how taxing it was on Nina and asked her several times if she wanted to stop but she refused, stating that she wanted to complete the vision quest. I never asked the Great Mother if she was channeling through Mrs. Jerrells, but I felt very confident that she was behind it.

Steve spoke, breaking me out of my contemplations. "Look, Chris, I like to think that you and I are more than just co-workers. When I first came to you and offered you this position, I knew and believed in your abilities without question. You must admit, you've been acting a little more aloof than usual. Are you alright with all the changes that have been happening to you? When is the last time you've looked at yourself in the mirror? You look like a rougher version of Johnny Depp; the hippie look! Your hair is down to your shoulders! You haven't shaved in several days and you are in desperate need of a shower," Steve commented with concern. He laughed, but I could tell his genuine worry for me; I felt it.

"I understand your concerns. I'm not going off the deep end if that's what you're worried about," I stated. "I just want you to know that I'm here for you if you ever need to talk. Dr. Green is also just a phone call away," he stated.

"Thanks Steve, but I got this," I replied. He gave me a hit on the side of my arm as he got up and headed towards the galley of the jet.

Steve returned with some sandwiches, fruit and juice. "Here, eat something," he said in a commanding voice. "I contacted Nina's supervisors and Dianna when you appeared to me in my dreams and gave them an update as you suggested."

"I'm just glad you retained the dream implant," I said. Then Steve became somber.

"Look, Steve, we are going to find her. And by the way, I'm taller than Johnny Depp," I quipped with a smile.

"You're incorrigible," he retorted, and laughed. It was good to see him laugh for a change.

Chapter 10

The Jemez Order

Steve received a phone call from the A.D. just as we were landing at the Santa Fe Municipal Airport. He wanted to know his whereabouts. Steve informed him that he was following a lead on the Navajo Reservation and would brief him on it later. I hated to wake up Nina, who was sleeping so peacefully, but Steve had to get back to Albuquerque and we didn't have time to waste.

"It's time to get up, sunshine." That was my new nickname for Nina, since her astral symbol was the sun. It took her a minute to figure out where she was again. She had been sleep deprived and wasn't used to it like the ViCAP team.

"Here's a large mocha latte, but you'll have to drink it as we leave. Steve has to hurry back to Albuquerque. Let's go," I said as I handed her the coffee. She was still a little discombobulated, but got herself together and we exited the jet.

"Wow, Steve. You really know how to show a girl a good time. Invite her on your jet, then kick her out before she's had a chance to get breakfast. No phone number, no let's do this again speech or anything," Nina joked.

She was never without something clever to say. It assisted in cheering Steve up. She gave him a reassuring hug and said, "Don't worry, we'll bring her back." It was nice having her around. She was a part of the ViCAP family now and I was a part of hers.

Jemez Springs was a resort town. It was filled with retreat hostels, spas, bath houses, bed and breakfasts and weekend getaways. If you wanted to relax and have fun in New Mexico you couldn't go wrong here. With its hot springs and hot sulfur springs. This was definitely paradise, but we were here for something else. As tired and overworked as we were; no one needed a little R&R as much as we did.

We checked into the Elk Mountain Lodge near the Jemez River in the Jemez Mountains. It was the cheapest we could find in Jemez. As much as I wanted to keep right on working, Steve was right. We needed to sleep for a few hours before we fell out. This was the best place for it. Nina couldn't wait to hit the sack, and I decided to get some real sleep for a couple of hours. My mind and body needed it.

I lay down on the bed and checked my phone messages. Most of them were from Dianna. One was from Dr. Green and one from Steve. He probably called Dr. Green after his concerns during our last conversation. He was on good terms with her and had to talk to her, as a stipulation of me working with the FBI. She just wanted to know how I was doing and asked if I could call her when I get a moment, which wouldn't happen anytime soon.

Steve's message was pretty much the same as before. He was concerned about me and the direction of the case. He also reminded me of the calendar date. It was the one thing that remained with me day and night. Not only was I counting down the days, but the hours and minutes. My focus, senses, physical agility and gifts were sharper now, after leaving Cherokee. My Spirit Guide's presence was strong, even in my conscious state. She was a part of me now, with and all her abilities and attributes.

Dianna's messages were pretty much repetitious, stating that she missed me and urging me to be safe. She left two messages per day, sometimes three. I hadn't spoken with her in several days or seen her in dreamscape. I'd been so busy. We hadn't physically been to-

The Jemez Order   *157*

gether in over two weeks. Hopefully this separation period was winding down. I gave her a call after checking my messages.

"Hello," I said.

"Hello, stranger. How are you?" she inquired in an upbeat voice.

"I'm doing well, and you?" I asked,

"I'm just missing you. I was beginning to get a little worried until Steve explained to me what was going on," she stated.

"I miss you too," I replied.

"How's Nina?" she inquired.

"She wasn't doing very well, but is asleep in her suite right now. We were up for three days with limited food and water. She wasn't used to it."

"Where are you now?" Diana asked.

"We're in Jemez."

"Oh, you're back in New Mexico! That's good; it isn't far from here," she replied.

We continued to catch up on the phone until I fell asleep while she was still on the line. I was truly exhausted this time. I woke up with my cell phone still on the bed and the battery low. Then I realized I had fallen asleep on Dianna. I quickly dialed her back and explained. She understood and we talked for a few minutes, after which she had to leave for the Residence Office. I was lucky to have someone so understanding.

Nina and I departed early the next morning. I began second guessing myself in the car on the way to the Jemez Order. After my last talks and texting with Steve, there was definitely cause for doubt. I was following up on dreamscape about a missing priest, whom no one including myself even knew existed. It was a suggestive implant by Kayah. The only one who thought this lead had any merit was Nina. I attempted to rationalize every angle that could involve the missing priest. Could the killer have experimented with the abduction of the priest first? Then I had to inquire why no one had reported it. This one did seem far-fetched.

158   *The Jemez Order*

"You seem to be staring into oblivion. What's on your mind?" Nina inquired. Her voice brought me back to a conscious state. I'm lucky she was driving the vehicle because I just completely zoned out, lost in thought.

"I'm sorry, what were you saying?" I asked.

"Are you ok?"

"Yeah, just thinking," I replied.

"About what?" she inquired. I didn't tell her of my doubts and remained silent.

She gave me a sideways glance and then broke the silence in her normal fashion. "Did you talk to Dianna last night or visit her in dreamscape?"

"Yes. We talked on the phone, but I fell asleep while speaking to her."

"Did you call her back this morning?"

"Yes," I stated without furthering the conversation.

"Do you want to talk about it?" Nina inquired.

"No. not really," I replied.

"Aren't you the loquacious one this morning," she responded.

"Please forgive me, Nina, but I just need a moment."

When we arrived at the Jemez Order, the first thing that caught my attention was the number for the address of the facility. It was the number 55, like the number the Kachinas wrote down in the dirt during my vision quest with the Great Mother. The facility was enormous and the surrounding private land that accompanied it was vast. It was designed to look like the old Spanish monasteries, but was completely modernized. It was truly a beautiful sight to see. You could tell a lot of money had gone into the building of it.

The priests were dressed plainly, donning the traditional black monks' robes. We inquired from one of the Monsignors where to find the head priest. He escorted us to the receptionist's desk at the business office. The Monsignor went behind the receptionist counter where the rest of the office was, and spoke to the receptionist. I could hear what he was saying as the receptionist picked up the telephone

The Jemez Order 159

and pressed one of the buttons on the business line. She spoke to another priest on the phone by the name of Monsignor Davis, and told him that there were visitors at the desk waiting to speak to him. I guessed he was the one in charge.

Apparently the panther's vision and agility weren't the only things she had imprinted on me. It was impossible to hear what the receptionist was saying from this distance, especially the person to whom she was talking on the phone, and yet I heard everything clearly. The Monsignor who had escorted us returned from behind the desk to tell us Monsignor Davis would be right with us and asked if we could have a seat. After 30 minutes, Monsignor F.D. Davis arrived through the same door we had used. He wasn't even in the business office the way we had thought.

He was a tall man, taller than me. He appeared to be in good shape, like he worked out. Then again, he did run a health resort. You could tell he was the alpha male of the priests. He had an air about him like someone of importance someone who demanded your full attention and respect.

"Good morning, I'm Monsignor Davis. How are you," he inquired with a friendly smile, looking at us.

"Very well, how are you?" I responded.

"Good morning," Nina replied.

"How can I help you?" he inquired.

"I'm Christian Sands with the FBI, and this is Agent Blackwater with Bureau of Indian Affairs. We are investigating a case and wanted to get some background information on the Jemez Order."

"Are we involved in this investigation?"

"We aren't at liberty to say at this point," Nina responded.

"Well, we opened the doors after the closing of the Servants of Paraclete Ministry. We purchased the lands and facilities thereafter. We aren't a part of the Archdiocese. We assist priests from all around the world get back on track. We are funded by donations. I wouldn't mind providing you with a tour, but I must remind you that certain areas are restricted due to doctor-patient confidentiality and legal privileges," Monsignor Davis stated. He seemed nice enough, perhaps I was wrong in my assumption. The Monsignor escorted us around the facility, explaining their mission and goal. He didn't get into specifics. He explained the differences between the Jemez Order and the Servants of Paraclete Ministry, and why the Servants had failed. Basically they didn't have the trained medical professionals the Order had. He went on to state the differences between psychiatrists and psychologists, which they had both.

"So you see, we provide clinical treatment of the symptoms as well as spiritual treatment," he added.

He continued to escort us around to the public areas: the dining hall, the prayer quarters, the church, library and the business center. They also had all the amenities of a resort fit for Jemez Springs; a hot sulfur bath house, fitness gym, full theater, hot springs area, swimming pool, sauna, Jacuzzi, basketball court, racquetball, tennis, bowling. Whatever your desired pleasures were, they accommodated them. They also had a full service staff.

Their staff included medical doctors, therapists and counselors. They had trainers, kitchen / wait staffers with chefs, maintenance staff and housekeepers. They even had a masseuse, but they weren't vain enough to have a spa with stylists and nail technicians. It was a religious retreat. Amongst the areas that were off limits were the treatment areas and private quarters. After we completed the tour, we sat down and questioned Monsignor Davis on the disappearances we heard about.

"We heard there were some priests who went missing from here," I asked the Monsignor. "No, that was a rumor. We've never had any priests go missing. We've never filed a missing persons report and there has never been a case investigating this, because there is no case." Monsignor Davis didn't appear to be upset in the least, but I was getting something totally different about his guise and demeanor deep inside my psyche.

The Jemez Order 161

When we left, I felt like someone who had just crawled out from under a rock. I had no idea of such places or of the existence of the Servants of Paraclete, which had been in existence since 1947. The Order and the SOP seemed to be some of the best kept secrets around. The Vatican was better than the CIA in regards to guarding secrets. We needed to conduct some quick research into the history of these groups. I thought I was just going to meet an old priest in a church and ask him a few questions, but this turned out to be something totally unexpected.

"Are you Catholic, Nina," I inquired in the car?

"Yes," she responded.

"Me too. Did you know about any of this?" I asked.

"Not a clue," she said, and then shook her head in disappointment.

"What about Monsignor Davis? What did you get from him?" I asked.

"He appears to be someone who wants to help people. We can't judge the church based on the actions of a few lost souls," Nina stated.

"Not just a few Nina. They have a multi-million dollar facility, and it isn't funded for a few incidents. This appears to be rampant and systematic.

"What sort of vibe did you get from the Monsignor," Nina inquired?

"I got the feeling like he was hiding something."

"Chris, is it wrong not to want to air your dirty laundry in public? Most of us would choose not to. That doesn't make them any different than anyone else. At least they're attempting to make a concerted effort to repair the problems."

"Yeah, but to what extent and at whose expense?" I asked.

"Are we investigating church transgressions or trying to find a serial killer?" Nina inquired.

"Not you too! Kayah set us on this path and my spirit guide sent me to see her. It has to tie in somehow." Nina went silent on me. For the first time she didn't have some quip, fast and clever comeback or rebuttal.

"Look, I know this defiles everything we have been taught about the church. I'm not trying to dig up any dirt and defame them, but if this leads me down some dark corridors and skeletons are found in the closet, I won't keep them hidden. I need to know if you are still with me on this," I asked Nina.

"Yes, I am," she stated, looking firmly at me as if to say *I will do it, but I don't like it.*

We stopped for lunch at a road side diner, which seemed to be the standard here. It'd been a while since we had a good meal. Nina always seemed to look good, even on limited rest. I could only imagine how I must have appeared. I had never taken my appearance into consideration until Steve mentioned it. At least I'd showered and changed.

"Do I appear different to you?" I asked Nina.

"You mean besides the wolf look?" she commented and laughed.

"No, I like it! You look sexy with the long hair."

"I didn't look sexy before?" I inquired, smiling.

"There you go, looking for more compliments," she said, smiling back. "Although, I would like to give you a shave. The scraggly beard doesn't do it. It makes you appear like a tatterdemalion," she further stated.

"Wow. Thank you for your bluntness!"

"What?" she said, and then gave me an alluring look.

"So how do we collect information on these alleged priests if no one has reported them missing, and we can't question any priests or medical staff at the Order?" she asked.

"Who says we need to get information from them? We can subpoena the non-confidential staff. You see how many people work there?" I replied.

"Excellent idea," Nina said. "I'll call Steve and get it approved," I stated and called him immediately.

"Hello, Steve, can you talk right now?"

"Yeah, how's it going?"

The Jemez Order 163

"Very well, but I need a subpoena to question the non-confidential staff at the Jemez Order," I stated.

"I can't do that, Chris. The A.D. will surely find out. Besides, I would need a judge to write it and we don't have probable cause for it. Chris, I'm really starting to worry about this new course of action. I don't know if I can back your play there. You might want to just sit this one out."

"Alright, Steve; I'll talk to you later." The pressures from the A.D. and the ticking clock might have been getting to Steve.

"How did it go?" Nina inquired.

"Not too well. We're on our own," I replied.

"What do you mean?" Nina inquired.

"Steve said he could no longer back us here."

"Well, we've practically been doing this on our own since we started," Nina stated.

"Hey, I understand if you want to quit, Nina."

"Are you kidding? We started this together, now we're gonna finish it together," she replied.

"So once again, how do we question the staff?" Nina inquired.

"Leave it to me. It will be plausible deniability for you from here on," I stated.

Later that day I created a fake subpoena.

We went back to the Jemez Order to question the staff. Monsignor Davis was surprised and perturbed this time with our actions. He even threatened to call their lawyers and the Governor. I had no doubt he would do so. The Order has enough money to make things very difficult for me, Nina, the FBI and BIA (Bureau of Indian Affairs). We conducted our interviews in private without the prying eyes and ears of Monsignor Davis. We hadn't completed all the interviews before their gang of lawyers entered and requested to see the subpoena, which I didn't give them.

"These interviews are over. I need to see your credentials and badges," the lead lawyer stated.

We said thank you to all of them politely, and left without showing them anything. The Monsignor already knew our names, so I guess that would have to suffice. We departed without getting the information that we were seeking. We did acquire the address and location of a soup kitchen operated by the Jemez Order. A staffer informed us that several priests helped out there. We drove down Route 4 from Jemez Springs to Jemez Pueblo, where the soup kitchen was located.

When we arrived at the soup kitchen they were just closing up for the evening. The kitchen was in an old abandoned warehouse that was partially renovated and converted. It provided more than enough space for the kitchen and dining area for the patrons. The sign over the entrance read: *This is the Jemez Order Kitchen- All Are Welcome.* There were two more signs stationed outside the front of the building; the one to the left of the door read: *This will be the site of the Jemez Order Mission Services.* The sign to the right read: In need of *volunteers.*

There was no one present when we entered the building. The Monsignors and patrons had already departed and a single volunteer was left to close and lock up. The Jemez Pueblo population was 30% below the poverty line, and the kitchen was fully utilized in this poverty-stricken area. Jemez Pueblo and Jemez Springs were like night and day in reference to income.

The young Latino man was putting up chairs when we entered the warehouse. He was a small fellow in his early twenties, weasel-like in stature. He appeared to be very nervous and jittery when we approached him.

"I'm sorry, but we're closed for the night. You have to come back tomorrow," he said in a hurried voice, not even looking up at us. "I'm sorry, but were not here for a meal," I said as he looked up and continued to work.

"Everyone is gone for the day. The priest won't be back until the morning," he stated.

The Jemez Order 165

"Perhaps you can assist us. I'm Christian Sands with the FBI and this is Agent Blackwater with the BIA. Can we ask you a few questions?"

"I don't know," he replied, his eyes skating away from us.

"Well, if you give us a few minutes, you'll find out, and we'll be on our way," Nina insisted.

"I don't know," he repeated. His last recourse was to settle for playing the *'I don't understand English well'* routine. I had experienced this ruse on numerous occasions when a subject didn't want to answer questions. He'd understood English perfectly minutes ago. There was something definitely off about this guy. Anyone could tell.

"OK, let me finish up real quick. I need to close the door, wait here for a second," he stated, in full command of the language again.

More than enough time went by, and he didn't return. We decided to look for him when we discovered several armed men at the entrance. They weren't here to welcome us, as the entrance sign stated. We were outnumbered and outgunned. We ran back to the sections of the warehouse that weren't renovated.

A firefight ensued; they began shooting at us, and Nina shot back. We ventured further into the depths of the warehouse to escape the mêlée of gunfire and seek cover.

"They've got us trapped back here," I stated, panting.

"I know, and I'm running out of bullets," Nina replied. They had us trapped behind some crates in the warehouse. This was another one of those times I wish I had taken a gun.

"Nina, look; do you see that? It's the transformer box. Can you shoot it out?"

"Yeah, but then we'll be trapped and blind," she replied.

"Yes, and they will be blind too. Do you trust me?" I inquired.

"Yes," she responded, looking me firmly in the eyes.

"Then shoot it out," I urged.

I was taking the huge chance that my other abilities had progressed also since finding my animal Spirit Guide. I was gambling that my ability to see in the dark was enhanced. My night vision was already better than most. However, it would have to be enhanced exponentially for me to see in here, once the lights went completely out.

"I just got this feeling, Nina; I can hear the panther talking to me." Then she shot the transformer box. Thick blackness closed in on us like a blanket. It took a minute for my eyes to adjust, but it worked. I could see amazingly clearly, like a cat.

"Did it work?" she whispered in inquiry.

"Yes. Be quiet and I'll get us out of here."

We barely escaped with our lives, leaving the assailants shooting at each other in the dark. The real question was who wanted us dead? Once again the Great Mother has been proven correct. If Nina hadn't been with me to shoot out those lights, I would have been dead and without my night vision, she'd never have escaped alive. We needed each other to complete this.

When we arrived back at the lodge, I asked Nina to join me in my suite. "I have something for you in my room," I stated.

"What is it," she inquired?

"You'll see," I replied. I pulled out an unopened bottle of Grand Marnier Cuvee du Centenaire 100 year from one of my bags. "I appropriated this from the jet. I was going to drink it with you after this was over, but now seems like as good occasion than any."

"Thank you. How did you know this was my favorite?" she asked.

"I pay attention," I responded.

"Yes, you do," she stated.

Nina looked a little rattled after the shootout. "Are you going to be alright," I inquired?

"Yeah; it's just that this has been the second gunfight that I've been in since taking this assignment. I never thought I would need a backup gun," she stated.

"I never thought I'd need a gun at all. Guess we were both wrong," I stated and poured two glasses of the GM as we toasted to being alive. Nina and I didn't talk about the 'who's and why's' of the attack tonight.

Nina eventually fell asleep while we were on the sofa. I placed a blanket over her and let her rest. I watched her for a minute or two, staring at her beauty. I reflected back on what had occurred at the warehouse. It was amazing how my powers, if you can call them that, were progressing. It seems the closer I became to my Native American roots, the stronger my abilities became. I decided to put on the Indian attire the Great Mother gave me. She had given Nina and me several gifts before we departed. The clothes weren't anything fancy or ceremonial. It was just a plain ribbon shirt, a pair of buckskin pants and some moccasins. Then I got the prayer rug from my bag.

I didn't utilize the peyote or other dream inducers. I didn't really need it, and I didn't want to go too far under with Nina asleep and gunmen attempting to kill us. I thought we were safe, miles away from the town of Jemez Pueblo in a secluded lodge in the Jemez Mountains. No one knew we were here except the receptionist who signed us in, and we hadn't seen anyone since we arrived. We hadn't spent any time there to be noticed. But I wasn't taking any chances

I heard my cell beep. I had several text messages and emails I had neglected for the longest time, and needed to acknowledge. They were from Steve and Dianna. The email message from Steve read: *What are you doing, Chris? The Governor called the Director. You used a fake subpoena posing as a Federal Agent. The A.D. has a warrant for your arrest for impersonating a Federal Officer, Fraud of a Federal Document, False Arrest when you detained and interviewed the staff of the Jemez Order, harassment, and breaking and entering into a Jemez Order Kitchen in Jemez Pueblo. There is no need to tell you that there's an APB out on you. There was nothing I could do to stop it. I told you to discontinue your investigations of the Jemez Order. Tell Blackwater to get back here immediately!*

Dianna's messages were pretty much the same as Steve's, asking me to turn myself in. *What's happening to you, Chris? I don't hear from you for days, and now this? You're wanted for questioning by the FBI. You need to turn yourself in, Chris. I don't think you should try to get in touch with me until you do.*

I had anticipated the Monsignor would carry out his threats when the lawyers arrived, but I didn't think this would be the reaction of Dianna. I couldn't think about this right now. I had work to do in dreamscape, so I flushed it from my mind. I sat down on the prayer rug, and began chanting quietly. I visited Gracie first to let her know that I was still searching for her and to calm her fears. The killer was taking care of her now, like the rest of the women he'd abducted. He was feeding her and bathing her. There were still no further clues or breaks in his calculating and meticulous regimen.

My next dream visit involved Monsignor Davis. This would be the first time for me to visit the dreams of a priest. I had never been that close to any priest to perform dreamscape. For that matter, I never had a reason. I didn't know if I should. Was this something sacred that I shouldn't violate, like holy ground? Then again, didn't priests do the same thing when they question people's psyches and dreams? Nonetheless, I wasn't a priest and still had some things to learn about shamanism.

I decided to leave it in the hands of the Spirit World. If I wasn't meant to go there, my spirit guide would let me know. The door to the Monsignor's dreams was wide open. His dreams weren't empyrean as I would have expected. In fact, they were dark and filled with dirty secrets.

I didn't want to see anymore. I had seen as much as I could take. I was raised as a Christian and looking into the darkness of his dreams made me jerk out of dreamscape. It was like when I was a kid, escaping the horrible nightmares in my past before I learned how to control my dreams. I was sweating and trembling, not from fear but from the disgust and abhorrence of it all. When I came out of the dream, Nina was still asleep. I went outside to catch a breath of fresh air after my unpleasant experience.

I came back inside after several minutes and decided to calm my nerves by getting into the Jacuzzi. The water always had a soothing and calming effect on me. I took off the Indian clothing and jumped in. The water felt excellent, I wished I had one of these in my home.

The Jemez Order   169

For about 30 minutes I just cleared my mind in meditation. I didn't think about anything, I needed to download and shut it all off.

"There you are." a female voice broke into my thoughts.

"Yeah, look; I'm sorry, you were asleep so I jumped in," I stated, embarrassed to be naked in the Jacuzzi. My clothes were clearly on the floor for her to see, including my underwear.

"Mind if I join you?" she inquired.

"But I'm naked in here."

"What was it you said last time I found you in the water? *I don't think anyone will mind.*" Then she disrobed and jumped in naked also. When it came to physique, she had the full package.

"I know what you're going to say. "Nothing I haven't already seen, right?" I quipped.

"No, that's not what I was going to say," she said. "I was going to say thank you for saving my life." she moved in even closer and kissed me. There was no use in fighting this any longer. I could not resist these fervent emotions. We made love in the Jacuzzi, the passion had overwhelmed us both. There was nothing or no one else in the world at this moment in time. Then we moved out of the water and continued on the floor. It was like the animal was coming out of me. I couldn't let her go, I just wanted to stay within her and lose myself in this ecstasy. We finally made it to the bedroom, and continued making love blissfully into the morning.

I was every bit of the non-monogamous animal that Asku and my Spirit Guide said I was. I liked to think that I was above animal magnetism and urges and could resist temptation, but apparently not. As good as I felt, another part of me was aching inside with regret and pain.

"Wake up, Nina, they're here!"

"Who?" she inquired, her voice filled with anxiety.

"I'll explain later, but we have to go!" I threw on the closest available items; the Indian clothing that was on the floor. Nina slipped into her military fatigues and threw on a blouse. We quickly stuffed our bags and departed. We could see vehicles heading up the mountain trail miles away. Nina stopped for a second outside and observed them.

"How did you know," she whispered, but I could still hear the cat in my head.

"We have to go, Nina. Take the battery out of your cell phone."

We jumped into the vehicle and went down the backside of the mountain through the Jemez National Forest. They couldn't view us leaving from so far away. They would also take the time to case the suite, which would put even more distance between us. They were under the assumption that they had the element of surprise on their side, but they were wrong. We drove for miles on Route 4 in the opposite direction of the FBI posse that was after us, until finally stopping at a gas station near White Rock.

"Those were all dark blue government issue vehicles heading up the mountain. Do you want to explain why the FBI is after us?" Nina inquired.

"It was Steve; that was how I knew they were coming. He knew I would feel his presence, or he hoped I would. That's why he came with them. He also had to give the appearance that he wasn't involved. I gave him no choice, he had to do this. The Monsignor called the governor, who in return notified the FBI director. Steve left me a text message last night, informing me about it. The A.D. put an APB out for my arrest. Dianna even left me a message to turn myself in. They're charging me with impersonating a Federal Officer, Fraud of Federal Documents, several counts of false arrest when I held the staffers, harassment and breaking and entering at the soup kitchen," I informed her.

"All spearheaded by the A.D., no doubt," Nina stated.

"You got it," I replied.

"He threw the book at you. Did he leave anything out?" she inquired. "Well, they can probably add fleeing a federal officer, evading arrest, and kidnapping you now." We both laughed.

"Steve's text also said that you should report to the ABQ HQ immediately," I told her.

The Jemez Order 171

"OK; that part I didn't hear," she stated.

"I just wanted you to be able to make the decision on your own. Either way, I will tell everyone you didn't know about this and I lied to you. I will also state that I informed you to turn off your phone as a ViCAP field procedure."

"You think they'll buy that?" she inquired.

"We've done that in the past and the team can attest to it."

"So what do we do now?" Nina inquired.

"The basics; find food and shelter," I replied.

"That's going to be difficult since we can't use our credit or bank cards," Nina stated.

"I've got enough cash on me to check into one of these roadside motels. It won't be the Ritz, but it'll do for now," I replied.

We drove a little further until we came to the Hampton Inn on Route 4. I checked in using cash and a fake name. I only booked one room for the two of us.

Half an hour after checking in, I emerged from the bathroom.

"Hey, let me take a picture of you. You look good in your Indian clothing. Thanks for shaving," Nina stated.

"I'm glad you approve," I replied.

"I've just noticed that you weren't wearing your glasses any longer," she said.

"Wow; as observant as you are, you're noticing it now? I haven't worn them since I left Cherokee. I don't need them any longer," I replied.

"I've always been able to look past the superficial and see a person's inner beauty," she responded. She always knew the right thing to say at the appropriate time. "So you've completely gotten rid of Clark Kent. Now I have my own little Superman equipped with night vision," Nina added with a smile.

"I wouldn't go that far," I replied.

Then she placed her hand on the side of my face. "Chris, just don't forget there's a place for Clark Kent in the world also."

"I understand," I replied. She was seeing the metamorphosis happening to me, more so than anyone. She was witnessing it firsthand. She had been there for me through it all.

I was now a rogue; a vigilante and a fugitive being hunted by the same people I used to chase and hunt people for. We couldn't use our credit or bank cards and were low on funds. There were two people that I could call. Dr. Green was one, but Steve knew her personally. They would expect me to contact her or my family in Atlanta, whom Steve knew I would never involve. The other person that was displaced from the FBI's radar was Dr. Banks. He wasn't a part of their peripheral. He was no longer my physician and a part of my past. We had limited contact now, so I gave him a call.

I used the pay phone in the hotel lobby to call Dr. Banks on his office phone. He didn't have a problem wiring me several grand until this was over. He told me how proud he was of me, and hung up the phone. He was the closest thing I had to a father growing up. Nina was seated at the table cleaning her gun when I arrived back from using the phone.

"So you never told me what you discovered during dreamscape," she inquired.

"Monsignor Davis is running an Ecclesiastic jail. The priests are prisoners there. He beats them with whips and lashes them like in medieval times. Some are even tortured. He's a sadist who enjoys it. There are priests in there for alcohol abuse, drug abuse and a whole slew of heterosexual and homosexual abuses, including the abuse of minors. Also, there are priests missing from there, but I didn't complete the dream; it was too dark even for me; him being a priest and all. I'm almost certain he sent those men to kill us," I said.

"Even if he did, there's no way of proving it in a court of law since this is all based on a dream," she pointed out.

"You haven't seen what ViCAP does once they build a case around my dreams. I usually acquire more evidence though, but first we have to do some other things," I replied.

The Jemez Order   *173*

"You mean staying alive and not going to prison?" she said with a smile.

"Yeah; that too, but first we need to collect the wired money from Dr. Banks, change vehicles and then strategize on our next moves," I responded.

We received the funds Dr. Banks had sent to the market's Western Union. We purchased some food and personal items while there. We hid the rental vehicle and purchased an old hoopty for 1000 dollars. It was an old Ford Bronco, and it would hopefully get us where we needed to go. Afterwards we returned to the hotel.

"Chris, I don't mean to be presumptuous, but is it over between you and Dianna?"

"I think so," I replied.

"I'm sorry; I know how much you felt for her," Nina stated. I remained silent. This was definitely not a conversation I was looking forward to having. This was another one of those things Kayah briefed us on about: the Eagles' directness. I knew the answers Nina was looking for and she had been there for me through it all, so I engaged in her questioning.

"Nina, I still have deep feelings for Dianna, but apparently they were a little one-sided after all. I don't know where you and I are heading, but I care deeply for you as well. I always have, as you've noticed. I'm willing to see what develops if you are."

"I was hoping for the same," she replied, then came to me and we kissed.

"This feels right. I can definitely get used to this," she said.

"I agree," I replied and kissed her again.

"Hey mister, we need to get back to strategizing. We have people searching for us and a killer to find. Do you think your abilities can help you see what the Monsignor knows about those missing priests now?"

"You're right. Look at you, practicing restraint," I said, jesting.

I pulled out the prayer rug and utilized the remaining peyote I had left. I would have loved to have Nina go with me, but we weren't certain of our surroundings and she needed to be on guard while I was under. I was going under deep this time, and would be out for some hours.

I woke up feeling depressed. It wasn't like the hangover depression I used to have when on the sleeping pills, but a feeling of emptiness from what I witnessed. Monsignor Davis was like an open book, easy to access. He didn't take the time to shroud his actions.

"I was mortified to see a priest acting in such a way, Nina. He's power-sick and thinks he's unstoppable. Not only did he commit grave atrocities in this Ecclesiastic prison, but he's had two priests killed that I know of. They were going to expose what was going on in the Jemez Order and he had them murdered. He had their bodies buried in the Santa Fe forest. This is how we'll get the evidence, Nina. I know where the bodies are buried. I even saw the faces of the men who committed these murders. Monsignor Davis spoke their names; Arelio Sanchez and Julio Gutierrez. These were the same men who were shooting at us. They are Monsignor Davis' henchmen."

"Apparently Monsignor Davis rescued them and their families from Mexico and gave them shelter. They became indebted to the Monsignor, so he manipulated them into doing his dirty work. He used their illegal immigrant status as a tool and a weapon. He threatened the deportation of them and their families if they didn't work for him. Monsignor Frank D. Davis is a true monster and is going straight to hell!"

"So let's go verify these graves and see if we can get the proof we need to connect these bodies to Monsignor Davis," Nina replied.

We arrived at the Santa Fe Forest under the shroud of darkness. It was eerie and ominous looking as we made our way to the location that had been given to me in the dreams of the sadistic priest. The sounds of the forest seemed more alive at night than during the day. It wasn't still in the least bit. Normally it grew quiet as one would pass through the forest, but this wasn't the case tonight. The creatures didn't fear us at all. This is when the predators come out to play and hunt. They were more interested in avoiding their natural enemies than us.

Nina was using a flashlight, but didn't really need it, because I, like most of the nocturnal creatures of the night, could see without it. As we made our way deeper into the forest the moonlit sky became covered by foliage. It was pitch black within its depths. The blackness seemed to absorb the illumination of the flashlight and its beams were limited like in a black hole in space. Then I felt it. I had never been in this place before, but I could feel the spirits of the dead priest hovering over the burial site. Goosebumps rose from on my skin.

"This is it, Nina. They're here. We need to finally put them to rest," I said as I began to dig.

Nina became a little edgy as I dug deeper into the earth for the bodies. I continued relentlessly. I had to verify that they were here and to release their spirits. It wasn't a windy night, but it seems the deeper I dug, the more the wind picked up until it was blowing like the gusts from a storm. The trees were moving feverishly around and the leaves were blowing about us. Something didn't want us to find these priests. It was as if the ground were cursed!

"What is it?" Nina shouted over the tempest.

"Something doesn't want us to release them," I yelled back to her.

Then the wolves came from out of nowhere, growling and snarling as if ready to attack! Nina pulled out her service revolver and quickly jumped from the hole I was digging. I joined her with the shovel in hand. The animals remained at bay watching us for several minutes, before they attacked.

Nina was a good shot, but my speed was tenfold by this point. I killed three of the wolves with the spade in less than a minute. There were six wolves lying dead on the ground before they retreated. Nina was breathing hard as I put my arms around her to calm her down.

"Perhaps we should return when it's daylight," she said.

"I'm almost there, Nina, give me a few more minutes," I replied and jumped back into the hole. I was even more emphatic about finding the priest after the incident with the wolves.

"There here," I yelled to Nina as I hit the lid of a wooden casket. At least they had the decency to bury them in a casket!

I pried open the lid as a burst of wind from within the casket rushed out and knocked me over. The windstorm has ceased and the two apparitions appeared in front of us. They didn't say anything, but had a look of contempt. I could feel that they were thanking us, and then they disappeared. Nina was rendered speechless with amazement. I placed the lid back on the casket and covered it with dirt. Now I had the evidence I needed to convict Monsignor Davis of these murders.

"But how does this fit in with the serial killer?" Nina inquired.

"That, I don't know, but I think Monsignor Davis can assist us with those answers. We need to go back there tonight and get those answers. It will be very risky and dangerous, but they won't be expecting us to come back with so many people looking for us. I'll use the shadows and the night as an ally. It will offer me cover and assist me in gaining access. I will use my panther abilities to get me in and out safely. I just need you to wait near the vehicle for me and alert me if anything is going on outside. I know the layout of the facility and campus from dreamscaping with the Monsignor. He also provided me with the access codes for the door and alarms."

"Your abilities are growing, Chris."

"Thank you, Nina. I just hope it's enough."

Later that night we drove to Jemez Springs. Before I exited the vehicle to go inside, Nina grabbed my hand. "Here, just in case you run into trouble," she said and placed her backup weapon in my palm.

"Thanks, Nina, but no thanks. I won't need it."

"Please; will you do it for me?" she asked.

"Nina, it goes against all my principles to carry that. Please don't ask me to."

"Alright, but be careful. And if you're not out in an hour, I'm coming in there after you," she stated firmly.

"No, I'll call you on the burner phones. I'll be alright," I said, and then kissed her before exiting.

The Jemez Order   177

Now it was time for me to let my nocturnal instincts lead me. I blended into the night and became a part of the shadows. In every corner where there was darkness or a hint of shadow, I slunk without being seen. I was camouflaged in it like the jet black coat of a panther. I watched as several men passed by me. It was like I was invisible, engulfed in the sunless corridors. I stealthily made my way through the facility with a noctivagant purpose; hiding in the lightlessness. I finally made it to Monsignor Davis' room. The door was locked, but I easily bypassed it with a credit card. I entered without being heard or seen. He was asleep as I spoke to him; unseen in the dark corner of the room.

"Monsignor Davis; I'm here to correct an injustice. Wake up," I raised my voice, just slightly so only he could hear me.

"Who's there?" he inquired in a startled and shaken voice as he jumped up from the bed. "Who is it?" he asked again? Then I stepped out from my piceous surroundings.

"What are you doing here? How did you get in here," he asked as his fears turned to anger, now that he knew who was in the room with him. I said nothing and just sat in the chair near his bed. "I'm calling the police," he snarled furiously as he turned on the lights and walked towards the stationary phone.

"Go right ahead. Make sure you tell them about Father Maize and Father Honanie," I replied. He paused with the phone's receiver in his hand.

"What are you talking about?" he asked in a low and hesitant tone.

"I'm talking about the priests you had murdered because they were going to expose you and the center for the atrocities and medieval practices taking place here," I stated.

"That's absurd!" he exclaimed. He still didn't make another move towards calling the police.

"You had Arelio and Julio kill them and bury their bodies in the Santa Fe Forest. You know the place, because I sure do," I said. Then he placed the phone's receiver back in its cradle and sat slowly on the bed. He had the stare of a condemned man.

"How did you find out?" he asked.

"It doesn't matter. Would you like to tell me what happened to the other three missing priests," I inquired?

"There aren't any other missing priests," he said.

"You might as well confess. The police will be here in the morning when I tell it all," I replied.

"You don't get it; there aren't any priests missing," he stated.

Then the unthinkable occurred. He got up from the chair he was seated in and walked towards the dresser, opened one of the drawers and brandished a handgun. I would have never thought a priest would be in possession of a gun. I knew he had others do his dirty work, but what would a priest need a gun for? He hesitated with the weapon in his hand and didn't say anything. For a second I thought he was going to use it on himself, but then he turned it towards me.

"You must really have a lot of enemies, priest. There's no telling what shit you're into if you need a gun. Have you really sunk that low? You're supposed to be a man of God," I stated.

"You have no idea who I am or what I'm capable of. You should have stayed on the run, Agent Sands. Now you've forced my hand," he stated, pointing the gun at me. I froze, unable to move, unwilling to believe the evidence of my senses.

Just before he shot me in cold blood, the lights in the room began to flicker. It wasn't just the usual flicker from a power outage during a storm or a power surge, but it was like watching an old black and white movie projector scattering the light. What happened next I can only try to describe the best I can.

Two apparitions entered the room. I could sense the immense fear on the priest as they did. I guess I would have also been scared, but I've seen far worse in my nightmares. The spirits were shifting back and forth visually, like the transparency of certain gases against the light. Then they took on the shapes of the Kachinas I saw in my dreamscape with the Great Mother.

"I don't think they're here for me, priest. I think it's time for you to pay for your transgressions," I drawled, looking at the fear in his eyes. He was no longer fixated on killing me. The blankness and the fear that covered his face said it all. It was time to pay the piper, and he knew it. He took his aim off me and directed it towards the apparitions. Then he began erratically firing toward the lifeless entities, as the bullets passed completely through them without any effect. He might as well have been shooting at the wall for all the good it did him. I dove on the floor when he began discharging the weapon.

Priests and security guards gathered outside Monsignor Davis' door after they heard the shots. They were yelling and asking if he was alright. The security guards attempted to break down the door, but they couldn't. It was closed by supernatural forces. There was no one getting in or out of the room. They shot at the lock and the door itself, but it was closed tight as a steel trap. Then things turned worse for Monsignor Davis. The Kachinas turned into the most hideous and unimaginable poltergeists. They began haunting his mind, as he dropped to his knees holding his head with the gun still in hand. He was definitely in agonizing pain as he began screaming from the depths of his soul.

I heard sirens, miles away in the distance. My hearing was extremely acute now from my panther imprinting. Monsignor Davis put the gun up to his head and shot himself, scattering pieces of his skull and brains to the wall, his limp body falling to the floor, lifeless. The Kachinas turned back into their Native American spirit form and blew the window to the room open. It was their way of telling me to exit. I was two stories up, but it wouldn't be a problem for me. The door remained shut tight as I made my way out the window. It closed behind me and locked itself from the inside. I made my way off the compound under the stygian veil of the night, blanketed by the tenebrous shadows. I remained noctivagous as I rejoined Nina back at the car.

"What happened in there? I heard gunfire but couldn't get in the door. Then security appeared, so I got out of there. Are you alright?" Nina inquired excitedly, standing outside of the vehicle. She was giving me the once over; scrutinizing my body from head to toe. She was checking for gunshot wounds or to see if I was injured in any other way.

"I'm fine, Nina. You did well. Now let's get out of here before the local police arrive." I stated and jumped into the car.

"So did you get what we're looking for?" she inquired.

"Yes and no," I replied.

"Are you going to tell me what happened?" she inquired.

"Well, for starters, two Kachina ghosts appeared and drove Davis to kill himself after he confessed to murdering two priests. He also said he didn't know about any other dead or missing priests," I informed Nina.

"I thought the two dead priests were the link?" she inquired further

"No, they were leverage. There are missing priests who are still alive. We need to find them. They are the key to this. They will lead us to the serial killer," I stated.

"So we didn't really accomplish anything here. We're back to where we started from," Nina said her teeth grinding in frustration.

"Did you really want me to stick a gun in the face of a priest and beat the information out of him?" I asked.

"Davis is far from being a saint," she retorted.

"What we did receive is a taped confession from Davis. I had my telephone on record the whole time," I replied. We had dropped the title Monsignor and his association with priests without effort.

"Will the recording hold up in court?" Nina inquired.

"Yes, with the other evidence I will provide; the names of the killers, motives and where the bodies can be found. The first thing I need you to do is drive me to the Residence Office. I need to drop off this recording and get a write up on this."

"You've really lost it now. Are you insane?" Nina inquired in a perturbed voice.

"No, but some would like to think so. I assure you, Nina, I know what I'm doing."

"You want me to drive you to the RO while the city is blanketed in a curfew, with wall-to-wall law enforcement officers searching for

The Jemez Order 181

a serial killer and you? Did I mention the city is encompassed with revolving check points and road blocks that change daily? You told me previously that you can't predict the future, so how are you going to predict where the road blocks will be?"

"I'll show you," I responded.

I retrieved the phone from my pocket and began to dial. Then I placed it on speaker mode while it was ringing.

"Hello, Steve, can we talk?"

"Give me a minute to get to a secure location... OK, how are you doing?"

"I'm fine, and you?" I inquired.

"Don't ask. I'm glad you sensed me coming in the mountains. It served two purposes. I needed to get the A.D. off my back and I hoped you would feel me coming. He had the nerve to ride along with us. The man really has a hard on for you." We all laughed at his comment.

"Yeah, I almost didn't feel you coming. I was asleep," I said, then looked at Nina and smiled, as if to say 'I told you so'. She nudged me on the arm and returned the smile. Then Steve pleaded, "Tell me you have some good news. They're ready to move on to preventing the next abduction."

"Yes, I have made some progress. First of all, Gracie is alive. Second, I've got a confession on this phone from Monsignor Davis, on the killings of two priests, made just before he killed himself. The bodies can be found buried in the Santa Fe Forest, off route 550. I'll write up all the details; the exact location of the burials and the names of Davis' accomplices."

"But why?" Steve inquired.

"It'll be all in the report. I'll drop it off tonight."

"Are you crazy?" Steve demanded in a raised voice.

Nina laughed out loud.

"Is that Nina?" he asked.

"Hey Steve," she blurted out.

"Hello, Nina. I have you covered with your bureau. I told them you were still undercover for me. No one else knows."

"Thanks, Steve," she replied.

"So you were saying that you're going to waltz your way to the front door of the Residence Office and place a parcel in the mail box, *like the Coyote*? Don't do it, Chris," Steve warned me.

"Steve, all I need are the locations of the checkpoints and road blocks."

"It's too risky. Why blow it now?"

"It's on the way, and you guys need to move on this. It's connected, as I told you. It's all coming together, Steve, but I don't have a lot of time. Do this for me."

"Alright, where do you want me to send it?"

I gave Steve the email address of a Gmail account that I rarely use, and isn't connected to me. They wouldn't be monitoring any internet traffic leaving the Field Office, but they would be monitoring and tracking all traffic coming in. It was protocol during such investigations. It would be even better if Steve could meet us somewhere, but the A.D. had an extremely tight leash on him after the news leak.

The only way to keep Steve's involvement from being suspected was to drop off the information in a sealed parcel addressed to him. My voice was recognizable on the recording. This information somewhat vindicated my investigating the Jemez Order, but it wouldn't cause them to drop the charges. I'd still be considered a vigilante and a rogue, now more than ever.

We drove back to the Hampton Inn to collect our bags and check out. We spent a little extra time there to do the write-up on the Jemez Order. I had to close some gaps in this investigation to get the heat off Nina and me. I felt bad about what happened at the Jemez Order because the only ones who would really suffer from this would be the families relying on the soup kitchen. The ill priests would just find another center. I'd have to revisit the charity at a later date and see if there was anything I could do to keep it open.

The Jemez Order   *183*

After completing the report we departed the hotel. We needed to retain the assistance of the night. Utilizing the hotel's computer, I received the email from Steve in reference to the checkpoints and road blocks. I trusted Steve, but even if the A.D. was monitoring him, we were on our way out the door.

I didn't have a problem in Albuquerque. Everything was set up the way Steve had informed us it would be. Nina parked a mile from the Residence Office. It was easy blending into the night and dropping off the parcel, easier than entering the Jemez Order Facility had been. There was more open space to maneuver and more obumbrate. *This must be how the serial killer felt as he snuck up to the front door of the Residence Office and dropped off his letter.*

Now came the hard part; finding and connecting these missing priests in the puzzle. I needed some big magic, so I drove us back to the sacred grounds of the Hopi Nation. Nina slept in the car on the way there. Now that I had settled some of the atrocities involving the Jemez Order, I needed assistance with the rest of this mystery. My quest had led me back to Kayah. This would be the best place to acquire additional noumena help for connecting with the Spirit World.

It was morning when we arrived at the Black Mesas of the Hopi Nation, Nina had slept through the entire journey there. We went directly to the Walpi Village to see the Great Mother. She was delighted to see us and was prepared for our arrival. We sat on her prayer rugs and thanked the Spirits for our safe travel back. Then we discussed our journey.

"The Fallen Ones, the priests, they were Hopituh Shin-nu-mu; Peaceful People of Hopi?" I asked the Great Mother, but already knew the answer. Nina didn't know and I wanted confirmation as well.

"Yes; the fallen ones are from the Black Mesa, Hopituh Sinom, the People of Hopi. Father Maize is from this village and Father Honanie is from the Kykotsmovi Village. They are both from great Hopituh clans. They were a part of the future of the Hopituh Shin-nu-ma," she replied.

"Why didn't you just vision quest with the Monsignor like you did with us?" I asked Kayah.

"It is different. Like you, I need a bridge to cross over into dreams. I have no connection with the White Devil or the white man's world. Father Maize's and Father Honanie's spirits had already passed. They came to me as Kachinas do, and informed me of you. I felt you and Nina's spirits because they are so strong in the spirit world. It was easy to form a bridge with you without having contact or connection with you, especially when your two spirits are together. It is like a beacon. It is hard not to pick up on the abundance of your spirit presence. Maize and Honanie needed you to find them and set them free. Their spirits were not at rest. They knew you could bridge the worlds that I cannot."

"I still haven't found the other missing priests," I told Kayah.

"This once again is the path only you can walk. Nina will be your Eagle protector overhead, but you must walk alone," she said.

"I have come here to ask the spirits to assist me on this path. I need to ask the fallen ones to assist me now that they are free."

"You have brought justice to the spirit world and the middle world. For this you will be rewarded. Usually there is a price to pay, but you have given up so much already, Spirit Warrior. You will be aided in what you seek," Kayah said.

"Thank you, Great Mother," I replied.

I left Nina with Kayah and ventured to the Kiva alone. I remained there for most of the day, chanting and, with the assistance of peyote, slipping into the dream world. When I arose from the Kiva several hours later there were all sorts of gifts laid out in front of it. The Hopituh had heard of what I had done, apparently, and wanted to show their appreciation. They were masterful artisans and their gifts were exquisite. There was pottery, baskets, woven clothing, food and drink. The people weren't present when I exited the Kiva. They were

The Jemez Order   185

shy and peaceful shunning the spotlight and standing clear of attention. They were uncannily similar to me in several characteristics. The night had come when I rose from the Kiva. I was just in time to hear the Great Mother bless the village. I loved this Hopituh tradition more than any. Her voice had such a profound, serene effect on me, it was soothing to hear her beautiful voice echoing over the village. It took me back to pleasant days of the past, when I was a boy and my mother used to say nightly prayers with me. Then she would read me a bedtime story before I fell asleep.

When the Great Mother completed the prayers, she joined me at the base of the Kiva. I felt ambivalent. I was elated and honored by the gifts, but saddened because I still didn't have all the answers I was looking for. Kayah attempted to calm me and told me not to get discouraged. She grabbed my hand and said, "They have shown you all you need to know." Nina was at Kayah's pueblo. I decided to remain at the Kiva for a while longer.

Chapter 11

The Dark Moon (howl of the Coyote)

The night is a totally different animal than the day. Man has feared
the night since the time when we were living in caves. When we were
afraid of what we couldn't see and the horrors that came when the
sun went down. This was when the predators came out to hunt. This
was a time when man was prey and you would find him curled up in
a corner in fear, hoping to make it through the night.

Things haven't changed much since the days before we discovered
how to use fire. We have always utilized fire as a protector. It protected us from the elements, predators and the night. We are still
afraid of things that go bump in the dark. We attempt to illuminate
the night for protection, but there are those few among us who grav-
itate towards it. They find comfort, ease and purpose in the dark.
The moon is their sun and the night offers protection. They see the
unknown things in the night and are the things that go bump in
the dark.

186

The Dark Moon (Howl of the Coyote) 187

I was on the run and Gracie was running out of time. My back was up against the wall again. Soon we would be coming up on the week when he kills the victim. I stood outside the Kiva and just starred at the night skies. The stars were gleaming and there was a quarter moon out. I spent a lot of time out at night, gazing at the different phases of the moon. I watched its cyclic progression while listening to the coyotes howl and sing to her brilliance. I lay back down on the mesa ground and continued to stare up at the sky until Nina found me, as she always did; my Eagle protector.

"Hello, you," she said with a warm and very pleasing smile.

"Good evening," I replied.

"How's it going?" she inquired and lay down next to me on the ground.

"Not so good, Nina. I can't get to him."

"Who, the killer?" she asked?

"Yeah," I replied.

"Kayah said you're trying too hard to see what you already see," Nina stated.

"I know, she mentioned something like that to me as well. It sounds like a riddle," I replied.

"Such is life," she said and held my hand. She knew I was feeling down.

"Did you see all the gifts the Hopituh left for you?"

"Yes, they're very nice."

"They provided me with gifts also. You should have been there when they were coming up. They were touching me, holding me and hugging me. I ate and drank so much my stomach is swollen," she said, laughing and placing my hand on her perfectly flat belly.

"Yeah, you're becoming a fatty," I replied. We both laughed and she hit me affectionately. She was athletic and very physical, even when she played.

"Even the council members came. They asked if you could pay them a visit before we depart. I think they want to thank you in person. It's beautiful out here tonight, isn't it," Nina commented, looking out at the calm and magnificent night.

"Yes, it is," I stated, staring at her beauty. Then she looked back at me and smiled. It was in her nature to be loquacious, so I let her continue until she swung on top of me and began kissing me under the beautiful, starry night.

"You're thinking about Gracie?" Nina inquired but knew the answer.

"Yeah, we're sharing the same starry sky and moon with the killer," I answered, and that's when it finally dawned on me.

"What is it," Nina inquired as I sat up from the ground.

"Kayah was correct; the answers are right in front of our faces. They have been there all the time. It's the moon, Nina. The killer is following the moon. We need to look at a calendar with the moon on it."

We got up and rushed to where the laptop was located in the pueblo. I googled for a calendar with the moon phases on it, then accessed my personal files. I juxtaposed the dates of the killings on the moon calendar and there it was, plain as day; the killer's schedule. It contained when he abducted the women and when he killed them.

"All the abductions occurred on the new moon of each month, or as the Native Americans call it, the dark moon. The only killing that I witnessed was Jessica. It occurred on January 16th during the full moon. Following this pattern, the other women were killed on the full moon as well. This means Gracie has until the 16th of February before he takes her outside and ceremoniously kills her."

"I have to call Steve and let him know."

"But how is this going to help find him? All we know is when he's going to commit this murder."

"Well besides telling us how much time we have to work with, we now have his pattern, He follows the moon, which means we have to research lunar followers and worshipers to see if we can make a match."

The Dark Moon (Howl of the Coyote)

"I'll access the BIA database and research anything pertaining to moon worshippers."

"Thanks, Nina. I'll call Steve and inform him so they can work on other possibilities as well," I said. This wasn't a big break, but I'd take whatever crack in the case I could find!

After I notified Steve of our lunar findings, I asked to be excused to return to the Kiva. I didn't want to dreamscape, but just meditate and reflect. I wanted to see if there was anything I might have missed in my hastiness. Nina insisted on being with me, so I let her come. I lit a fire in the Kiva. It was a cold night on the Black Mesa. I laid out the prayer rugs and sat in a lotus position to meditate.

Several hours went by as I continued deep into the night, with Nina curled up beside me. I dreamscaped occasionally to check in on Gracie, and then continued meditating. It was becoming as fluid as Asku and Kayah had said it would be for me to traverse the different realms. I no longer needed the assistance of sleeping pills or peyote, but I still had some lessons to learn on reading signs and symbols.

I saw morning approach in the opaque sky above. I was getting sleepy, so I placed more wood on the fire to sustain it while I slept. I lay down and snuggled behind Nina with my arms around her, to ensure her warmth when the fire subsided.

When I woke, Nina was no longer within my arms, but up and waiting, as usual. She was an incredibly caring and patient woman.

"Good morning, sleepy head. How are you?" Nina inquired.

"Starving," I replied.

"Yeah; me too. Let's say we drive to Tuba City and grab a meal," she suggested.

"Sounds like a winner to me, but I have to see the Great Mother before we depart," I replied.

"Did you find out anything last night," Nina inquired.

"Yes; a lot of things were illuminated for me. I heard the howl of the Coyote. I know who he is; *he is like me!* I'll explain everything when we talk with Kayah."

We exited the Kiva and went down to Kayah's pueblo. Kayah, like Nina, was already up and waiting for us. We sat down in front of her on the rugs she had waiting for us.

"I am enlightened, Great Mother. I needed to slow down and refocus. I have spent so much time in the Spiritual Worlds that I have neglected the signs and symbols of the Middle World. It all makes sense now. Only two of the Kachina Spirits appeared at the Jemez Order. The Kachinas you've shown me when we first met in the dream world are illustrations of not only the two dead priests who were found, but of the third missing priest. Monsignor Davis mentioned that there were no more missing dead priests. The third priest escaped and is alive."

"Each dream is particular and unique, Cheveyo. Learning how to read and interpret them is just as important skill as being able to receive them. Until now you have visited and received dreams from Middle Realm, from the Earth, but receiving and interpreting visions from the Upper and Lower Realms is different. When you are channeling you're utilizing the spiritual world. There is an old Hopituh saying: *Give the Navajo corn and he will eat for a day, but give the Hopituh seeds and a plow and he will not only eat forever, but he will also feed the Navajo.*"

"I have heard this before in a different context, Great Mother," I responded.

"You must learn how to utilize the tools given to you, Cheveyo," she replied.

"The third priest is the one I am chasing. He appears in the Spirit World because he is like me. He is able to use the night as I do. He is able to evade and not be seen. He knows of me and that is why he carefully shields himself from my visions. I believe him to be a Shaman, and his spirit guide is the coyote. What can you tell me about the coyote, Great Mother?"

"He is a powerful adversary. He is more powerful than most because he is underestimated in his strength. What he lacks in physical prowess he multiplies in intelligence, which is his greatest tool. He

The Dark Moon (Howl of the Coyote)

is cunning and clever. He is the true trickster; a master of deception and disguise. If he is a Shaman, he will be difficult to find and just as difficult to defeat. He will fool and trick you. When the coyote howls at night he will continue to do this, from one spot continuously for an extended period of time. This is to fool the other animals of his whereabouts. Once they relax, thinking they know of his location, he sneaks away and observes from another to pounce on prey and avoid enemies."

"He is a loner, but is also opportunistic. He will travel with other coyotes, no more than three or four to a pack. He is most dangerous in a pack with support, but he is also more reckless and careless. He takes uncalculated risks while in a pack."

"You will never see him by day, only by sunrise and sunset. He is active at night, like you Toquer Shoo-coots. You trick him in order to catch him," the Great Mother stated. "He appears with the other Kachina Spirits, but he remains unknown. I do not know his identity. He keeps it shrouded from me also. He is powerful in the spirit realm," Kayah added.

"So we've been attempting to track a shaman all this time?" Nina said in astonishment.

"Yeah, that's why he is so similar to me. That's why he covers the victim's eyes. He doesn't want others with vision quest abilities to see him. The eyes are not only windows to the soul, but window to the psyche and to our dreams. It isn't called vision quest for nothing. I think we are looking for a cult comprised of other escaped priests in which one verifiably is a shaman. Monsignor Davis confirmed that 'they' are not missing! That is probably why Jessica said it felt like there were several hands on her before they killed her. There actually were several hands," I stated.

"So how do we locate them?" Nina asked.

"We remain on the course we first took; we look for the priests at places they congregate," I said.

"Seriously? You can't narrow it down?" she inquired.

"It already is. We start with the NAC-NA, the Native American Churches of North America. We begin with all the ones within the radius of our crime scenes, but first we need the coyote footage at the scenes of the abductions. I have a theory I need to look into. I'll call Steve and see what he can do."

"Are you going to brief him on this new discovery?"

"Not yet. He has a lot on his plate and I don't want the A.D. to mess this up. We're dealing with a small window of time and a narrow margin of error."

Nina and I thanked the Great Mother for all her assistance and she wished us luck and a safe journey. We stopped by the Hopi Tribal Council Facility in the Kykotsmovi Village on the way to Tuba City. The council was extremely thankful for what we did for the Hopituh Shin-nu-ma and joined us for a meal in Tuba City. The council picked up the tab and asked if we could return at a later date. They wanted to honor us with a celebration for uncovering the truth of the missing Hopi Priests in Jemez. We agreed and departed.

Steve sent the coyote footage to Nina's GOV.com address, since it was considered government property. I checked the footage while Nina drove. Steve also included a message about Monsignor Davis: *Monsignor Davis was discovered dead in his room at the Jemez Order Facility. It was confirmed that he committed suicide. The FBI found two bodies exactly where you said they would be and arrested Arelio Sanchez and Jose Gutierrez in the killings of Priest Maize and Honanie. The rumors have started that you might be connected to the serial killer.*

I was wondering when they would get around to that again. The killings had been going on before I even came to Albuquerque and never mind the fact that I have an unblemished track record for solving some of the FBI's worst crimes. They always thought it could be an officer of the law. I guess I'm a dead ringer for the profile; young male, pretty much isolated, a loner treated as an outcast, with mental health issues. The serial killer and I had more in common than they could ever fathom.

The Dark Moon (Howl of the Coyote)

"They found the buried priests and arrested Sanchez and Gutier-rez. There are also rumors about me being involved with the coyote because of the way I dropped off the parcel without being seen," I briefed Nina.

Our next stop would be to visit the Native American Churches. There were three NACs in the radius of the serial killing abductions; one in Tuba City to which we were en route, one in Chinle and one in Window Rock. They were all on the Navajo Nation Reservation. In our questioning of the staff we would be looking for anomalies in answers to eliminate and narrow down our suspects. This was our big break in the case. I could feel the pieces coming together.

The NAC / NA differs in practices from church to church, but the one thing that they have in common is that they're peyotist.

There wasn't a service being held at the church when we arrived, but the doors were open, so we let ourselves in. We weren't expecting a warm reception. We haven't received one yet and the news of the FBI on Indian Lands had most of the Res in an uproar. The Hopituh just wanted justice for the fallen priest and to vindicate the Coyote Society of having anything to do with this killer, who called himself by their name.

We met with a young parishioner when we entered the Native American Church of Tuba City. She was cleaning the aisles. Nina spoke to her in Navajo. None of the leaders were present for questioning. We'd probably fare better questioning her anyway; she seemed receptive. We began by asking her preliminary questions leading up to the core of the interrogation. I didn't understand Navajo, so Nina conducted the interrogation. We inquired if she heard anything about missing women in the big cities, and asked if she had noticed anything strange or peculiar around the church or the Reservation.

Then we moved towards a more priestly line of questions. We asked if any of the priests were healers or seers. She stated that they didn't have any at their congregation. They were peyotists who practiced snake dancing, and she escorted us to the snake room. She answered all our questions without difficulty. Suffice it to say they weren't the church or priests we were attempting to locate. She did state that there was talk about great healers in Window Rock. We thanked her and departed.

We decided to keep Window Rock for last and went to the NAC in Chinle. When we arrived there they were holding mass. We waited in the back aisle and observed the peyote ceremony. They had a so called healer in their midst, who didn't really have the gift, and snake dancers. I held my laughter out of respect, but inside I was cracking up at the charlatan healer. The snake dancers appeared to be authentic. After the mass we introduced ourselves and attempted to question the leaders. After the peyote consumed during the ceremony, they were more than cooperative. These weren't the priests we were looking for either. We waited for several hours, but didn't observe any suspicious activities and departed for Window Rock.

It was getting late when we arrived at our destination. There were several parishioners and two of the church priests in a meeting when we arrived. We were asked to wait until the meeting adjourned. We bided our time thinking if we cooperated perhaps they would in return. When their meeting ended we spoke to priests; Roanhorse and Wauneka, who were willing to meet with us without parishioner bouncers. We met with them separately and inquired the same questions we asked in Tuba, but this time the answers were more intriguing. Everything we asked one priests the other would contradict. One priest stated that he hadn't heard of the abducted women and the other stated the opposite. It was clear that they weren't expecting us or the questioning.

We informed the priest that we knew who the subject was that we were looking for, and were just attempting to tie up some loose ends. One of them boldly stated, *"Good luck with that."*

The priests we interviewed from the other churches had inquired about how they could assist us. Roanhorse and Wauneka didn't seem to care in the least about getting involved. They also fit the profile. They spoke of their healer, who also had the gift of seeing, but he

The Dark Moon (Howl of the Coyote)

wasn't present at the time. I sensed we were definitely in the right place.

We inquired about the whereabouts of the other priest and they stated that he was attending to the flock; visiting the homes of the parishioners. Nina was forward enough to inquire which houses would we find him at. Both priest were opposed to giving us information in that regards and stated that it's was private affair visiting the homes of the parishioners. The priests were beginning to get agitated by our questioning, so we decided to leave well enough alone and departed. We couldn't afford to have the reservation police find us here harassing the Navajo when I had warrants out for my arrest. I touched as much as I could while there since they didn't offer to give us a tour, nor did we expect one; especially after the interrogation. Hopefully I could pick up something in dreamscape from my contact.

We decided to stay in Window Rock and investigate further. We wanted to attend one of the Masses and meet with the healer. We had to wait until the following day to attend the services. Therefore we checked into the Quality Inn off Hwy 264. Nina and I finally had a little time to relax. We decided to take a shower together and made love. Afterwards we rested in bed together. Nina checked emails and I looked at the coyote footage.

"What exactly are you expecting to find in this footage? We've all seen it a thousand times," Nina said.

"I know, but we weren't looking for the right thing," I replied.

We continued to check the footage of the coyote together. Then I researched for videos of coyotes in the wild. I spotted the anomaly I was looking for. After countless observations of the coyotes in the wild, I confirmed my suspicion.

"It is just as I thought," I said with enthusiasm.

"What is it, Chris?"

"This isn't a normal coyote in any way. He is abnormally larger and his gait is completely different, see?" I said to Nina.

"Yes; it is, but what does that mean?" she inquired.

"He walks like a man would walk on four legs, imitating a coyote. I never thought I would witness one, but this shaman is a shape shifter," I stated.

"Yes; it does have an abnormal walk," Nina replied, as astonished as I was after carefully scrutinizing the coyote and comparing it to others.

This shaman was more powerful and experienced than I'd expected. He had abilities I couldn't begin to fathom. How did I defeat such a man? How did I tell this to anyone? Who would believe me even if I showed it to them? Nina was a believer because of her background and history with shamanism.

"So what's the plan?" Nina asked.

"First I would like to sleep on it, and then consult the spirits. Perhaps I can find some enlightenment there," I replied. Nina wanted to keep her watchful Eagle eyes open, but I convinced her to get some rest. We both needed it and fell asleep on the bed together.

When morning came we couldn't wait to go back to the Window Rock NAC. I didn't receive much from dreamscaping last night. It was as if there was a shroud covering the church. All I could see was darkness. This was no doubt the work of a skilled Shaman. The church was closed when we arrived. There was an itinerary on the door for scheduled activities including the services. The worship wasn't until 10:00 and the work study was at 11:00. We were early, but decided not to add breaking and entering on the list of felony charges. Therefore, we went to have breakfast nearby. Gracie wasn't inside anyway. I would have felt her presence. We needed to speak to the healer and perhaps some of the congregation when they arrived.

After eating we returned a little before 10:00 and waited outside the church. We observed the priests Wauneka and Roanhorse at the door, greeting the parishioners as they entered. After all congregation was inside and the doors closed, we exited the vehicle and entered the church. The mass was similar to the other peyote masses we'd observed in Chinle and Tuba. They presented a snake charmer who danced with several snakes on his arms and passed the peyote pipe.

The Dark Moon (Howl of the Coyote)

Towards the end things got interesting as Priest Roanhorse addressed the parishioners.

"As you know and can tell by now, Father Tsosie isn't present. I know you have brought your sick tribesmen with you today so Father Tsosie can heel them, but he couldn't make it today. It saddens me to tell you that Father Tsosie felt the doubters before they even arrived here. He is a great seer and knew that the evil ones, who don't believe, would be with us. He can't perform his healing with those who don't believe in attendance. It requires pure faith in order to work. You know who they are. I'm sorry you brought your sick clansmen all the way here, but until the evil ones are gone, Father Tsosie will not be healing any longer."

Then we heard the rumbling of the entire church as they looked towards the back at us. The priests were igniting the flames of a mob. There was nothing Nina and I could do. The church was filled with an angry and upset congregations. This was our cue to depart. As we got up from our seats, so did several of the parishioners. This was becoming ugly quickly. There is nothing like the will of a zealot to incite rage. Once at the door we ran to our vehicle. The crowd ran after us and threw things at the vehicle as we drove off.

About a half a mile down the road we noticed several vehicles speeding up from behind us in pursuit. It was the parishioners, no doubt. Nina sped up as well. There was no way we would be caught in any type of conflict with a mob of Navajo who could possibly be armed. It was a no-win situation. Our only recourse was to flee.

We flew past a speed trap set up by two hidden Reservation Police cruisers. We were doing about 30-40 miles per hour over the speed limit in what would be classified as reckless endangerment. When the police cruisers became involved with sirens sounding and flashers illuminated, the parishioners ended their chase. With the mob dispersed, we pulled over and I was arrested on sight. There was an FBI BOLO out on me throughout the reservation. Nina attempted to use her BIA credentials to straighten out the matter, but to no avail. They didn't arrest Nina and let her follow us to the police station. I was detained at the Reservation Station until the FBI arrived. It only took about 40 minutes before they showed up. They sent Ortega and Burkhart.

"Well if it isn't the infamous Christian Sands. You are really making a name for yourself in Res. Territory. They say you are already a part of Hopi lore, Cheveyo. You do realize we are running out of time to find her," Ortega stated, his sarcastic tone setting my teeth on edge. Just when I was beginning to like Ortega.

"I'm the one who gave you guys the moon schedule, remember?" I stated.

"Oh yeah, you did, didn't you. So, how are you going to find her from in here?" he asked.

"Look, Ortega, if you're here to gloat, save it!"

"No, I'm here to get you out. The Great Mother says you still have work to do. She asked me to keep a watchful eye out for you, so I monitored the Res radios. I'm here to help," he stated to my surprise.

"So you're just going to waltz me out the door?" I asked.

"Well I would prefer it if you just walked out on your own, but if you need a dance partner, Agent Blackwater is in the lobby also," Ortega quipped.

"Are there other agents coming to pick me up?" I inquired.

"No, I took care of all of that. I told the Residence Office it was a false report and that I had everything under control. I figured Steve knew what you were doing, so I notified him. Now let's get outta here and find Gracie," Ortega said.

We drove out of Window Rock and off the Reservation as fast as we could. We checked into a hotel in Gallup, New Mexico to hide out until things died down a little. We needed to collect our thoughts and strategize. Nina couldn't believe what Ortega did for me and neither could I. Ortega reserved a hotel room for us, since I appeared to be as wanted as the Coyote these days.

"You guys should be alright here for a while. I'll leave Agent Burkhart here with you in the next room. I need to check back in with Residence Office. They're going to get suspicious if I don't. I'm going to drive back and meet up with you tomorrow morning. Call

The Dark Moon (Howl of the Coyote) 199

me if you need anything or feel the urge to leave while I'm gone," Ortega stated and departed.

The priests had really outsmarted us. They had the reservation police, the FBI, a whole congregation of religious zealots and perhaps the entire reservation out to get us. We were exhausted from the near mob attack and the arrest. We just needed to rest for a few hours so we lay down on the bed together staring at the ceiling. Then we both began laughing at the same time. It started out as a chuckle then it grew into a full-blown gut-busting laugh. We were laughing at ourselves and the way we ran out of the church.

"Did you see the way they all turned around and looked at us?" Nina giggled.

"I thought the old lady was going to tackle us at the door," I replied, laughing as well.

"I never thought I could run so fast," Nina said.

"I couldn't believe it. When I saw you just flat out dash, I was like, what the hell? This girl can run!" We laughed so hard there were tears in our eyes.

"I've been thrown out of bars and nightclubs before, but that's the first time I was thrown out of church and run out of town! You really know how to show a lady a good time, Chris," Nina said, just barely getting it out while laughing so hard. I was rolling in the bed at that point.

She really did know how to make light of a bad situation. She masterfully turned a frown into smile. That's when I realized how much I adored her. I stopped and wiped the tears from my eyes and just looked at her.

"What?" she inquired.

"Nothing," I replied.

"No, what is it?" she asked.

"I was thinking about how incredible you are."

"You're just now noticing that?" she said, smiling.

"No; I'm just noticing how modest you are," I replied and we started laughing again. Then I held her in my arms. I dismissed the outside world and kissed her like there was no tomorrow.

"Wow, where did that come from?" she asked, but before she could continue I quieted her with an even more passionate kiss. She made up for all the bad in my life. She was the one constant, ethereal and beautiful light in my dark and dismal world. She was truly God's gift to me. She was my savior and companion. How very lucky I was to have her. We fell asleep while on the bed and I took the opportunity to do some dreamscaping. Agent Trace Burkhart was next door, so I felt safe while she slept and I went under. I needed to check on Gracie's status.

Early that morning, before sunrise, I was wakened by the sounds of Nina screaming. I jumped up, startled and bewildered by what I saw. There were dozens of rattlers in our room. I didn't hear or feel them while asleep. I'm most vulnerable while in dreamscape. I can't hear or feel anything in my external surroundings; luckily, once again Nina had been present to wake me! She held on to me tight as I assessed the situation. Her weapons were out of reach! I grabbed the bowie knife Asku had given me from its spot the nightstand.

"Listen to me, Nina; I want you to stay on the bed."

She was frightened and still holding me tight. I grasped her face and directed her eyes towards mine. "It's alright; I'm going to get us out of here. Just look at me."

The snakes were on the bed now. She curled up in a fetal position. I wrapped my arms with pillow cases, then grabbed the Deer Horned blade and went to work! With the speed and agility of the panther, I killed the snakes on the bed first. Then I carved my way through the ones in the rest of the room with lightning fast speed. I had never used a knife like this before. You would have thought I was an expert in Escrima, the Filipino Martial Art of knife fighting. I was a killing machine, displaying grace and precision with the blade in my hand.

Nina continued to fix her sight on me. She had calmed down and now fixated on what she was witnessing. She was enamored by the

The Dark Moon (Howl of the Coyote)   201

speed and graceful show I was putting on. When it was over I looked
around the room and surprised myself. I couldn't believe I had killed
so many in so little time.

"Are you OK?" I asked Nina. She nodded, and then asked, "Did any
bite you?" She was coming back around now as she took the pillows
off my arms and began assessing me from head to toe. I hadn't been
bitten. The snakes were fast, but I was faster. Then it hit me.

"We'd better check on Burkhart. We made a lot of noise for him
not to hear it and come immediately over," I stated. Nina looked at
me and without saying a word we rushed to the door together. She
was back, and fearless as ever.

We knocked on the door several times, taking turns calling out
Burkhart's name. There was no answer at the door, so we displayed
our credentials to the hotel management and had them open it. When
the door was opened we discovered Agent Burkhart lying on the
bed, dead. Nina checked his pulse and vitals, but there was nothing.
After a careful inspection of the body we didn't find any offensive or
defensive wounds. It was as if he had died of a heart attack in his
sleep! There was no sign of struggle of any kind in the room. Nothing
was out of order or disturbed, not even the bed. Burkhart had lain
down on the bed fully clothed and died that way.

We informed the hotel's management staff that we would take care
of everything and that this was an FBI matter. I telephoned Steve
immediately and briefed him on the situation.

"Will you notify Ortega about Burkhart?" I urged. "Nina and I are
going to go off the radar for a while. I think it's best that way."

"Sure, I'll call him after we hang up," Steve said.

"We've scrutinized the body, Steve, and as far as we could tell he
died in his sleep from heart failure, but the forensic team you send
can give us a better evaluation."

"So, off the record now, what do you think happened? Because you
and I know Burkhart was in excellent health," Steve replied.

"It was the Coyote, Steve. He got to him in his sleep. Burkhart had
the dying look of fear on his face. The Coyote is like me, but more

powerful. He is a Shaman with the ability to manipulate dreams. That's why it's been so hard to track him!"

"But how was he able to establish a connection with Burkhart without some sort of previous physical contact or some items of his?" Steve inquired. Steve was on point as usual, and his question was rational and sound.

"I have a theory, but I'd rather not share it until I'm completely certain about the assumption. We're getting closer, Steve. That's why he tried to kill us. He knows who I am and that I'm on his trail," I replied.

"Will this provoke him into killing her sooner, though?" Steve asked.

This is the reason why investigators are dismissed from cases they are emotionally invested in. Steve was no longer thinking like an investigator or profiler. He was thinking with his emotions. Under different circumstances he would have never posed such a question.

"No, Steve; he won't deviate from his regimen. It is a part of his signature; his MO. Following the lunar calendar is essential to his ritual and sacrifice. We still have until the 16th. Besides, it is his belief that we are inferior to him, physically and mentally. He doesn't fear us in the least, so there's no need to deviate in his plans."

"OK, you guys need to get out of there. Make sure management leaves the door locked until we get there. Chris, I have faith in you; now go get that son of a bitch by any means necessary!"

We gathered our belongings and briefed the hotel management on the necessary details for both rooms before departing. There was no time to lament our fallen brother. We had to worry about the living right now, and her time was running out.

"He knows we're here, like Kayah prophesied. He can feel our combined spirits. You know what this means, Nina? We are there. We will find her," I stated. Nina was rendered speechless by the carnage that had taken place. I was used to killings, but had forgotten that she doesn't witness this amount of homicides in her duties at the BIA.

The Dark Moon (Howl of the Coyote) 203

We drove to another cheap hotel off the main road, just to gather our thoughts and clean up. Neither of us would be able to go back to sleep after a morning like that. Once we were resettled, I engaged the spirit world while Nina kept a watchful Eagle Eye over me. She was a fearless Federal Agent with outstanding fighting skills I'd witnessed on several occasions, but the snakes had gotten to her. I know she was used to snakes from her background, as I was, growing up in the mountains and hills of North Carolina. I think it was being taken by surprise while asleep is what had her shaken. The Coyote was very clever.

After several hours in dreamscape, I felt the coyote's spirit as he has felt ours. He couldn't hide for long, we were too close! Though I still couldn't breach his shroud it was comforting to know we were getting close. Gracie was still alive, but despair surrounded her. She had given up hope. There was nothing I could do to comfort her.

We finally took turns sleeping for about four hours. We slept together as couples do – in each other's arms. We couldn't afford to be caught off guard again because it would probably be the end of us. It was easy for Tsosie to pick up on our spirit energy. Yes, Roanhorse gave us his name. They do get sloppy when they run in packs. Now it was time to trick the trickster.

"So he can find us whenever he needs to by the brilliance of our spirits. I think it's time we set a trap for him. Let him get over-confident and we flank him, like castling in chess. We allow him to invite himself into your dreams and while he is there, I'll enter into Roanhorse's dreams. I've got enough of a connection with that snake now," I stated.

"How do you know he'll take the bait," Nina inquired.

"He will. Like Kayah stated, it's almost impossible not to feel us together and be drawn into it. The Great Mother showed me a thing or two during vision quest which will allow me to leave my dream shadow behind with you and astrally project into another dream. It is what she did with us when we first dreamed of her. We were together, but shared different dreams with her instead of one."

"How will Tsosie be able to reach me in dreamscape without any physical contact?" Nina inquired.

"It's my assumption that he will make contact with you the same way he was able to reach Burkhart. If he's able to reach you, it proves my theory as well," I stated.

"Which is?" she asked.

"It will all illuminate itself, Nina. I don't want to speculate. Let's just let it play out for now. We have a sound plan and, with a little luck, we can pull it off."

We grabbed something quick to eat and then settled in, as if to go to sleep, but this time we would be dreamscaping. If we sat down on the prayer rugs, Coyote would discover the ruse as soon as he entered her dreams. It didn't take long before our adversary took the bait. I wanted him to see me asleep and lying next to her, as I dreamed about her. Then I stepped into another door, like Kayah taught me, and visited Roanhorse. Roanhorse and Wauneka were Tsosie's apprentices. They weren't shamans, as they didn't have the gift, but he was teaching them the journeyman's way of the craft.

I proceeded through the shadows of Roanhorse's dreams. I didn't force any issues just in case Tsosie had a greater bond or connection with his apprentices as I had with Nina. I saw them at the Jemez Order being tortured by Monsignor Davis and the priests. They were brutalized by the Order, then they became administers of the torturing. They found delight and joy in it. Davis used their sadistic illness to his advantage, just as he used everyone else around him. When their appetites became too excessive, Davis expelled them from the Order! Davis also felt Tsosie was a threat to his power. Then I sensed Nina was in distress and had to cut my dreamscape visit short.

Tsosie was a treacherous trickster and caused Nina to have nightmares when he entered her dreams. He had her dreaming of snakes. He touched on the one thing that scared her recently and exploited it. I returned and broke the bond. It wasn't Nina who couldn't hang, it was me. I didn't want to see him hurt her in any way. I loathed him with every fiber in my body.

The Dark Moon (Howl of the Coyote) 205

"Did you get the location?" Nina asked wearily as I woke her from the nightmare.

"No," I replied.

"So why did you break the connection?" she retorted.

"I felt you in distress," I replied.

"I was alright. You forgot I can prevent anyone from entering my dreams if I don't want them there," she said in an upset and irritated voice.

"No, I didn't forget, Nina, I just couldn't take him being anywhere near you any longer."

"That's sweet, but it's not going to help us save Gracie or catch Tsosie," she said, and then kissed me.

"There has to be another way to get him; just like we just fooled him that time. We can do it again," I stated.

"You do realize tomorrow is the full moon," Nina stated.

"Yes. Ortega reminded me of it," I said, then went over to Nina and held her in my arms. I thought of Gracie's plight, but refused to give up on her. I gave my word and I was going to save her, one way or another.

"You know I've always found that if I table a problem for a while and revisit it with a fresh mind, I have a better perspective on the matter at hand. Perhaps we're overthinking this," I told Nina.

"What do you have in mind?"

"Nothing spectacular; let's just go for a drive and listen to some jazz to clear our heads," I replied.

It was a gorgeous day in New Mexico. The sky was clear and the sun was shining. There wasn't a hint in this beautiful day of the horrors that tomorrow could bring. We drove down to the Bandera Volcanic Ice Caves. We listened to classic jazz on the MP3 player in the car. Coltrane was playing as we drove down the highway. We went through some Thelonious Monk, Dave Brubeck and Miles before turning our listening attention towards progressive jazz; Acoustic Alchemy and Return to Forever Band.

We attempted to enjoy the sights of Bandera as the rest of the visitors and sightseers. It would have been a pleasant excursion under different circumstances, but we couldn't escape the accumulating stress that loomed over us. Therefore we grabbed a bite to eat while there and then headed back up to Gallup. It was a quick respite from the chaos of our life, but the desperation was still present. We were no closer to finding Gracie than we were with the rest of the abducted women.

On the way back we listened to Chemical Composition's jazz CD *'Excitement Within the Trojan Horse'* which gave me an idea. It could prove be a fatal risk, but we were running out of time and options. It was a chance I had to take.

"I have an idea on how to finally put an end to this nightmare," I said to Nina while driving.

"Excellent. Let's hear it."

"Kayah has been correct in every way about the Coyote. He and his minions are careless together and we have to beat him at his own game. We have to trick him in order to beat him. Let's use the old Trojan Horse scheme to get into their camp," I stated.

"And how will we go about doing that?" Nina inquired.

"We have to let them abduct me," I replied.

"Chris, you have been brilliant in your strategy up to this point, including all of the calculated risks, but this one is way too risky! What if they just kill you on the spot? What if we don't get there on time or you can't inform us of where you are? There are just too many what ifs," Nina exclaimed. Her jaw was set in a posture of extreme stubbornness.

"I know it's risky, but we don't have a choice. Besides, they are abductors. That's their profile. They don't kill on the spot. They are like most coyotes; they always take their prey back to the den. Once I'm inside I will dreamscape through Roanhorse and alert you of where they are located," I told Nina.

"This is excessively risky and assumes too much, Chris."

The Dark Moon (Howl of the Coyote) 207

"I know, Nina, but it's Gracie's only hope. I saw her again last night and it wasn't looking good. They've began making preparations. They've covered her body in these Aramaic symbols. If you come up with something better, let me know, because we've run out of time."

What began as a pleasant drive on a nice sunny day quickly turned gloomy and silent. I had known Nina would be opposed to me sacrificing myself. I knew how deeply she felt about me. She was better at expressing her feelings than I was. I was more of a touchy feely person who expressed himself through actions and physical contact. The rest of the ride back to Gallup we quietly listened to jazz without conversation. She was upset with me, but she knew what I was doing made sense and that there was no other way at this point.

When we got back to the hotel, Nina broke down and began to cry. This was only the second time I'd seen her cry. The first was in the swimming pool when she professed her feelings for me. She was strong and optimistic about everything except for this.

"Nina," I said aloud as I went over to her and placed my arms around her.

"I don't want you to go. What if something goes wrong," she said, interrupting me.

"Nothing will. You will fulfill the prophecy and rescue me as foreseen." Then I wiped the tears from her eyes and kissed her. "I believe in you, Nina. I wouldn't be doing this if I didn't have complete faith in you. I know it's asking a lot. I'll be placing my life and Gracie's life in your hands. You're the strongest person I know and I know you can do it."

Then she placed her head on my shoulders and continued to hug me. We lay on the bed together, hugging each other for about a half an hour. Eventually Nina regained her strength and wanted to go over the plan, so she could be precise in her rescue.

"I need to break into the church and get caught by the priests. Then they'll surely take me back to their lair. They won't have much time for anything else. They'll consider me a trophy." I didn't tell

Nina about their sadistic history with the Jemez Order. If I told her she would insist against this course of action.

"I'll arrange to get myself caught tomorrow after the church service. After I'm caught I will notify you through dreamscape of the location where they are holding us. I'll retrieve it from Roanhorse. I need you to be ready to accept the information, so just relax on the bed and meditate like I've shown you. I'll come to you in dreamscape," I said.

"Alright, just be careful," she replied.

"I will. Now, let's meditate and dreamscape together," I stated.

The next day, I snuck into the church while they were conducting services and hid in the basement. I would make my presence known at the completion of the service. While in the basement I searched for signs and clues that would lead me to the location they were holding Gracie. I would have gratefully accepted a minute hint or miniscule clue and run out of there with all due haste, instead of the alternative; being captured by these sadistic killers.

When the service ended I made my presence known by knocking over a vase they had in storage. Wauneka caught me. He, along with two other zealots, beat me in the basement and then took me to Roanhorse, who continued the beating. Then they blindfolded me and tied me up. I spent countless hours bleeding on the basement floor before they finally transported me to another location. Perhaps my plan was working and they were taking me to the lair where Gracie was located. On the other hand, maybe they were taking me to a dump to murder me and dispose of my body.

Chapter 12

CHACOANS OF CHACO CANYON

The Chacoans are the original or Ancient Pueblos (Anasazi). They were the great architects and master designers. They gave birth to, and passed on wisdom and knowledge to their Pueblo descendants; the Aztecs, Acoma, Hopituh, Jemez, Keres, Taos, Tewa, Tiwa and Zuni. They were archaeastronomers who built ancient observatories like Fajada Butte and Hovenweep Castle near the Four Corners. They were solar and lunar worshippers who built, aligned and scheduled their culture around solar and lunar cyclic events.

They created buildings to capture the power of the sun and moon as well as solar and lunar calendars and clocks like the Sun dagger petroglyphs and pictographs. They were also believed to be the descendants of the Pleiadians (People of the stars, extraterrestrial beings). The Hopituh called them Chuhukon (Chacoan) which means Pleiadian - 'Those who cling together'. The Navajo name for Pleiadian is 'Sparkling Sun' or home of the Black God. The color black was associated with royalty and supremacy.

The Black God was ruler of the Upper Realm. The Anasazi built elaborate roads and highways with astronomical symbols and solstice markings. Some believed them to be landing strips for their Pleiadian

*relatives others believe them to be roads leading back to 'Shipapu' –
the dimensional doorway of their place of origin.*

I was in the Kiva with Gracie. I could feel her presence. I was
blindfolded and tied up; thus far my plan was working. I tricked the
Coyote into bringing me to his lair. Kayah had stated that I had to
trick him at his own game of deception, and it was working. I didn't
need my eyes to figure out where we were. I had a bond now with
Roanhorse and Wauneka that the Coyote was apparently unaware
of. He was becoming sloppy or he just didn't care at this point! The
only way to break this bond would be death, and I was sure that's
what they had in store for me.

"Gracie, can you hear me? Gracie!"

"Yes, I can hear you. Is that you, Christian? Am I dreaming again?"

"No, Gracie; I'm really here."

She sounded weak and delusional. She was exhausted from dehy-
dration no doubt.

"Are you alright?" I asked her.

"I didn't think you would find me," she said her voice sounding
weak.

"Don't talk now, Gracie. I'll get us out of here."

Then Roanhorse and Wauneka came into the Kiva and carried me
out. I was taken into another structure. They threw me in a room and
began beating me again, while I remained tied. They spent about 30
minutes –which seemed like an eternity – beating me until I passed
out. While I was unconscious I reached out to Nina, who was ready
to receive me in dreamscape. I showed her through their minds where
I was located. I don't know how long I remained unconscious, but
they revived me later with a bucket of cold water. That's when Tsosie
arrived.

"Who told you to beat him like that? How long was he out for?"
Tsosie demanded. Then he turned to me "You have been a tremen-
dous obstacle in my plans, Cheveyo. You have been a bad boy and
now I must reprimand you for it." He was speaking to me as if I were

a child and deserved to be punished. They strapped me down to a table. I guess they were about to torture me some more.

"Is this what happened to you at the Jemez Order, Tsosie? Yes, I know what happened to all of you there. I saw it when you were visiting Nina's dreams, the nightmares that you were causing her. I snuck through the backdoor of Roanhorse's subconscious while you were busy with Nina. I knew she could handle you. She has a strong spirit and a lot of experience in vision quest." I was attempting to get into his head and purchase a little time before they killed me. Then my heart sunk when I felt the presence of someone who shouldn't have been there.

"Agent Ortega, you can come out now, you've assisted them long enough. You've tossed suspicion on the Coyote Clan, your own people and everyone you could think of to divert it from the real culprit," I stated. He removed blindfold. This confirmed that he intended to kill me.

"How long have you known?" he inquired.

"I suspected at the jail. The Great Mother would have never confided in you, Ortega. That's why she asked me to investigate the Jemez Order. She knew of your corruption. Also, you called me by my spirit name; Cheveyo. Only a few people know me by that name and the Great Mother would have never shared it with you. You gave Tsosie the connection he needed to kill Burkhart at the hotel."

"I applaud you, Cheveyo. You haven't disappointed me. You've lived up to your reputation," Ortega stated with a smile and clapped his hands in approval.

"So when were you recruited, Agent Ortega?" I inquired with a saddened heart.

"It's more like when did I recruit them? I was a Reservation sheriff at the time the first priest began going missing, but no one was interested in a few missing brown priests. My brother was one of the first to disappear when it was the Servants of Paraclete Ministry. Nothing was done and nobody listened. It was a cover-up. The Archdiocese

212   *Chacoans of Chaco Canyon*

might have changed the name, but it remained the same. Now a few gringo girls go missing and they send a team of specialists," he replied.

"So you justify the killing of all these innocent women because of church atrocities?" I demanded, laying it on the line.

"These atrocities have been happening to my people since the Spaniards came to the Americas."

"And what about Gracie? I've exposed the Jemez Order. You don't have to continue," I replied.

"They are the necessary sacrifices that will forever keep our lands safe and prosperous."

"Tsosie has brainwashed you with his mind games," I retorted.

"No. He is a great Shaman. He was one of the priests who managed to escape. He walks with the Kachinas," Agent Ortega stated.

"*He is the Kachina who doesn't speak!*" I thought to myself.

"Yes. He told us you would come and everyone would feel the strength of the Chacoans once again!" Ortega stated.

"So you blame it on the Coyote Clan, the Hopis and whoever you could to deflect suspicion from yourself," I replied.

"You should have left when you were given the opportunity," he retorted.

"You mean after you attempted to kill us with the snakes?" I said.

"He wanted to give you a chance to live since you are of Indian heritage," Ortega replied.

"You're insane," I replied!

"No, Cheveyo; he isn't insane. He is like you. Both of you have the half blood. You have great potential, Cheveyo, and I would love to have you with us, but the white man's world has tainted you. I know your dreams. You don't know who you are or where you belong. Sorry it had to come to this," Tsosie stated.

"Now I see why the Great Mother didn't trust you to investigate the missing Hopi priests, Ortega. The Hopis and the Coyote Clan didn't accept you, so you found your own clan with these maniac priests," I said, baiting him. He glared for a moment his hand balling into a fist. He hit me before and stalked out, trailing behind his Shaman master.

Chacoans of Chaco Canyon

Roanhorse and Wauneka were sloppy and careless, but meticulous when it came to torturing me. They began cutting me repeatedly. This was an old and painful torture trick where the victim died slowly from wounds and loss of blood, but not before feeling every knife slice. Then to solidify the deal with irony, they threw salt on my wounds. The salt added to the pain tremendously. It also slowed the bleeding. They wanted to take their time. They were all sadists and received pleasure from injuring others; it was like some sort of rush or high for them. I only hoped Nina would make it here in time. I passed out again. They left me tied to the table, unconscious, and went to prepare for the ceremony.

In dreamscape, I reached out to Nina. "Steve; I have the location of the serial killers. They've formed some kind of cult. They're in Chaco Canyon. They have Chris and Gracie. I'll text you the location. I'm on my way there now," Nina said into her cell phone. She would arrive before Steve and the FBI.

Nina parked a mile from where they were keeping us. It was dark outside, but there was a full moon which gave her good visibility. There were several cult members congregating outside. She saw the priests carry Gracie from the Kiva and tie her to the sacrificial post. Gracie was naked and covered in Aramaic writings and symbols. She remained blindfolded and gagged. There was firewood surrounding the post. Then the three priests who were dressed in Kachina costumes called the cult to order. The priests chanted and danced around Gracie. The other zealots formed a circle around her as they joined in the chanting. They hadn't lit the fire yet.

Nina was a natural fighter and utilized my bowie knife and the stealth of a Cherokee Warrior to take out many of the zealots standing guard outside. She was quiet, deadly and on a mission. She had been taught well by her tribe. She was like a warrior princess, clearing a path to the structure they were holding me in. My connection with her was acute. She entered the building unnoticed; they were all outside at this point and busy with Gracie. I was elated to see her. Although I knew she would find me, I hadn't been sure if I would be alive. Kayah had said she would rescue me and I was depending on the prophecy.

"Chris, I'm here. Wake up. This is no time to sleep." Her words dragged me up from the depths so the dreamscape image of my beloved merged with the corporeal one. "Are you alright? Are you able to move?" she inquired.

"Yes; I knew you would come," I replied.

"We're surrounded and they have Gracie tied to a stake outside. She's naked with all sorts of writings on her body. They're going to burn her at the stake," Nina stated. Then she pulled out her Beretta 9mm.

"Here's your knife," she said. It still had blood on it. "But I suggest you use this." She handed me her spare Glock.

"You used this?" I asked.

"Yes," she replied. This was the second time the bowie knife had saved my life, as Asku had predicted. "Whatever you do, Christian, don't shoot Gracie. I know it's been a while since you've used one of these."

"That's just it, Nina; suppose she gets wounded in the crossfire?"

"We have no choice. They're out there chanting, ready to torch her. We need to strike now and take them by surprise," she replied.

The cult members were scantily dressed, almost naked, as they moved back and forth in rhythm to the chant. Tsosie and the other two priests, Roanhorse and Wauneka, continued their ceremonial Kachina dance, circling the stake were Gracie was bound. They hadn't noticed their fallen brethren on the perimeter yet. They were too excited. The cult and the chanting became louder and louder as they seemed to lose themselves in the euphoria.

It was different than I recalled in my dreams of Jessica. This was a bigger production; perhaps was intended to be the last of the killings for a while.

"They must be following the folklore about the seasonal appearance of the Kachinas," I whispered as we watched the crowd. It was all clear to me now. "The abducted women are sacrifices to the Great

Chacoans of Chaco Canyon

Spirit Massauu. This is the end of the season. They will appear again next season and start the killings all over again."

"No. This ends here, Chris," Nina stated emphatically.

"OK, Nina, but let me distract them. We'll split them up. You're a better shot than I am, so I'll lead some away and make it easier for you. You get in a position where you can direct the gunfire away from Gracie."

"Can you run in your condition?"

"Don't worry about me. I'll give myself a head start before I let them notice me," I said.

"Alright, Chris, but be safe," Nina replied, and kissed me.

I took a position near the parked vehicles about 10 yards from where the ceremony was taking place. I couldn't see Nina from where I was located, but what I did observe totally took me by surprise. I fixed my gaze on Tsosie the whole time while I was taking position. The cult was in some sort of transcendental state. I was certain they were all high on something. Tsosie took off his clothes and continued circling the stake. His irises began to change color and became a golden yellow. They glowed. Then he fell to the ground on his knees, as if he was having spasms or a seizure.

The cult backed off from him further. It was harder to see through them while he was on the ground. There was only the light from the fires and torches and the moonlit sky, but my vision was as clear as a panther's. Tsosie began to shift into the largest coyote I've ever seen. I couldn't believe I was witnessing what I thought to be true. It was one thing to view the size of the coyote on camera, but he seemed even larger in person. The coyote continued circling. Roanhorse and Wauneka grabbed torches from the surrounding fires. They were preparing to light Gracie on fire.

I began shooting in the air. About half of the zealots and Roanhorse directed their attention towards me. They followed me over to the vehicles and began shooting in my direction. Then Nina began her assault. She picked off the other armed zealots, one by one. I wasn't doing badly either. I could hear Steve and the sirens approaching in the distance before anyone else, as I led my group further into the darkness. I was like a cat playing with its prey, as I maneuvered them away from all the lights and fires burning. They were under the impression that they were stalking me, as I utilized the night as a panther would and began my assault.

My night vision was acute as I killed them silently with my bowie knife. They never heard me coming. I slit their throats one after another. Then they heard the sirens begin to close in. That's when they panicked and began to scatter.

Now the hunt was on for Roanhorse. He attempted to flee, but there was nowhere for him to hide. Not only was my vision extraordinary, but I had a psychic connection with him now. I could feel where he was located as I meticulously hunted him. He ran further into the night, opposite the sacrificial gathering. The police were there and he wanted to get as far away from them as he could. He could feel me on his heels as he ran panicking through the moonlight. I was calm and cool in my chase. He was out of shape and became winded soon. I caught up with him. He was bending over and breathing hard. He couldn't see me as I spoke to him from the darkness.

"Did you really think you could escape this," I asked, surprising him as he swung up with the look of fear and shock. He immediately began shooting wildly in the direction he thought my voice was emanating from. He was shooting erratically into the open air of the night. I moved stealthily to another position and spoke again. He swung in that direction and began shooting wildly until he fired the last bullet. I heard the click of the hammer with no discharge and moved in closer, so he could see me. I was covered in blood. It was the blood of his fallen brothers that I stalked and killed, as I was about to do with him.

"So how does it feel; the killings?" he asked.

I was silent now. There was nothing left for us to discuss. I had to put down this mad dog.

"Don't tell me it didn't feel good killing them. The way you stalked them, me; it's in you like it is in us! You're a hunter. The thrill of it gets you off, doesn't it? Yeah, you enjoyed it," he stated, bending over to catch his breath further. I just stood there covered in blood, watching him attempt to talk his way out of the inevitable. Then he dropped the empty gun and pulled out his knife. It was probably the same one he used in torturing me.

"Ok then, let's get it over with," he stated and stood up from his bent position.

I would have elected to be a gentleman about the situation and let him rest further, but since he was in a rush to die, who was I to deny him? I was feeling overconfident and cocky about my chances of killing him. I was faster and stronger than him from the Panther imprinting. Even if he wasn't exhausted, I didn't think he would have posed much of a challenge. It's like the panther took over when it came time to fight or kill. I had all her instincts and skills. He was right about his assumptions as well. It had been gratifying killing the others, and I would take great pleasure in killing him. They had beaten and tortured me endlessly, had hurt and terrified Gracie. I was usually devoid of emotions when I approached these cases, but this one had become personal, very personal.

We danced around each other for a couple of seconds, scrutinizing each other before making a move. We needed to feel each other out and rate skill levels and weaknesses. I knew he enjoyed knives, so I had to be careful. I couldn't over-exert myself in my condition either, as I had taken a good beating from them previously. It was one thing to catch someone by surprise, but totally different squaring off with him in front of you. Then he lunged at me, but I was faster than him. He was good in his recovery, though.

It was clear that Roanhorse was no amateur with a knife, but he was underestimating me and careless as usual. I cut him on the arm as I escaped another one of his attacks. He was the aggressor in this mêlée. Then I diverted another one of his swings, I was pouncing around him like panthers playing in the wild with each other, except he didn't match my agility or speed. He became enraged and erratic at that point, and rushed at me like a bull would a matador.

I sidestepped him several times, outmaneuvering his swings and advances until finally cutting his throat in one of his wild lunges. I left him bleeding out on the ground for the coyotes and other animals to feast on during the night.

I returned to the ceremonial grounds. There were several cult members lying dead, and then I saw the Coyote in full form, watching from the distance. Tsosie had remained transformed during the mêlée. He was snarling at me with huge fangs and approaching me in the attack stance, with his back hunched. I didn't have the energy or the strength for this fight. I would surely die in the attack. Then Nina began firing on him from afar as the FBI descended on the scene. I fell to the ground as Tsosie fled.

"Don't let it get away! That's the killer; that's Tsosie," I yelled as the agents restrained me. The coyote continued into the dark plateau of the night as Nina ran over to me.

"I know I shot that coyote twice and he just kept right on running. I've never seen anything like it before. How do you kill something like that?" Nina inquired, excited and out of breath.

"With something that contains the same amount of magic as him," I replied.

"What happened to you?" Nina asked looking at the blood on me.

"I led Roanhorse and several other zealots north of here. They're all dead. What about Ortega and Wauneka?" I inquired.

"Wauneka and several zealots died in a gunfight near the Canyon's entrance with Max and a few other agents," she stated.

"And Ortega?" I asked.

"He left me no choice. I asked him to put down his weapon. I had him zeroed. There was no way for him to win, but he drew on me anyway. It was either him or me. It was like he wanted to die. His last words were 'the Chacoans will rise again!'"

The FBI rounded up the remaining cult members were attempting to flee the scene. Steve freed Gracie from her bonds and covered her up with a blanket. I spotted Dianna amongst the Federal Agents.

Chacoans of Chaco Canyon   219

She approached me, but didn't really know what to say. She had abandoned me when I needed her the most.

"Good job, both of you," she said, speaking to Nina and me with a saddened face, and then departed. The FBI agents pulled me up from the ground where Nina and I were sitting, and handcuffed me.

"Wait, take those off of him. He's not a criminal," Steve protested.

"He is, until a judge says otherwise," the A.D. replied.

"You do realize what he's done for us, don't 'you? He sacrificed himself for Gracie and this whole bureau. He has been beaten, tortured, discredited, defamed and hunted, and this is how we are going to treat him?" Steve inquired, looking at the A.D. over the top of Grace's head. She remain snuggled in Steve's arms.

"Take off the cuffs, but drive him directly to the Residence Office and place him in the holding cell," the A.D. commanded. Steve stood up at that point and looked directly into A.D. Pollin's eyes and stated: "No, he isn't; this man is a part of my team. He's wounded and he is going directly to the hospital." Steve climbed into the back of the emergency vehicle with Gracie and Nina accompanied me.

Max Maurice and several other agents discovered a mass grave of charred bones near the sacrificial site. Tsosie had escaped, but was number one on the FBI's most wanted list. His picture and face were circulated nationwide. Now that we knew who he was and what he looked like, it wouldn't be long before he was caught.

The FBI covered up Ortega's involvement with the murders. It was just too big of a scandal. The cover-up was used as leverage by Steve to secure leniency for me. It was a trade-off. Ortega had officially been shot in the line of duty and was given a hero's burial with star, military salute and flag. His family was given full benefits. Only a few knew the truth of his involvement. I avoided prison on several felony charges, but was institutionalized at a Government Mental Health Facility for psychiatric evaluation. It was better than jail. I was suspended indefinitely until the doctors agreed to release me.

While in the hospital, I had police guards standing outside my door. They weren't there for my protection, but to ensure that I didn't escape. I could have at any time, but remained. There was nothing wrong with me, but I'm sure every patient in here would tell you the same thing. I wasn't complaining, though, because I needed the rest and relaxation. Those stressful, sleep-deprived nights took their toll. I had lost weight, was dehydrated and looked like a zombie. I would visit Nina in dreamscape some nights and on occasion, I reached out to Asku or Kayah. But most nights I just used the dream catcher that Asku gave me, so my sleep wouldn't be interrupted.

I was tracking the Coyote from the hospital with the assistance of Carlyle Jenkins, my tech savvy FBI colleague at Quantico. He placed an ongoing search engine on any news regarding coyotes and synced it to my laptop. I was still credible at Quantico; in fact, I was considered a hero. I was the man who saved the FBI; at least it's reputation in the intelligence community. I monitored the internet closely for any sighting of coyotes. This thing was far from over. Tsosie was still out there and waiting to regroup to start this killing spree again in the next season of the Kachina and likely also plotting his revenge. I was thinking more on the latter.

My Spirit Guide, along with Asku and Kayah, counseled me to stay on course for the imminent threat. I continued following the lunar cycle. If the Coyote was going to attack, it would be on the dark moon as before. The abduction would be very personal. He wouldn't risk going after Gracie again, she was heavily guarded, but he would risk going after Nina. She was near to me and had assisted in bringing down his cult. I was convinced that he would go after her!

An abnormally large coyote was captured several days later in the Chuska Mountains and taken to an animal shelter. Two days later the coyote escaped. There were no signs of a break-in. It was him; I could feel it. He was going after Nina. I could sense she was in danger.

It was a rainy night in the District Maryland and Virginia. There was another dark moon in the sky tonight. It was the type of moon that the coyote used while abducting young women. Everything appeared to be darker than usual with the rain falling. I used my abilities to manipulate the dark and maneuver in the shadows of the night to procure my escape from the guarded hospital. I made it to Nina's condo in Southwest D.C. I remained unseen in the shadows and waited in the falling rain. Then he appeared from out of nowhere; a huge coyote silently walking in Nina's parking lot. This time he wouldn't out-maneuver me.

I was just as stealthy as he was, and stayed downwind. I had my sacred bowie knife out and ready to strike. Between one heartbeat and the next, I lost him amongst the vehicles. I became irate and searched frantically. I couldn't afford to lose him, Nina's life depended on it. Then I caught sight of him again turning the corner of the building. I ran swiftly but carefully, attempting to remain unseen. When I reached the corner of the building I saw his tail as he walked between two vehicles. He was following Nina's scent.

He made it to her vehicle. Luckily she was inside her condo. He hit the side of the vehicle hard and set off the alarm as he ducked out of sight. Several tenants came to their windows and looked outside to see if it was their vehicle's alarm sounding. The alarm was silenced after a few minutes. He paced back and forth and hit the side of the car again. This time the blinds were disturbed for only four condo windows and the alarm was cut off. He was narrowing down the tenants one by one.

He activated the alarm again, this time only one set of blinds opened. He looked up as I did. Now he knew where she lived. He hit the vehicle again. He was going to lure her outside. I had to stop this. Every time the alarm went off I moved closer without him noticing. The loudness of the alarm hindered his hearing and threw off his other senses. Besides, he appeared to have tunnel vision and focused on two things only; Nina's vehicle and staring up at her window.

After the fifth or sixth hit, I was close enough to make my move. The darkness of the night and the rain worked against him. He didn't see me nor hear me =. His focus was obscured by his hatred of Nina. I pounced on him with the agility and lightning speed of a panther, just as Nina was exiting her building to check on her vehicle! We wrestled like wild animals. He was using his teeth and I was using the bowie knife. Nina must have heard the growls of an angry dog and the sound of us hitting the vehicles as we wrestled. We continued setting off alarms in the struggle. Wrestling with the panther had prepared me for this. I stabbed him several times, but he kept coming.

We were both covered blood when he backed off. Neither the coyote nor the panther are known for their stamina. I thought he backed off because of his injuries, and perhaps he was as tired as I was, but this wasn't true. He'd spotted Nina standing squarely within sight. She was standing still under an umbrella, unarmed and in shock at what she was witnessing. She watched the large coyote with a bloody mouth and blood all over him, snarling at her as he'd been snarling at me the night she shot him.

He hunched his back as his yellow eyes reflected the luminance of the dim parking lot lights under the dark and rainy moonless night. She had on white short shorts, a white cut off t-shirt and Timberland boots. When he took his attention off me I caught my second wind and pounced again. This time I got a clean cut, like a panther going for its prey's throat. I put the knife in deep and kept it there as I moved it around, severing the jugular. The coyote let out one last yelp as injured dogs do, and fell motionless on the wet ground. Then he turned back into a man; back into Tsosie. Nina ran to me where I lay between the vehicles in the dark. She wrapped her arms around me.

"Chris, you're going to be ok, I'm here." We heard the police sirens in the background. One of the neighbors must have called the police when they heard the commotion. Tsosie laid there naked, dead with several stab wounds and his throat cut.

"I told you I didn't like guns," I said to Nina, then I passed out. I had sustained several traumatic contusions and bite wounds.

They couldn't explain the huge canine bites I had sustained or why my flesh was found between the Tsosie's teeth. They also couldn't explain why he was naked in the middle of Southwest D.C. with no transportation. They refused to accept the reasons I gave them. I didn't get charged for killing Tsosie since he was a wanted serial killer, but I was slapped on the wrist for escaping a Federal Mental

Chacoans of Chaco Canyon 223

Institute and excessive use of force. Can you believe it? A.D. Pollin still manage to charge me. In the end, all the charges were dropped and the case dismissed. I was mandated to go directly to a mental institution for a nervous breakdown (stress disorder and depression). They didn't believe my story about Tsosie's transformations they never had and nothing would change their minds. They said I was attacked by his large dog that escaped again.

So that's how I ended up here at the Northern Virginia Mental Health Institution in Falls Church. Perhaps I should have been a little smarter about the way I explained the events that occurred, but so much for hindsight. Steve and Nina knew the truth, but played the bureaucracy game a little bit better than me. I had to appease the A.D. and prevent any further incarceration, so I was sent here by court order, but without police guards this time. I was being treated for a mental breakdown, depression and bipolar disorder. I guess I was a bit exhausted and battered by the case. I just wanted to close the books on this one, so whatever I had to do, I welcomed. It was nothing compared to what I had already endured.

My employment as a consultant with the FBI was terminated due to my mental instability. This was bogus because they already knew of my psychological profile when they hired me. I was given a full pension, as if I was a government employee. I received a classified visit from POTUS (President of the United States) and the Director of the FBI. The visit was kept a secret and I received a medal.

Nina received a huge promotion in GS ranking and was given the same medal as I was, to add to her collection of medals, plaques and awards for outstanding service and exemplary duty. She was also given a month of vacation to recuperate. As I stated, she was smarter than I was about explaining the events that occurred. She said she saw me wrestling with a large dog and Tsosie. I didn't blame her. I wish I had said the same thing.

The entire ViCAP team was honored and received medals for outstanding service and plaques for duty beyond the cause and given time off. They also received special thanks from the president. They were recognized in the media this time, but their names weren't mention by the Director.

I spent a full year at the Mental Health Institution in Falls Church. I remained a patient of Dr. Green, who continued to treat me at the hospital. Nina visited me almost every day. Steve came on the weekends without fail. He even brought Gracie to visit once. She couldn't wait to thank me in person for what I did. My mother came from Atlanta, Georgia with my sister and niece on two occasions. Amber came several times and brought her mother and son. Max visited me on Sundays, so we could watch basketball together on the television.

I received several phone calls from Paul, who transferred out of the unit after being shot. He and his family thought it best if he got a desk job at a Field Office. He received his choice of any office in the country. They decided to go back home to Houston. I still joke with him on the phone as to why he didn't decided to go to Honolulu, but that was Paul; he was down to earth and simplistic. He was a true blue Longhorn.

I heard from Dianna once while I was in the hospital, and she sent me a card. She knew I was with Nina. We were friendly towards each other, but she regretted all that had taken place and felt bad about her actions. We talked and I told her that there were no hard feelings on my side.

I caught up on a lot of reading and playing chess while at the institute. I was allowed to have one instrument while there. I chose the cello, of course. I could only play during certain hours of the day; between 1pm and 6pm, which didn't really give me a lot of time, since they filled our day from 8am to 4pm with classes and counseling. Therefore I played from 4pm to 6pm most days.

I was nearing the end of my stay at the hospital. One day while playing chess in the recreation room, as I often did between the hours of 7pm and 9pm, I sensed her coming. I got up from the table and looked out the window. It was Nina, coming to take me home; back to her cabin in the Smokey Mountains of Cherokee County. Once again she was rescuing me from the darkness.

The End.

Forever looking up and longing to be in the clouds. Climbing and making your home in the highest of trees to be close to the sky. Transcending the three worlds; the Night, the Earth and the Sky. The Guardian of the Realms.

See You Soon; "The Shaman Prince"

CONTENTS

1	The Gift and the Curse	3
2	A Dream Within A Dream	9
3	Silent Night	23
4	The Crossroads	32
5	Out with the Old and In with the New	49
6	Home of the Brave	72
7	Fall from Grace	89
8	The Talisman	100
9	Kachina	131
10	The Jemez Order	155
11	The Dark Moon (Howl of the Coyote)	186
12	Chacoans of Chaco Canyon	209

Made in the USA
San Bernardino, CA
21 June 2017